HEARTSTAR

HEARTSTAR

Book One: The Key Made of Air

Elva Thompson

HeartStar
Book One: The Key Made of Air

iUniverse books may be ordered through booksellers or by contacting:

iUniverse
1663 Liberty Drive
Bloomington, IN 47403
www.iuniverse.com
1-800-Authors (1-800-288-4677)

ISBN: 978-1-4917-0138-6 (sc)
ISBN: 978-1-4917-0139-3 (hc)
ISBN: 978-1-4917-0140-9 (e)

Library of Congress Control Number: 2013914333

Print information available on the last page.

iUniverse rev. date: 02/23/2015

CONTENTS

For we do not wrestle against flesh and blood, but against principalities, against powers, against the rulers of the darkness of this age, against spiritual hosts of wickedness . . . Therefore take up the whole armor of God, that you may be able to withstand in the evil day.

—Ephesians 6:12-13

ACKNOWLEDGEMENTS

The author wishes to thank: Scott and Trisha Bischoff, Nancy Church, Rainer Gruterich, Iam Saums and Sara Nason for their love, support and encouragement. A special thank you, to my dear friend Randy Hutchinson for his untiring commitment to HeartStar, and the thousands of hours he spent reading and re-reading the text.

Thank you to iUniverse for their professionalism, support and enthusiasm throughout the publishing process.

DEDICATION

This book is dedicated to the Living Earth.

CHAPTER ONE
Saturday, 16 April
PRESAGE

The doorway to the chapel shivered; the wood splintered, and with a mighty crash, the door blew inwards. Her friends had told her to run. They were expendable. She was not.

When the screaming began, she was already running in terror through the cobweb-festooned archway and down the dank torch-lit staircase. At the edge of the catacombs, she paused and listened, her ears primed to catch every tiny sound.

Above her in the church, she could hear the terrified squeals and shrieks of her companions. She wanted to scream too from the horror of their pursuit but knew instinctively that her only hope of escape depended on her silence. Taking a shallow breath of the lifeless air, she looked into the shadowy catacombs with a sense of dread.

The ceiling quivered and groaned, and small stones showered down upon her head, shaken loose by some ponderous weight moving above her. The stinging sensation jerked her from stupor, and wrenching a firebrand from its holder on the wall, she fled into the necropolis. The walls began to vibrate with a low, ugly sound and the floor humped and rolled beneath her feet, but she kept running.

Skulls poured from the walls, blocking her path, and skeletons fell from recesses, reaching for her with outstretched arms. A bone knocked the torch from her hand, and she was alone in the dark. Losing her footing, she fell head first into the waiting bone pile.

Emma Cameron woke up screaming. A cold wind blew in her face, and she was drenched with a film of perspiration. Gathering her senses, she looked up at the open window banging on its hinges. Switching on the bedside light, she got up and closed the window.

She turned back towards the bed and glanced at the clock. It was half past five. She'd better get a move on. Jim Lynch, her partner in the market-stall business, would be picking her up at six. Grabbing her bathrobe from the back of the door, she made her way to the shower.

The hot water made her feel better but did nothing to dispel the terror of her dream. The nightmare had filled her with dread, and returning to her bedroom, she sensed an aura of menace still lingering in the room. She peered nervously in the dressing-table mirror. Her emerald eyes were swollen, surrounded with shadows, and her heart-shaped face was drawn and pale. "You look like shit," she said to her reflection and dabbed make-up on her cheeks to hide the freckles that looked more like age spots than Celtic heritage and thirty years of sun exposure. She brushed back her long red hair and tied it in a ponytail and then put on a T-shirt and a pair of jeans.

When she got downstairs, the cats were crying and scratching at the door, so she let them out and watched uneasily as they fled into the misty hollows of the garden. Were they running from her nightmare too?

She felt a strange reluctance to go back inside. Her house felt alien, as if another power had taken up residence there without her knowledge. Telling herself she was imagining things, she went back to the kitchen to make a strong cup of tea to calm her nerves and sat listlessly down at the table.

Her father had died nine months ago, leaving her The Goblins in his will. Emma had mixed feelings about moving back into her childhood home; the eighteenth-century thatched cottage had always held a hint of terror for her as a child, but being on the verge of homelessness after her divorce, it had come as a godsend.

The house had been unoccupied since her father's death, and the two-acre garden had been neglected and overgrown. When she had moved in at the end of September, she asked her neighbours Dave and Maggie Forbes if they knew of anyone to help her get the place in order. They suggested their friend Jim Lynch, and she used the small sum of money she had received with the house to hire Jim and pay for the repairs. He had fixed the plumbing and restored the greenhouses and grounds in under a month, but the supplies were so expensive, even in the DIY stores, that they had almost drained her cash. Needing an income and seeing Jim also was out of work, she had suggested that they utilise the glasshouses and go into the market-garden business together. He had jumped at the chance, and things had started well, but the government's new austerity measures took a lot of money out of people's pockets, and their business had suffered as a consequence.

A few minutes later, she heard Jim's van pull up outside.

"Mornin', Em," he said cheerfully as he came into the kitchen.

Jim Lynch was a tall blond man in his late thirties with an athletic physique; bull neck; broad shoulders; long, ruddy face; and impish, tawny eyes. His hair was tied in a single braid that reached halfway down his back.

"What's up?" he asked with concern upon seeing her haggard face.

"I had a terrible dream and woke up screaming," she replied, gently pressing the right side of her face with her fingers. "And my jaw's bloody painful."

"What's that from?"

"I must have been grinding my teeth all night."

"You sure you don't want to go back to bed? I can 'andle the market on my own."

3

"No!" she answered quickly. She warmed her trembling hands on her teacup. "I don't want to stay here on my own. The house is getting on my nerves."

"Well, 'ow about I make some breakfast? 'Avin somethin' to eat might make you feel a bit better." Jim took off his jacket.

Emma nodded. "I would, if you're going to make it. There's fresh tea in the pot."

"So, what was it about the nightmare that frightened you so much?"

"I was being hunted, and everywhere I tried to hide . . . it found me. All I remember is running and my heart pounding." She shivered. "It's left me a bit shaky."

"What was 'untin' you?" he asked, taking eggs and butter out of the fridge.

"I don't know," she said slowly, "but it sapped my energy inside and out. And it was trying to absorb me when I woke up. Whatever it was, it wanted me dead. I'm frightened. I think there's something in—" Her cup suddenly slipped out of her shaking fingers, spilling tea over her jeans. "Shit! That's all I need," she exclaimed, looking down at her pants. "Now I'll have to change."

She went upstairs, and when she got back, Jim set two boiled eggs in front of her. "Do you want your toast cut up into soldiers like mine?"

Emma gave a little laugh. "For crying out loud, I'm not a bloody invalid."

"I'm just tryin' to be 'elpful! And I did make you laugh." Jim chortled, smearing thick layer of butter on his mutilated toast. "Hmm, should've done this before I cut the bread," he said, examining his buttery fingers.

Emma laughed again. She was feeling better now that Jim was there. He was a great support to her. Being a Taurus and anchored to the earth, he was a perfect complement to her airy Geminian traits—and he was a vegetarian too, so there were no dietary issues when they ate together.

After clearing away the breakfast things, they got ready to leave. "We'd better get a move on," Jim said, looking at the clock, "otherwise we'll miss the night nurses on their way 'ome from the 'ospital. I'll meet you in the van."

"Coming," Emma said, and grabbing a scarf and jacket off the peg, she locked up and followed him outside.

The church clock in Oakham chimed seven when they pulled into the market square. "Another grey day," Jim remarked as he opened the back of the van and pulled out plastic crates full of honey, nuts, and grains.

"Gosh, the road is quiet," Emma said, looking along the nearly deserted high street. "I hope we take some money today. The bills are due."

"Money is tight," Jim agreed. "I 'ate to see what the electricity bill is. The 'eater's been on in the green'ouse for days."

The morning dragged on, and trade was poorer than usual.

"It's almost noon and there's no one about," he said dolefully, looking around the square. "I could do with some comfort food. 'Ow about you?"

Emma nodded. "Me too."

"I'll pay." Jim took a bank note from his pocket. "'Ere's a tenner. Go and get a bite to eat at the White Lion. I'll 'old the fort. Grab me a toasted cheese."

Emma walked along the high street past the quaint and brightly painted shops to the junction. There were only two pubs in easy reach of the market, and their normal haunt, the Horse and Jockey, had been closed for several weeks since a kitchen fire.

The White Lion was on the corner where the high street met Blood Lane. The seventeenth-century coaching inn stood sheer to the street, and its wide covered archway on one side led to a tiled courtyard and stables round the back. The building reeked of intrigue and decay, and behind the sagging brick, Emma sensed a brooding presence frowning from the latticed windows at the cobbled street below.

The pub door opened and two middle-aged women stepped outside accompanied by warm and savoury aromas from the dining room. "Hello," they said, smiling and holding the door open. "Are you going in?"

Emma nodded and, quickly dismissing any misgivings she might have about the pub, stepped inside.

The room was crowded with locals, some sitting on stools at the bar and others at tables eating lunch. A group of actors from the playhouse dressed as Georgian fops in frock coats and frilly shirts were leaning on the bar having a drink before the afternoon performance. Noticing a couple gathering their shopping bags to leave, Emma made a beeline for the table, almost colliding with the waitress who scurried in the same direction.

"Sorry!" the woman exclaimed. "I'm run off my feet. Sit yourself down. Now what can I be getting for you?" she said, giving the table a quick wipe. She took a pad from her pocket and jotted down Emma's order. "I'll be right back with your wine."

Within minutes, the waitress was back with a tray. "Your drink," she said as she set the glass on the table. "Your food won't be a minute."

The landlord came out from behind the bar and stoked the fire. "Getting a bit chilly in here. There's nothing better than wood heat," he said to the customers at the bar.

"Strange how it got cold all of a sudden," one of them said. "There's a draught coming from somewhere."

Sipping her wine, Emma looked around. An older man with thinning hair sat down with a group of friends at the adjoining table. It was Joe Smith, the village blacksmith, though she hardly recognised him. His haggard face was grey and the air around him held a pall of fear that seemed to saturate the room. Almost immediately the crowd thinned out, and she watched uneasily as most of the regulars downed their pints and left.

"Your sandwich," the waitress said, putting a plate and cutlery in front of Emma.

"Well, Joe, what's going on?" a man said with concern. His friends leant closer, and Tom, the postman, lit a cigarette.

Compelled to listen to what Joe had to say, Emma inched her chair nearer to their table and eavesdropped on the conversation.

After taking a furtive look around the bar, Joe turned his haunted face towards his friends. "I 'ad a bad fright on my way 'ome from 'ere last night," he said hoarsely. "Me and Betty got to the last streetlight in the village, the one before the pathway to the ruins, and without warnin', Betty stops dead. I nearly tripped over 'er. She was starin' forwards into the darkness and growlin'. Then she backed away and 'id behind my legs. I knew somethin' was up and it weren't good, so I tried to turn round and go back to the village, but the air got so cold I couldn't move. Then the streetlight went out and we was alone in the dark." A long silence followed, and Emma noticed that Joe was staring into space.

"Joe? Joe!" Tom gently nudged his arm. "Are you all right?"

Joe glowered around the table. "Alone in the dark . . . no, we weren't alone. Everythin' started glowin'. I could 'ear 'oof beats and a rattlin' sound." There was another long silence.

"Joe! What happened next?" Wally, the butcher, asked nervously.

"A little man came dashin' towards me," Joe muttered. "'E was dressed old-time-like, runnin' as if all the 'ounds of 'ell was chasin' him. 'E 'ad long red 'air, and 'is face was green. And then—Oh! For pity's sake." He buried his face in his quivering hands.

Tom put his hand supportively on Joe's shoulder. "You all right, mate?"

Joe violently pushed him away and glared at his friends. "A coach came out of the darkness. It was made of bones, and the driver . . . 'e 'ad no 'ead! 'E was 'oldin' it in 'is 'and!" He gave a terrified shriek and jerked back in his chair.

"What's going on over there?" the landlord shouted from behind the bar. Joe's friends went quiet and looked awkwardly at one another. They got up and said goodbyes in Joe's direction, then nodded to the landlord and hastily left the pub.

The atmosphere was charged with malice and foreboding. Emma shivered; as crazy as it seemed to her rational mind, she felt spiritually connected to Joe's story, and it frightened her. Deciding not to stay a moment longer, she drained her glass and headed to the back door, leaving her untouched sandwich on the table.

Stepping out into the courtyard, she held her breath in astonishment. A soft green light lay over the tiled yard, and the brick outbuildings gleamed a warm red under a stunning turquoise sky. Across the yard, she saw a swaying sea of golden daffodils growing by the garden wall. The brilliance of the flush caught her eye and then captured her whole attention.

CHAPTER TWO

TREVELYAN

From a world outside of time and space, Trevelyan shadowed Emma. The mortal shared his faerie resonance, and there were so few humans left now that carried the gift of second sight. He needed Emma's help desperately; she was critical to his plans. He sensed her thoughts. She had been uneasy all day. 'Twas true, he had sprung the latch on the window and blown the air to make it bang against the frame, but he had to wake her. She was in great danger and he could wait no longer. Resonating with the vibration of Emma Florence Cameron, Trevelyan of Wessex stepped into the human world.

A figure about three feet high emerged from the flowers and glided towards Emma. He was perfectly proportioned, had smooth olive skin, reminiscent of a Mediterranean complexion, and was elegantly dressed as a Georgian-style gentleman in a dark-blue velvet frock coat, breeches, a lace shirt and cuffs, cream stockings, and buckled shoes. His silver hair was tied back with a dark ribbon, and on his head sat a fancy blue tricorne hat with two rows of silver braid around the edges. *Must be one of the actors from the theatre*, Emma thought as he approached.

He smiled, and she heard a voice speaking in her head. "Emma Cameron, I need your help."

She was just about to answer him when a straggler from the bar rudely nudged her aside. "What are you doing standing in the way of the door like that? Are you daydreaming, lady?" he asked. His raspy voice and his hot breath on her cheek brought Emma to her senses.

"Sorry," she said, moving aside so he could pass.

The courtyard suddenly became grey, and a cold wind blew through it. Gone was the sun, the gladness, and the vibrancy of the daffodils. Rubbing her eyes, Emma looked around the courtyard wondering what was going on. It was empty now, and there was no sign of the little gentleman she'd seen. Had she imagined it?

Jim waved when he saw her. "Did you remember my sandwich? I'm starvin'."

"Sandwich! Oh! I'm sorry. I heard a horrible story in the bar and totally forgot about your sandwich and mine," she said, remembering that she'd left hers on the table. "Joe the blacksmith, do you know him?"

"I've 'eard of 'im, but I wouldn't know 'im from Adam if I saw 'im."

"He used to shoe my horse. He was in the pub. I hardly recognised him. He was sitting hunched over at a table telling his friends about something he'd seen on the way home from the pub last night." Emma paused for a moment and then went on to tell Jim what she had overheard.

"Oakham's a queer place and no mistake," Jim replied. "My uncle Jack lived in the village all 'is life, and growin' up 'e told me a lot of stories about local people seein' phantom coaches and the like. There was a big fight between the Round'eads and the Cavaliers by the old church, so I'm not surprised Joe saw somethin' by the footpath to the ruins."

"Do you know anything about the history of the ruins?"

"Not much. I know the chapel was built in the twelve 'undreds on an old Roman site. It's a place I avoided as a kid. Uncle Jack told me that a few years back, when the council was doin' a bit of clearin' around the church, they dug up some coffins. Some of the people 'ad been buried alive and 'ad tried to scratch their way out; 'ad wood splinters under their fingernails. I didn't sleep well for weeks after 'e told me that."

"Oh God!" Emma gasped, internalizing the feeling of suffocation.

"Oakham's a spooky place. I don't 'old with them people that say ghosts and the like are all rubbish. I 'aven't ever seen anythin' supernatural myself round 'ere, but that don't mean nothin'. Plenty of others 'ave."

"Something strange happened to me on the bridle path a few years ago near those ruins. See the scar on my lip?"

"Yes, I can see it," Jim said, peering at her face. "What 'appened?"

"I was riding my horse along the track, and as I got level with the ruin, a rose briar struck me in the face. The scratch was deep and bled like hell. Something was laughing as the thorn ripped through my flesh." She looked at him with haunted eyes. "I heard it as plain as day. Something was out to hurt me, and hearing Joe's story brought it all back again." She rubbed her hands together nervously. "I know this is going to sound crazy, but while I was listening to Joe's story, I felt that I was connected to it in some way. I was so preoccupied when I left the pub that I'm not really sure about anything that went on, but I think something happened to me in the courtyard."

"'Ang on a minute, Em," Jim said, moving away to help a customer at the stall.

"Nice few quid, there," he said when he returned, putting the money in his apron pocket. "You were sayin'?"

"I left the pub by the back door," Emma continued. "There was a strange light on the courtyard, and then I saw a little man coming towards me. He must have been from the playhouse because he was dressed in the same period costume as the other actors in the bar. Anyway, as he got up to me . . . he disappeared."

Jim raised an eyebrow and cracked, "Disappeared, eh! 'Ow many did you 'ave to drink?"

"I said I don't expect you to take me seriously, but that's what happened."

"Em, Joe's story rattled you, that's all. You were already on edge from the nightmare. You were probably mistaken and 'e dodged round you."

"Yes, but he called me by name," Emma responded.

"Everyone knows you at the market."

"They don't know me as Emma Cameron."

"Come on, Em. You're stressin' over nothin'."

"Perhaps you're right. And I'm sorry again about your sandwich."

"Just as long as you're not tryin' to put me on a diet." Jim laughed, turning his attention to a broken bag of dried figs that had fallen off the stall.

The sky stayed cloudy as the afternoon dragged on.

"It's after six," Jim announced, looking at his watch. "Looks like rain. Let's pull the stand down and go 'ome. There's no point in 'anging round 'ere." In a few minutes they were packed up and ready to leave. Emma disappeared for a moment and came back with a bunch of red roses.

"Roses!" Jim exclaimed, starting the engine of the van. "We only took thirty quid today, and that barely pays the petrol. And you spent business money on flowers!"

Emma flushed and said awkwardly, "You know how much roses mean to me."

"Well, let's 'ope things pick up, or we'll be washin' dishes somewhere. Can't eat roses, you know."

They drove along the twisty lanes in stony silence. Emma was still smarting from Jim's reprimand. She was the one who had put up the initial investment for the stock, and a couple of quid wasn't going to break them. But he was right, she admitted to herself. Every penny added up. Trying to make amends, she asked, "Would you like to stay for dinner?"

Jim smiled. "That would be nice. I've got a few things to do in the green'ouse, so it'll fit in nicely. Appreciate it, Em," he said as they pulled up in her driveway.

"I'll take the flowers indoors and then go with you," she said as they headed to the kitchen door. She put the roses in water and a pecan roast from the freezer in the oven and then joined Jim outside.

On the way to the greenhouse, Jim stopped in astonishment at the broad beans. "They were only two inches 'igh yesterday. They must be all of six today," he said, pulling thoughtfully on his earlobe. "It must be all the 'orse shit I dug in."

Emma stared at the beans, aware of a nebulous green glow around them. She knew it was an energy field and wondered if Jim could see it.

"Jim, don't think I'm daft, but I can see a light around the beans."

"I'm glad you said that," he said, staring at her in confusion. "I thought I was seein' somethin' that weren't there. What the 'ell is it?"

"It's an aura," Emma said. "There are electromagnetic fields around everything in existence. My grandma Emily taught me to see them. By looking at the colours around animals, people and plants, even stones, she could tell if they were sick or healthy."

"You mean a stone's got an aura?"

"Yes, everything in this world has an energy field, including us. Our emotions colour our auras too. Haven't you heard the expressions 'green with envy', 'red with rage', 'in a blue mood'?"

"Sure."

"These phrases are actually subconscious acknowledgements of auras."

"Well, I'm buggered."

"I don't think you'd like to be buggered, Jim." She sniggered, nudging him in the side with her elbow.

"What's wrong with 'bugger'? My mum and uncles say it all the time."

"It means 'to sodomise'. It's old English."

Jim's eyebrows shot up in surprise. "Oh! No, that's not a nice word. I'll tell Mum." He laughed. "I can just see the look on 'er face when I tell 'er."

"Just like the look on yours, eh!" Emma chuckled.

When they got to the greenhouse, they were in for another shock. The radish they had planted a week ago had matured and pushed up from the ground. "This ain't natural," Jim mumbled, staring at Emma nervously. "The glow's in 'ere as well."

There was something about the quality of the light that was similar to the beans, the courtyard, and the little man who had emerged from the flowers; it felt the same.

"They're the size of golf balls," Jim said, staring at them. "I 'ope they're not woody."

"Try one," Emma suggested.

"I don't like to, Em," he said warily. "As I said, it ain't natural for things to grow that fast."

"Then I will." She bent down and pulled one up, wiped it on her jeans, and bit into it.

Jim watched her anxiously. "Well?"

"It's very good," Emma said, smiling. "And they're ready."

"'Ere, give me an 'and to pull some, then. The Red Lion will buy as many of these as we can bundle up. That'll really 'elp us financially. Thank you," he said loudly to a radish.

When they had finished, Emma went back indoors and poured herself a large whisky. The glow she'd seen in the courtyard was the same green light that was now evident in the garden. The little man she'd seen had asked her to help him, and she wondered who he was.

It had gone seven by the time the roast was cooked and ready to be served. Emma had just finished laying the table when Jim came in from the greenhouse. "For starters we've got twenty bunches. I've put them in the van, and I'll drop them off to the Red Lion on my way 'ome." Taking the band from his hair, he redid his ponytail and then sat down to eat. "What we got 'ere, then?" he said, looking eagerly at the food.

"Pecan roast, salad, fresh bread, and butter from Dave and Maggie next door."

"Did they call round?"

"They must have while we were in the greenhouse. The butter was on the table when I got back, and they left twenty dozen eggs for next week's markets too. Strange we didn't hear them."

"You'd 'ave thought they would've 'ung around," he agreed. "Or come lookin' for us in the garden, seein' the van's in the driveway." He sniffed. "Gosh! This smells good." He tucked in. "I didn't used to care what I ate, just as long as it didn't 'ave a face. But you changed all that white-bread and baked-beans business. Your veggie cookin's the best in the world." His tawny eyes glowed with warmth and appreciation.

"I don't know about that," Emma replied, "but thanks."

After they had finished eating, they retired to the sitting room. Jim laid a fire and put a match to it, and soon it was blazing. "I'll bring in some more logs," he said, going to the door, "and then I'll 'ave to get off 'ome. I've a few jobs I've gotta do for Mum."

A few minutes later, he was back with a basket of wood. "This should keep the fire goin' for a while." He put the carrier on the floor. "I'm off now. I'll see you tomorrow. Let's 'ope what's goin' on in the garden keeps goin' on."

After Jim had left, Emma made a cup of tea and took it with her to the sitting room. Settling into a chair by the fire, she thought about what she'd overheard in the pub and tried to figure out what had frightened her. She had still been freaked out from the nightmare, and she wondered if she'd read more into Joe's story than was actually there. The dark window caught her eye, and for some reason she was afraid someone was looking in. Putting down her teacup, she got up and closed the drapes, shutting out the night.

CHAPTER THREE

FORESHADOWING

The logs crackled merrily in the fireplace as Emma sat back down on the sofa. Her eyes roamed to the familiar things from her childhood: The studded velvet wing chairs and Chippendale sofa with its high scrolled arms and graceful lines. The oak bookcase with its sphinx-shaped pull-backs and elegant bracket feet flanked by the matching pair of delicate, hand-carved walnut lowboys that were her favourite little tables. The room was womblike, and she felt safe and comfortable in its warm, closeted embrace.

Then she remembered the roses. They were still in the kitchen. Downing her tea, she got up and went to get them.

When she was growing up, her father had always changed the roses in the hallway on Saturdays, ready for any visitors on Sunday morning. It was tradition, and lately she had followed in his footsteps. Now, the roses had become a ritual of remembrance—for Daddy.

Taking the faded blooms to the kitchen, Emma carefully shook off the petals into a large china potpourri crock that had been her grandmother's, and after a quick look round to make sure everything was in order, she put out the lights and went upstairs to bed.

The next morning, the phone rang at six o'clock. The call was from Totally Nuts, the health-food shop in Basingstoke; they wanted to buy some organic salad vegetables. Emma was so surprised by the order that she forgot to ask them how they had got her number.

"I've had two requests for salad already today, Jim," she said gleefully when he arrived. "One from the Coach and Horses for their restaurant and the other from the health-food shop. I wonder what's going on."

Jim thought for a moment. "Must be the mystics fair that starts tomorrow. Most of them think out of the box, so there would be a call for fresh organic food."

The orders flowed thick and fast all morning. Jim came in for lunch and, sitting down at the table, said, "Want to 'ear somethin' strange?"

"What is it?" she asked, putting an onion quiche on the table.

"Well, it's nothin' really. It's that I've got twenty-four bunches of radishes in the delivery van, and there's still tons in the green'ouse. I don't remember plantin' all those radishes, but I must've done." He thumbed his chin thoughtfully. "The spinach and lettuce are ready as well. I can 'ardly believe it. What do you think is goin' on?"

"I don't know. But I wish they had the mystics fair every week," Emma said. "We wouldn't have to worry about buying roses then!"

"No need to be sarcastic, Em," Jim said with a hurt expression. "I was only tryin' to point somethin' out that's all. Anyway, we've got almost five 'undred quid's worth of orders in the invoice book and countin'."

"That's wonderful!"

"If you don't mind me askin', what's this preoccupation with roses?"

"I don't know," she replied defensively, toying with her salad. "It was something Daddy always did, and the hallway looked so bare, so I thought I'd start doing it." There was an awkward silence.

"I was just wonderin', that's all." He smiled. "This quiche is wonderful."

"The sun's out," Emma said, looking through the window. "We can do a bit of gardening this afternoon, and when we're done outside, we'll do some packing for the market."

It was nine o' clock by the time they'd finished packing the dried fruit and nuts. "Better be goin' 'ome now, Em," Jim said as he put the spare bags back in a box. "I'll see you tomorrow. Let's 'ope the weather's as nice as it's been today." He gave her a hug and let himself out the kitchen door.

Emma locked it behind him. She had a nightcap and then went off to bed. Her dreams were a blur of familiar images of the house, but the hallway in particular seemed to hold unpleasant connotations. When she woke, she had the distinct impression she had experienced more than she could remember.

The orders for vegetables flowed thick and fast in the days that followed. Emma was so busy picking and bunching produce that the strange episode at the White Lion quickly faded from her mind.

Saturday's market was almost empty, but a steady line of regulars came to their stall. At noon, trade began to taper off.

"You 'ungry?" Jim asked, counting the cash and putting it in a money bag.

Emma nodded.

"As there's a bit of a lull, why don't you go and get some lunch? Grab me a toasted cheese and onion sandwich to go—and don't forget this time!"

"I won't," Emma said as she walked away.

She decided to have lunch at the Greenery. The cafe was down the street a ways in the opposite direction from the White Lion. She had walked about two hundred yards in a funk before she realised she had lost her bearings. A pub sign creaked eerily above her in the windless air. Emma looked up and saw the white lion trampling on a crown. The sudden realisation of where she was shocked her. This was the very place she had wanted to avoid.

Turning to go, she glanced up at the inn. The red-brick fascia was warm and welcoming, and the diamond-pane windows glittered gladly in the sun. There was such charm about the place that Emma wondered why she had thought it unfriendly and forbidding. She turned the doorknob and went inside.

The bar was filled with the regular market crowd, and after ordering a beer, a toasted cheese sandwich for herself, and one for Jim to go, Emma sat on a stool at the bar next to Tom, the postman.

"Terrible thing about Joe and little Betty," Tom said to the landlady, sliding his empty glass across the counter.

"Old Joe. He won't be shoeing horses anymore, bless him. This place just isn't going be the same without him," she replied.

Emma turned to Tom in dismay. "Joe Smith, the blacksmith? What happened to him?"

"The milkman found him dead early this morning, and his little dog too," Tom said, picking up his fresh pint. "They were lying in the ditch by the bridleway to the old ruin. It was the same place he saw them ghosts. I was in here last night with Joe, and he was acting strange and nervous like; kept looking over his shoulder. His wife was away visiting her sister. I said to him, 'Why don't you come home and stay the night with me and Doris?' But he wouldn't hear of it. He was still here when I left. He must have died on the way home." Tom was quiet for a minute. "Some folks in the village are saying that those devils he told us about last Saturday came to claim him." He took a big slurp of beer and belched loudly. "Perhaps when he was telling about them evil things he saw, one of them was listening and decided to shut him up."

Emma felt icy fingers creep up her neck and crawl across her scalp. The waitress put her sandwich and Jim's takeaway box on the bar, but she was too preoccupied with Joe's death to notice.

A few of the patrons were leaving through the back entrance, and instead of going out the front door, Emma got up and followed them distractedly into the sunlit courtyard, leaving the sandwiches behind.

The moment she stepped outside, the sun went behind a cloud and the light dimmed. The red-brick outbuildings with their sagging roofs seemed threatening and surreal. Shrinking back into the doorway, she hammered on the door, and getting no answer, desperately turned the handle, trying to get in. It was locked. There was only one way back to the market.

After taking a couple of strides across the tiled yard, Emma got the impression that something was observing her every move, like a hawk watches a rabbit before it strikes. With a deep breath, she made a headlong dash across the courtyard to the cobbled street ahead.

Her toe caught the edge of a broken flagstone and she fell, slamming her head against the pavement and scoring her hands and knees. Heaviness smothered her, pinning her body to the ground, chilling her blood, and crushing the air from her lungs. Her throat constricted and her breath came in short, choking gasps. She was about to pass out when the pressure abruptly eased. The weight was gone. She struggled up and stumbled across the yard and out into the street then ran for her life, not stopping until she reached the noisy bustle of the market square.

The smile on Jim's face faded as she walked up to him. "Em! Are you okay? Did you fall over?" he asked, eyeing her torn jeans.

"I got frightened in the yard behind the pub," she said, clinging to him. "I knew I had to get out of there, and I tripped and fell trying to get away."

"Look, there's Ada Jenkins across the way." He pointed to a portly woman buying geraniums at the plant stall opposite. "No doubt we'll be 'er next stop. I'll ask 'er to give you a lift 'ome. All right?"

Emma nodded.

"Nice radishes," Ada said as she approached the stand. "I could see them glowing from across the way. I'll take three bunches. My

Bertie loves radishes. He'll be pleased as punch. Give me some lettuce as well."

"Ada, would you mind givin' Emma a lift 'ome?" Jim asked as he put the produce in her basket. "She fell down and scraped 'er knees."

"Of course," Ada replied kindly, patting Emma on the arm. "Are you all right, dear?"

Emma nodded. "Just a bit shook up, that's all."

"I'll be over as soon as I can," Jim called as Emma limped away with Ada Jenkins.

Emma was still shaky when Ada dropped her off. "You sure you're all right, Emma? I could run you to the emergency room at the hospital if you want. Or how about you lie down and I'll make you some strong sweet tea?" Ada offered.

"No thanks. I'll be all right, though the side of my face is sore." Emma gingerly touched her cheek. "I'll be fine once I get into the house."

Once inside, she went straight to the bathroom and gently pulled off her blue jeans. The wounds on her knees were deep and starting to bruise, and it took a good ten minutes to clean the grit from them and apply a stinging antiseptic. When she was finished, she put on a pair of loose trousers and went downstairs to the sitting room. Turning on the wall lights, she lay down on the settee with the cats. The next thing she knew, Jim was leaning over her, gently shaking her arm.

"Em, it's me. 'Ow are you feelin'?"

"I must have fallen asleep. What time is it?"

"It's after four. I lit the fire. It was a bit chilly in 'ere and I didn't want you gettin' cold. 'Ere's a cup of tea, love." He pointed to a tray on the sofa table. "My mum swears by it. Sweet strong tea for shock."

"You sound like Ada," Emma mumbled, sitting up and rubbing her eyes.

"Must be an old lady thing, and 'ere I am advocatin' it." He chuckled and perched on the end of the settee, putting his arm around her shoulder. "Oh, Em. I thought you were goin' to the Greenery, love. 'Ow'd you end up at the pub?"

Emma wrapped her hands around the warm china teacup. "I don't know," she said slowly. "It was so strange. I walked in the opposite direction, and suddenly there it was. The pub looked so inviting I couldn't stop myself. I had to go in . . . and there's something else that's unnerved me."

"What's that?"

"This morning, Joe and his little dog were found dead by the footpath to the ruin, in the exact same spot where he had those awful visions."

"No shit!" Jim nervously rubbed the back of his neck. "'Ow'd it 'appen? Do you know?"

Emma shook her head. "No, but it's scared me. I know it's irrational, but I can't get Joe's death off my mind. I think whatever killed Joe . . . killed Emily."

"Now, come off it, Em!" Jim said sharply. "Your grandma was really old and died of an 'eart attack. 'Ow can you believe what 'appened to 'er 'ad any bearin' on Joe? Be sensible! Put them silly notions out of your 'ead."

"That's not what Emily's friends told me when I went to Scotland for the funeral last month," Emma fired back. "They said she was killed by a witch on the first day of spring and that the look on her face was so dreadful that the priest who found her was admitted to hospital for his nerves."

"A witch! Come off it." Jim pulled on his earlobe and stared at her. "That's all old wives' tales and superstition. Pull yourself together. That priest's nervous problems might not've 'ad anythin' to do with Emily. You're makin' assumptions, and I think you're takin' this too far."

"Jim!" Emma said indignantly, looking him straight in the eye. "Emily was a herbalist and healer. She knew a lot of things about old wives' tales, as you put it, that happen to be true."

"'Ave it your way, Em," he said, getting up. "I've got things to do." From the corner of her eye, she saw him disappearing into the kitchen, and she followed him, curious to see what he was up to.

On the table were some fresh vegetables, a box of pasta spirals, a bottle of soy sauce, and a recipe book.

"What's all this? Where did you get this cookbook? It's not one of mine," she said, examining the cover.

"After I packed up, I went lookin' round the market," Jim said as he dropped some pasta into a pot of boiling water. "I found *Vegetarian Cuisine* at the stand sellin' second-hand books, so I bought it. And as we took in over nine hundred quid today, I thought I'd make us vegetable rotini for dinner tonight." He came to the table and pointed out the recipe in the book. "It's a nice cookbook all right. It only cost a quid, and you can't beat that for a bargain."

"We took nine hundred pounds! Are you serious?" Emma's eyebrows shot up in surprise at their sudden change in fortune.

"That's why I'm back so early. I sold out of eveythin'." He grinned. "Yep! I couldn't Adam and Eve it."

Emma winced but said nothing. She loathed Cockney rhyming slang.

"After you left, people appeared from everywhere and I sold out, lock, stock, and barrel. It's the best day we ever 'ad. We can pay a few bills and put a little away. Dave from next door'll be back next week. You know 'ow he likes to run the market, sell 'is eggs and butter. Maybe we can take a break for a few days. Go to the coast or somethin'."

"We need new tyres on the van," she reminded him. "The ones we're driving on are barely legal. I'll just put them on my credit card and be done with it."

"Sure you want to do that?" He gazed at her. "Pay all that bloody interest? Let me do a bit of phonin' round. I can get us some second-'and ones pretty cheap, good ones, mind, just to get us by. It's off season at the coast, so accommodation will be pretty cheap as well." He picked up a wooden spoon and handed it to her. "'Elp me 'ere a minute and stir the veggies. This is the first time I've ever made anythin' like this. I 'ope it tastes okay." He drained the pasta into a colander.

"It really smells delicious, Jim," Emma said as she stirred.

Dave and Maggie had done her a real favour when they had recommended Jim, she thought, and she'd come to depend on him an awful lot, perhaps too much. He was a giver, not a taker, and she wondered why he didn't have a girlfriend. He wasn't gay. She knew from little hints he dropped that if she had encouraged him romantically, he would have moved in on her straight away. She didn't want to hurt his feelings with an outright rejection, so she made sure not to lead him on. They were friends and it was going to stay that way.

"Em!"

"What?" she said, turning round.

"I thought we'd celebrate with this." He brought out a bouquet of roses and a bottle of champagne from behind his back.

"Oh, Jim! Thank you!" She put the roses in a vase and fetched two long, narrow glasses from the cabinet.

Jim popped the cork and filled the glasses. "To us!" he cried, clinking his glass against hers.

After dinner, they took their drinks to the sitting room. Jim put a Debussy CD on the stereo.

"Thank you for making dinner, thank you for the roses, and another thank you for lighting the fire," she said, sinking into the sofa. The haunting strains of the music stole around the room.

"'Prelude to an Afternoon with a Faun', your favourite," he said as he sat down beside her. He slid his arm along the top of the couch and rested it lightly on her shoulders.

The grandfather clock in the hallway chimed eight bells. "Is there anythin' you need me to do before I go?" he asked, brushing his fingertips down her neck. "Or, do you want me to stay?"

"No. I'm going to be off to bed here pretty soon," she said, shrinking away from his touch. "I'm tired. All the champagne has gone to my head."

"Well, I'd best be goin' then." He gave her a peck on the cheek and lingered for a moment on the sofa, and then with a sigh, he got up and left.

Emma went into the kitchen to tidy up. She adored Jim to bits, but she wasn't interested in him physically. He was too rough and ready, and too young. She preferred older men—men with soft manners, cultured voices, and finesse. Besides, she knew that sex was the best way to ruin a business partnership and was determined to steer clear.

There was a quick knock on the kitchen door. *Jim must have forgotten something*, she thought. Opening the door, she gasped. Standing on the step was the little man in Georgian attire she'd seen in the courtyard at the White Lion the week before.

CHAPTER FOUR

SPIRITUAL DYSTOPIA

"Miss Emma, permit me to introduce myself. Trevelyan of Wessex, at your service. May I come in?" he asked in a soft, lilting southern brogue. Emma stared at him curiously. Wessex was the old Saxon name for the southern and western shires of England. Was this little man an actor at the theatre? If so, what did he want with her?

"May I come in?" he enquired again with a smile.

She suddenly realised he was sitting at the kitchen table. Having no knowledge of how he got there, she stared at him uncomfortably. "Excuse me! I don't remember inviting you in."

"Forgive me, but I cannot pass your threshold without an invitation, and did you not indicate with your hand that all was well and I could enter?" He looked at her questioningly.

"No!" Emma answered, shaking her head in confusion. "I don't think I did. I don't know how you got in here, but you need to leave." She pointed to the door.

"I've only just arrived, and we have things to discuss."

"We having nothing to discuss, and you need to leave." She was getting irritated with his cheek. "I think you're playing games with me, and now that you've had your little joke, you'd best be on your way."

"Little joke, eh?" he hissed. "I can assure you, this is no jest. I came to warn you."

"Warn me! Now come off it. I've had enough of this," she said firmly, coming to the table. "Out you go!" As she grabbed his sleeve, a full-body shockwave pushed her backwards. Slowly straightening up, she gaped at him in horror.

"Don't be accosting me in such a threatening manner, m'dear," he said, but not unkindly.

"Tell me what you want and then leave, please."

There was a suspenseful interval of silence. "Emma," Trevelyan said at last. "I was your grandmother Emily's friend for many years. Annie, as I called her. She had the second sight, and I was her mystical inheritance from Faerie."

Emma stiffened. Annie had been her grandmother's middle name. How did he know that? And was he truly from the Otherworld? She thought about the shock when she touched him. Perhaps he was telling the truth, but Emily would have told her about a faerie friend if she had one. "If what you say is true, then why didn't Emily tell me about you?"

"Suffice to say, m'dear, 'twas I who forbade her to tell you about our relationship."

"That's a very convenient answer. Tell me, why?"

"Let us just say that the time was not right. Now that Annie is dead, I left Scotland and came south to introduce myself to you."

"I'm sure she would have told me about you. We kept no secrets from each other," she said doubtfully.

"Annie had many secrets. She knew well the cup and ring marks in the stone, and the special places on the moor where faeries gather, and . . . other things that are not so lightly shared. But I don't have time to beat about the bush, and neither do you," he said with an ominous gleam in his eye. "Your grandmother Annie was murdered, and those responsible for her death are hunting you. But we will not speak of it here in your home." He looked around the room. "Walls have ears."

"This is ridiculous," Emma retorted. "You'd better keep your play-acting for the theatre. Is Trevelyan of Wessex your stage name this time round?"

"Emma, I am not from the playhouse, I—"

"I don't care where you're from," she interrupted. "I really think you should leave. You're frightening me."

"Frightening you?"

"Yes. Now please go."

"Emma," he responded, disregarding her protestations, "Annie was murdered, and so were Joe and his Betty. If you don't heed my warning, you are next."

Emma gasped and swallowed hard. His words resonated with her anxieties about Emily's death, and fear twisted like black smoke inside her. She stared at him nervously. Although he looked solid enough, she sensed a strange, almost fluid energy in his demeanour. Where did he come from? And how did he know so much about Emily and Joe?

As if he was reading her mind, she heard him say, "Accompany me to my house. There I will explain everything. And Emma, m'dear, I have something for you that belonged to Annie."

Emma's lips tightened. "But I have to go to your house before you'll give it to me, right?"

"Yes, m'dear."

"I'm not going anywhere with you," she answered back. "If you have anything to say to me, you can say it here."

"Alas! That is not possible." He took an eyeglass with a long silver handle from his waistcoat pocket and turned it slowly in his fingers.

Emma had an urge to run out of the house and get away from him, but instead she retreated to the sitting room and poured herself a large brandy.

A host of mixed feelings welled up inside her as she gulped the liquor down. How did he get into her home? And what was she doing hiding from him? And was he even real? Pouring another drink, she peered around the door, hoping he was gone, but he was still sitting at the table. For a moment she didn't know what to do. She knocked back the brandy, put the glass on the sideboard, and walked back into the kitchen.

"Ah! M'dear, you have decided to join me, I see," Trevelyan said affably.

Emma was having none of it. "Say what you have to say, and then leave."

"As I said before, I need you to come to my home," he said softly, twirling the eyeglass slowly in his hand. Emma gazed at it. The silver holder caught the light; it was really very pretty.

"My home is only a short distance down the lane. Just a little way down the lane," his lilting voice continued. "Shall we go?"

The spinning eyeglass painted silver spirals in the air. "Where do you live?" she asked, reaching out to touch the spirals as they danced in front of her.

"Not far, m'dear. Come along," he inveigled, moving to the door.

She followed him outside, along the garden path, to the back gate, and then onto the tree-covered bridle path beyond. Trevelyan stopped in the middle of the stony lane and faced her back gate.

"Emma!" a voice called, bringing her to her senses. She realised that she was standing in the lane without a clue how she had got there. Turning her head in the direction of the sound, she saw Dave from next door walking his dog, Minstrel.

"Hello, Emma," Dave said cheerfully as he came alongside her. "What are you up to standing in the lane all on your own? Are you daydreaming, or is it dusk-dreaming?"

"All on your own?" Dave's words hit Emma straight between the eyes. *What about Trevelyan?* she thought uneasily. Why couldn't Dave see him? Perhaps he'd left. Convinced Trevelyan was a hypnotist, she chanced a quick glance where he had been, hoping he had disappeared, but to her disquiet, she saw him smiling at her in amusement.

Minstrel barked excitedly and wagged his tail. "He's behaving strangely," Dave remarked. "Look at him."

Pricking up his ears, the red setter sniffed the air and then bolted forwards, passing the gate and continuing along the lane.

"Minstrel!" Dave called, sprinting after him. "Got to go, Emma!" he shouted over his shoulder.

"Wait!" Emma wailed, but Dave had disappeared. She tried to follow but was glued to the spot like a fly on sticky paper. From the corner of her eye, she could see Trevelyan looking at her.

"Come, Emma. There is nothing to fear, I promise you," he said calmly. "Come!"

Despite his assurances, frightening thoughts flashed through her mind with bewildering rapidity. "You hypnotised me, first to get into my house and now to get me out here," she said angrily. "You've tricked me! I'm going home, without you!"

"Home, m'dear!" he exclaimed. "Yes, we are home! This is an entrance, a gateway betwixt our houses. Come!" He held out his hand.

He's a bloody madman, Emma thought, taking a step backwards, *and he's talking nonsense.* "That's my back gate and my house, not yours."

The gate opened noiselessly, and before she could stop him, Trevelyan took her by the hand and led her into the garden.

"Emma Cameron, welcome to my home," Trevelyan said, fluttering his fingers. "This is the realm of Faerie, an enchanted, timeless land where what was, what is, and what will be walk together hand in hand."

Gasping in awe, Emma looked around. A soft green daylight now lay upon the garden—her garden, but it was exceptionally invigorated. The trees and bushes in the hedgerows were a-flower with dog roses and bramble, and the flower borders rioted in waves of unknown colours, creating faerie-bows in the soft magenta sky. The tension in her shoulders began to fall away, and her body was buoyant, suddenly liberated from the tugging gravity of home.

Then a sudden pang of fear spoiled the paradise. Home! Emma thought of her cats and Jim. What if she couldn't get back to them? Trevelyan had kidnapped her, and all the beauty might be glamour, a contrived vision to blind her. He had taken her outside of time to the Otherworld, and she couldn't get back home, without his help. Was she caught in a child's fairy tale? Imprisoned in the house made of sweet things, waiting to be sacrificed by a demon?

Taking a deep breath, she rounded on him, "You've kidnapped me, and I demand you take me home!" She tried to sound forceful, but her lower lip quivered.

Trevelyan waved his eyeglass and disarmed her protestations with a smile. "Take you home, m'dear? You are home. Why, you're just inside your gate. See for yourself. Your house is yonder."

"No. This may be your house, but it isn't mine. I want you to take me home."

"As you wish, m'dear," Trevelyan said, walking away along the pathway to the house.

Emma's head was spinning with conflicting thoughts and feelings. Events had overtaken sanity, and she wondered for a moment if she was dreaming. Emily had told her that in a dream, she had to face the fear, head-on.

"Wait!" she shouted after him. "Are you an evil wight from the Unseelie Court of Faerie? I know you put the glamour on me."

"Faith! Emma," he said, turning back towards her. "No, I am not from the Unseelie Court. 'Tis true that I had to coerce you into my world, and I apologise for that. But, the end in this case justifies the means." He gazed at her kindly. "All I ask is that you bear with me for a while, and then I will return you safely to your . . ." he hesitated. "Your version of reality."

My version of reality, Emma thought. It seemed so far away now, and if she was mad or dead, or both, it didn't matter anyway.

She watched Trevelyan walk on towards the house but didn't try to follow. Everything around her was the same but as different in its quality as chalk and cheese. How could it be her house? she asked herself. Unless . . . she had a house in Faerie.

After a while of wonderment, she walked slowly along the path, and with every step, the dreamlike quality of her surroundings deepened. The beamed walls of the house gleamed with a richer, deeper hue, and the golden thatch was neatly netted and smothered by climbing roses. Everywhere she looked there were flowers, full of butterflies and bees, and she marvelled at all the fantastic colours she had never seen before.

Going up the steps to the front door, she noticed with surprise that the sign on the house no longer read "The Goblins" but now said "The Sylphs" instead.

The entrance was open, and upon stepping inside, she saw a crystal vase of white roses on the table in the hallway, but she knew the ones she had put out in her hallway were red. Emma gazed at the flowers. They had just been cut; she could see the dew still glistening on the velvet petals.

She found Trevelyan in the sitting room. "Come and sit over here," he said, pointing to her favourite window seat. She sat down on the settle in a daze, trying desperately to adjust to her bizarre situation.

"Would you like a black-raspberry brandy?" Trevelyan asked.

"No thank you," Emma replied, remembering Emily's warning not to eat or drink anything from the Otherworld. Trevelyan may have apologised, but he had abducted her, after all.

"As you wish," Trevelyan said, giving her a sidelong glance. "Tell me, was it your intention to go to the White Lion today at lunchtime?"

"How did you know I went to the White Lion today? Were you stalking me?" she asked, eyeing him warily.

"Stalking! What an odious term!" Trevelyan threw his hands up in the air and gave a derisive laugh. Emma gave a little gasp. The black hole of his mouth was filled with stars, and a shudder passed through her as she realised how utterly alien he was.

"If stalking it was, m'dear, then it saved your life," he said, sitting down beside her.

"Saved my life!" Her eyes went wide with incredulity. "How? What are you talking about?"

"I see from the look upon your face that you do not believe me," Trevelyan said, "but a spell was cast against you today. It drew you to the White Lion and tried to murder you in the courtyard. When you fell and scuffed your knees and hands, they bled a little, and with the blood, a try was made. I was observing you from Faerie, and seeing you were in danger, I rushed to your aid."

Emma shivered, remembering the smothering weight that had pinned her to the ground.

"'Tis the truth, I tell you, as unfortunate as it may be."

"Why me? What have I done?"

"You're special, m'dear."

"Special? In what way?"

"You carry a gene that originates in my world, and because of our kinship, we have a great work to attempt together. 'Tis the reason I glamoured you into Faerie. Forgive me, m'dear, it was a most ungentlemanly thing to do. But now you are here, the vibrations are such that they will quicken your memory of who you are. Then your faerie power will be triggered."

Emma stared at him, her anxiety mounting. She had been tricked and taken away from her reality by a strange little man who had insinuated himself into her life, and now he was telling her a cock-and-bull story. Somehow she had to find a way back to her reality, to her home. Wherever it was.

"Emma!" His voice brought her to attention. "Annie wanted you to have this," he said, handing her a ring.

Emma's blood ran cold as she looked at the gypsy wedding ring with three diamonds set into the gold. "Where did you get this?" she asked accusingly.

"I took it from Annie's finger before they buried her. As I already said, she wanted you to have it."

"You took her wedding ring from her corpse!" Emma stood up, almost knocking him over. "Did you murder Emily?"

"Faith!" Trevelyan said indignantly. "I have told you before. I do not belong to the Unseelie Court of Faerie."

Emma took a deep breath to bring herself back from the verge of panic. Things were going from bad to worse. "All you've done is frighten me," she said at last. "You tell me Emily was murdered and I'm next on some demon's hit list. Then you give me her ring that you took off her dead body. I've had enough. I want to go home now."

"M'dear, I'm not trying to frighten you," Trevelyan answered gently. "I'm trying to wake you up. There is much you need to know, and there are many questions to be answered."

"Be that as it may, I still want to go home. Now!"

"As you please, m'dear," he said calmly, waving her to the door with a sigh. "Let me walk you to the gate."

With no more ado, they left the house and followed the path to the gate, which opened silently as they approached.

"Farewell, m'dear. Until our next meeting." With a tip of his tricorne hat, Trevelyan disappeared.

Emma found herself standing by the back gate. The lane was silent and dismal, and the failing light spoke more of death than life. Gone was the joyous light of Faerie and the gladness of its air, and she felt heavy and depressed as she walked back along the pathway to her house. She suddenly realised that the fear she had felt wasn't coming from Faerie but from herself.

Once inside the kitchen, she glanced at the clock. Only five minutes had elapsed since she'd left with Trevelyan, but she knew he'd taken her out of time for a lot longer than that. She got out the tobacco from a drawer and rolled herself a cigarette and then went to the sitting room. The fire in the grate had burnt down, leaving a bed of glowing coals. She pulled a chair over to the inglenook and sat smoking for a while, dwelling on the unfathomable sequence of events that had overtaken her. The happenings of the last few days had rushed in on her with such force that she didn't know fact from fiction anymore.

The coals in the fireplace began to turn to ash, and the room felt gloomy. Stubbing out her cigarette in the ashtray, she took a last look round, put the guard before the fire, and went upstairs to bed.

The window had come open again and the room was cold and draughty. Shivering in the unexpected chill, Emma shut the window, locked it, and closed the curtains. She put on her cotton nightdress, switched off the light, and got into bed.

She lay there in the dark trying to sleep, but her mind raced with thoughts of Trevelyan and how her understanding of reality had suddenly been shattered. She felt tense and stressed, and after a few minutes, she got up. There were sleeping pills in the medicine cabinet left over from the time of her divorce, and she took down the bottle from the cupboard in the bathroom. There were three pills left. One would have been enough, but she decided she'd take two. That would knock her out. Putting the tablets in her mouth, she slugged down a glass of water and then went back to bed. Her dreams were frightening and ugly. She stared at her hands as Emily had taught her and tried to wake herself up.

She was outside in the dark. It was raining, and a bitter, biting wind flattened her cotton nightdress against her naked body. She watched as her foot automatically jerked forward, followed by the other, and in terror, she realised she had no control over her body as it lurched across muddy fields. Her toe hit a rock and she went sprawling in the wet mud. Struggling up, she looked around. She was on a track, and a few yards away, glimmering in the gloom, was the ruined chapel. A scream escaped her throat when she realised where she was—just a hundred yards away from where Joe had died. She tried to turn and run but found she could scarcely lift her feet.

A brilliant violet mist rose from the soggy ground, clawing up the broken masonry around her, swirling above her head, and blocking out the stars. The dazzling light slowly coalesced, and she felt the foul-smelling air rhythmically contract and expand. Desperately, she tried to force her feet across the fallen stones, but still she couldn't move. She was trapped.

A soft voice in her mind commanded her to run. The terror that held her spellbound broke, and she ran, rushing blindly back along the bridle path towards the pub. Reaching the road, she found a telephone box and ran in, slamming the door behind her. Emma dialled the operator to reverse the charges, and after an agonising wait, the call went through.

"Jim! Help!" she screamed into the phone when he answered. "I'm in a phone box opposite the White Lion . . . Hurry . . ."

Her words were garbled, and there was a lot of static on the line. "Emma! Where did you say again?" he cried in alarm, rubbing the sleep out of his eyes.

Then the phone went dead. Scrambling out of bed, he shoved on his shoes, raced downstairs, and, throwing on a jacket over his pyjamas, went out to the car.

Jim drove as fast as he could to Oakham and prayed that he'd heard Emma's words correctly. He screeched to a halt outside the pub, grabbed a flashlight from the glove compartment, and got out of the car. The phone box across the street was lit up, but it looked empty. He ran to it and pulled the door open.

Emma was crumpled on the floor. Jim bent down and pulled her to him, and she struggled feebly in his arms to get free.

"Help me, Jim!" she cried desperately.

"Thank God you're all right, Em," he said as he helped her out of the phone box.

The mephitic air grew frigid as they stumbled across the road, and a purple mist curled around their ankles. "'Ang on, Em. The car's right 'ere." Jim opened the back door and slid her onto the seat.

Once she was safely inside, he got into the driver's seat, locked the doors, and turned the key in the ignition. The engine turned over slowly and then petered out. Jim frowned. He'd only had the battery a couple of weeks, and it couldn't possibly be flat. Unless something was draining the power. Turning the key again, the engine sputtered into life, and after switching on the lights and wipers, he drove slowly into the fog.

By the time Jim got to the bend by the flower shop, the fog had vanished and the road was clear. After a few miles, he turned south onto the main road and then east along a narrow tree-lined lane that went past Emma's house. The road ran straight for a little ways and then took a sharp bend to the right. Suddenly, in the headlights, he saw a small figure standing in the middle of the road. Jamming on the brakes, Jim swerved through a farm gate and jolted to stop in a hedge. Light flooded the road. An engine roared, coming towards the car, and a horsebox hurtled past.

A tremor of fear shot down Jim's neck, leaving a dull throbbing pain in its wake. He closed his eyes and took a deep breath to steady himself.

"What's happening?" Emma asked feebly. "I felt a big jolt. Did we hit something?"

"Nothin', love. Just goin' a bit too fast, that's all," Jim answered, trying to sound reassuring.

Cautiously, he pulled back into the lane and drove on slowly, looking left and right to see if there was any sign of the strange figure. There was nothing—the road and ditches were empty.

Jim hardly knew how he got back to Emma's, and he heaved a sigh of relief as he pulled up the driveway.

"We're 'ome, Em," he whispered as he helped her out of the car.

She staggered forwards and fell down. "Oh! Jim, my feet hurt."

Gathering her up in his arms, he took her inside the kitchen and sat her down gently on a chair. "I'll get you a blanket. I won't be a tick." He was soon back with a comforter and a large glass of brandy. "Slam it," he said. "It'll warm you up."

Putting the blanket round her, he squeezed her shoulder supportively. "Better start thinkin' of gettin' out of your wet nightdress before you catch cold. Want me to run you a bath?"

"Later," she said, managing a smile.

Emma gulped the liquor down, and her breath caught as the fire hit her throat and stomach.

Jim found a plastic bowl and filled it with warm water. "I'll be off, then, to get some logs to build the fire," he said, setting the bowl on the floor next to her.

"Thanks again, Jim," Emma said. "You're a real brick, do you know that?"

"I know you'd do the same for me if I was in your position." He smiled. "That's what we're 'ere for, to 'elp each other."

"Would you get me a bottle of tea tree oil before you go outside?"

"There," he said, coming to her side. "One bottle of tea tree oil for the lady. Now I'm off."

Shaking the oil into the water, Emma breathed in the pungent aroma and soaked her feet. They were cut, bruised, and very tender. The soreness was almost calming; the physical pain anchored her in reality. She laughed inwardly, almost hysterically. *Reality! What's that?*

She tried to remember what had happened after she took the sleeping pills and why she had left the house, but she could gain no fresh insight. One thing was for sure: a voice in her head had saved her from an evil creature at the ruins bent on her destruction. She shifted awkwardly in her chair; every joint in her body ached. Her bones felt like brittle metal ready to break into a million pieces.

"'Ow's the feet?" Jim said, hurrying by with a basket of wood.

"Better, but I haven't stood on them yet."

"A roarin' fire and another tot of brandy and we'll be well away," he said supportively. "I'll 'ave the fire goin' any minute. There's nothin' like a fire to warm the cockles of our 'earts."

CHAPTER FIVE

THE SAPPHIRE STAR-GATE

Jim soon had the fire roaring in the grate, and returning to the kitchen, he saw Emma carefully examining her feet.

"I got your slippers and dressin' gown 'ere, Em," he said, laying them over the back of the chair next to her. "'Ave you stood up yet?"

"No, but my feet are clean and I'm home safe, thanks to you." Looking at him with troubled eyes, she said, "When I woke up and found myself at the ruin, I was terrified. Still am. I think it has everything to do with my nightmare."

"Why do you say that?" Jim asked.

"The terror I felt at the ruin was the same as in the dream."

"What 'appened? Can you remember anythin'?" He stared at her anxiously.

"No." She shook her head. "I couldn't sleep and ended up taking two sleeping pills. The next thing I knew, I was at the ruin."

"You ever sleepwalked before?"

"Never."

"Maybe you should go and see your doctor," he said uncomfortably. "You might 'ave an imbalance of some kind."

"You mean I should see a shrink. You think I'm crazy, don't you?"

"No, Em. I don't think that, but you can't be wanderin' around in the middle of the bloody night, not knowin' where you are."

"I'm frightened, Jim," she said, her eyes filling with tears.

"Everythin' will be all right. Now, I'd best go and check the fire," he said, getting up. "I don't want to burn the bloody 'ouse down."

"Could you put the kettle on? I could really do with a cup of tea."

After Jim had gone, Emma got dressed. The kettle soon came to a boil, and she hobbled over to the sink, made herself a cup of tea, and took it with her to the sitting room.

She was scared. An unseen world was taking over, to the point where she wasn't sure of anything anymore. The magical attacks Trevelyan had warned her about were manifesting themselves. First Emily, then Joe, and now her. There was no doubt in her mind that it had been a near miss for her at the ruin. The soul-sucking horror that had lured her out into the night had been thwarted for the time being, but she knew it was waiting for another chance to destroy her. She wondered about the soft voice she had heard telling her to run. Had it been Trevelyan's?

Even though she had her doubts about him, she realised that he had never harmed her. He had taken her back to her world when she had asked, and he had given her Emily's wedding ring. Twisting the gold band on her finger, she looked into the fire of the diamonds and wondered what Emily had thought about Trevelyan and why she had never told her about him.

"Want a top-up?" Jim said, coming into the sitting room with a tea tray. He put it down on the table next to her and then pulled up a chair and sat down beside her.

His face was taut and strained, and she said, "Don't be worrying about me. I'll be all right."

"Actually, I was thinkin' about somethin' else, and it may 'ave some bearin' on what's goin' on. I wasn't goin' to tell you straight away, 'cause of the shock you've already 'ad, but . . . we nearly got killed on the way 'ome from the ruin."

"Is that what that jolt was?" she asked nervously.

"Yes. I saw somethin' really strange in the road."

"What did you see?"

Jim didn't answer straight away, and Emma felt a sense of expectancy come over her.

"I saw a little man, dressed old-time-like, standin' in the middle of the road," he said hesitantly. "'E 'ad 'is 'and up for me to stop. Em, 'e was so close that I 'ad to swerve violently to miss 'im. Thank God there was a farm right there. I skidded through the gateway and landed in the 'edge." He thumbed his chin. "The little man you saw outside the pub last week, what did 'e look like?"

"He was about three feet high and dressed like a Georgian gentleman with a three-cornered hat."

Jim gave a nervous little cough and swallowed hard. "Sounds like the same geezer. 'E saved us from collidin' 'ead-on with a speedin' 'orsebox. One of those big, wide kinds, like a coach. But what gets me is 'e disappeared. I mean, just disappeared!" Jim shook his head and leant towards her. "By rights, 'e should've been as flat as a bloody pancake. I looked for 'is body. Not that I felt a bump or anythin', but 'e would've definitely been mashed by the 'orsebox. I didn't find anythin'." He tugged nervously on his earlobe. "Do you think I saw a ghost?"

Emma pulled off the blanket and sat up. "No, Jim, you didn't see a ghost. From your description, it sounds like you saw Trevelyan."

"Who?" Jim looked startled.

"Trevelyan of Wessex is his name. It's the same little man that I saw in the courtyard at the White Lion, and . . . and he's not from this world."

Jim's eyes widened. "Well, if 'e's not a ghost, and 'e's not from 'ere, where is 'e from, then?"

"He's from the hidden world of Faerie. And he took me there."

He was stupefied. "Come again?"

"After you left last night, he came to the house and took me to his home in Faerie."

There was a long silence. "I don't know what to think," Jim said at last.

"I don't know what to think either," Emma agreed.

"Okay, so why didn't you tell me about goin' to . . . Faerie land?"

Emma shook her head. "It only happened a few hours ago, and what with everything else, I haven't had any time to tell you. Anyway, you wouldn't have believed me, just like you don't believe me now."

"Well, I wouldn't 'ave believed you. I mean, it's 'ard to believe. But now that I think I've seen 'im myself . . ." He leaned back in his chair and looked at her pensively. "Is there any chance that this Trevelyan creature could be responsible for all the weird shit that's 'appening? I mean, 'e 'as kind of ingratiated 'imself to you, ain't 'e? Maybe 'e's got some awful agenda that you're not aware of."

"I thought about that myself," Emma admitted. "But I don't think so, and now, from what you've told me, I'm inclined to think that he really is trying to protect us."

"Yeah, that may be, but from what?"

"Good question. If he shows up again, I'll ask him."

"Anyways," he said, looking at the fire, "I've got to bring some more logs in."

No sooner had Jim disappeared through the door than there was a twitch in the air, and Trevelyan appeared beside the sofa table.

"How are you, m'dear?" he asked soothingly, gliding to her side.

"Shaken up. Sore. And frightened," she said, looking him in the eye. "I walked in my sleep to the old ruins not far from where Joe died. There was something terrible waiting for me there, and I'm scared stiff it's going to happen again." She took a shallow breath. "I heard a voice telling me to run. Was that you?"

Trevelyan nodded and laid his hands on her feet. "Emma, rest assured, 't will not occur again." Taking her hands, he helped her to her feet. Emma was expecting pain, but there was none. "There, m'dear, your feet are as good as new."

She glanced at her soles. They were completely healed.

Trevelyan perched on the arm of the sofa and reached into his waistcoat pocket, bringing out a silver necklace with an oval, orange stone set in the centre of the chain. "I want you to put this necklace on," he said. "The gem is enchanted, and once you are wearing it, only by magical command will it come off. The vibrations of the topaz will protect you from dark things that stalk you from the shadows."

Taking the necklace from his fingers, Emma fastened it round her neck. It was snug to her skin, and running her finger along the chain, she noticed there was no longer any clasp.

She heard the kitchen door close, and Jim came into the sitting room with a basket of logs. Stopping short, he dropped the wood and stared at Trevelyan in surprise.

"Em! That's 'im! The little bloke in the road!" he cried.

"Jim, this is Trevelyan of Wessex."

"At your service," Trevelyan said graciously, moving to Jim's side and putting out his hand.

"Jim . . . Jim Lynch," he stuttered, bending over to shake Trevelyan's hand. "But 'ow did you slip by me and get in 'ere?"

Trevelyan smiled. "Why, sir, I am the space between all things, and space, as you know, is invisible," he said mysteriously. "And so 'twas easy to slip through your space unnoticed."

"Oh!" Jim exclaimed, flabbergasted by the whole proceedings.

Trevelyan's face took on a serious expression. "Now, we must get to our business, for the river of time is flowing, and as each second passes, the peril grows."

"Peril! What peril?" Jim asked, glancing uneasily at Emma.

"Both of you are in mortal danger," Trevelyan said, meeting Emma's eyes. "There is much you need to know." He looked slowly around the room. "There are eyes in the ceiling and ears in the walls," he said in a low voice. "Many are dreaming in some forgotten time, but there are others—spies of the enemy on the watch. Therefore, I think 'tis best we go to the Otherworld."

As Trevelyan spoke, a cloud covered the sun, and Emma noticed that it made no difference to the shadows on the walls.

"Now 'ang on a minute," Jim protested. "I don't know about this."

The air trembled. The room took on a brighter, sharper hue, and Emma knew immediately where she was: in the other version of her house, in Faerie. Jim was sitting in the chair by the fireside, and his eyes flitted around the room. Catching Emma's eye, he said warily, "I dunno what to make of this, Em. Somethin's really changed 'ere."

"You're in the world of Faerie. This is the same place that Trevelyan brought me to," she said, trying to reassure him. Sooner or later he would have to come to terms with the shifting of realities, as she was learning to do.

"And where the 'ell is Faerie?"

"Right where you are sitting!" Trevelyan exclaimed. "You are in the same space as you were, but now everything has changed its speed, and we are in the Green Dimension." Catching Jim's worried eyes, he went on. "All is brighter, happier, is it not?"

Before Jim could answer, a King Charles spaniel bounded through the open door and ran to him with joyful barks. "Chloe?" he said uncertainly, gaping at the dog.

"Yes, Jim. Little Chloe lives here in Faerie with me," Trevelyan said. "I knew you would be overjoyed to see her, and she you."

With a flood of passionate tears, Jim picked up his long-time little friend. "'Ow is this possible?" he sobbed. "She died a year ago . . . got run over by a car." He hugged her close and rubbed his face against her fur.

"Ah, Jim. Death, like life, is an illusion," Trevelyan said softly. "Only love is enduring. It cannot ever die." Picking up a carafe of liquor and three crystal glasses from the sideboard, Trevelyan brought them over to the sofa table. "I think a tot of brandy is in order," he said, pouring the drinks and giving them each a glass.

"To your good health! Brandy's good," Trevelyan said, clinking his glass to theirs.

Emma smiled. "It's too good!"

Jim took a gulp and then, holding Chloe on his knee, gazed out the window at the garden.

A brooding silence fell over the room, and Emma knew that the time was at hand for answers. "Trevelyan," she said, putting down her glass, "something or someone is out to kill me. It's happening just like you said it would. Why?"

"So, you finally understand that your life is in danger," Trevelyan said, taking out his eyeglass and peering into the glittering green lens. "Come. Let's all go and sit in the window seat and see the sun shine upon the faces of the flowers. There, in the light of Faerie, I will tell you of the dark, and fear will come. I say to you, withdraw from thought, for thought is the root of fear. And if you do not fear, the enemy is impotent."

Emma and Jim followed him across the room and sat on the window seat.

"The adversary has been searching for you since your birth, m'dear." Trevelyan sat down beside Emma. "While Emily was alive, we made an emerald shield around you as a safeguard. But after the darkness took her, you were left without protection. I knew evil would be tracking your faerie vibration in an effort to destroy you, and that is why I came south, for you are now laid bare to the enemy, and the onslaught upon your spirit has begun."

Emma stared at him. "You and Emily were protecting me?"

"Yes. We hid your faerie light within the green ray and left no clues of your true identity and heritage. But Emily is gone, the shield is broken, and the enemy of life has found you."

Emma blanched. "Who is the enemy? And why me?"

"I will answer your second question first," Trevelyan responded. "You, Emma Cameron, are one of the twice born. You are not completely human. Your true home is in High Faerie."

"What!" Emma nervously rubbed her hands together. "Not totally human! But that's impossible!"

"No, m'dear, it is not. Let me explain. Long ago, the Danaan wizard Ke-enaan had a vision of the future, of a time when the enemy would make war upon the Green Dimension, desiring its obliteration. He called a council in High Faerie, and four warriors were chosen, one from each direction, to go to Earth in the time of the vision to thwart the enemy's purpose and their plans. That age is now upon us." He laid his hand upon her arm. "You, Emma, are one of the four, and you are the only one, for the warriors of Earth, Water and Fire are dead."

Trevelyan's words chilled her. How she wished she could wake up and prove this all a dream.

"Dead! How?"

"They were captured and destroyed by the enemy. You are the last of the twice born, of the fourth estate, Air."

"If what you say is true, why don't I remember it?"

"Because the moon stole your memory at birth," Trevelyan answered, showering her with green sunbeams from his eyeglass.

The moon, Emma thought. She didn't have much recollection of her early years apart from one memory that had never left her. It was dark; she was a baby in a playpen on her mother's bed. Hovering outside the window was a huge full moon, and she distinctly remembered gazing at it. There was nothing more to the memory, she was too small for any kind of thought, but she never forgot the image. Now she understood—the moon was taking her memory of Faerie.

"Keep away from the moon. Its light spies for the enemy," Trevelyan said. "Know that at one time there was no moon. The enemy had not yet brought it into being to trouble the world of men."

"No moon!"

"Yes, Emma, no moon. Hard to believe, what!"

"That's a bit far-fetched," Jim said doubtfully.

"Far-fetched, eh! Look to the myths and legends of the world. There was a time of no moon when the three worlds were one. The spying light came at the time of the Separation."

"The Separation?" Emma enquired. "What is that?"

"To understand the nature of this evil, we must go back a million years," Trevelyan replied. "To a time when your Earth was part of Faerie and High Faerie. A great evil befell the physical plane of Earth. Shape-shifters from the abyss used dark magic and a black cube to penetrate your world. Serpents they were in the guise of men, and they slithered into the dreams of Earth's chieftains, making promises of power and victory against their enemies. Many of these leaders spurned the dark invaders of their minds, wanting only peace, but others, chiefs of lesser tribes, desired power. Then, in dark rites spoken on lonely hilltops and in shadowy groves, evil men in their lust for earthly power summoned the enemy with human sacrifice.

"Blood soaked the ground and hallowed stones, the seas rose in torment, the wind howled, the earth shook, and fire rent the skies. In a tumult of blood, Earth disconnected from the higher realms.

"At this, the time of the Separation, a sapphire from High Faerie was lost and left behind on Earth. That pentagonal jewel is a star-gate to all the worlds. Whoever commands it has power to open the portal to all beings, to those of light and of darkness. Of late, its radiations have shone forth upon the ether and become visible, not only to High Faerie but to the demonic realms as well."

Rising from his seat, he laid his hand on Emma's arm and said softly, "Now, if you both will come with me, I have something to show you."

Jim and Emma followed him out of the sitting room and into the hallway. Moving behind the rose table, Trevelyan put one hand on the wall and lightly touched the upper left-hand corner of the alcove with the other. As he did so, the plaster seemed to implode in a honeycomb pattern. To Emma's surprise, another wall appeared behind it, and about a foot off the floor set into the second wall was a dark, arched wooden door.

"Come!" Trevelyan said, turning the door handle and gesturing for them to follow.

Walking through, Emma found herself enclosed in the centre of a sphere, a pink nimbus of light with no edges. Before her was a miniature wooden coach painted in rusty red and dark green with golden trim.

"Look well, my friends," Trevelyan said, gently pulling back a blind on the window of the coach.

Kneeling beside him, Emma and Jim looked through the window. Sitting on the plush, red velvet seats were two beautiful porcelain dolls clothed in silk and satin.

"Behold!" Trevelyan said. "The likenesses of two from High Faerie: the Lady Niamh and Lord Caiomhin,[1] rulers of the House of Air in the fifth density of dimension."

Mesmerised, Emma gazed at the figures. A touch of familiarity harped on the edge of her consciousness, insistent with a sense of old acquaintance. "Their faces look familiar," Emma said, after a while. "I feel I should know who they are."

"They are the rulers of Gorias," Trevelyan replied. "The emerald High Faerie city of Air. They are your kin."

Trevelyan's words evoked vivid impressions in Emma's mind. For a moment she was free of her mortal coil, immersed in images streaming from somewhere other than conscious thought.

"Alas!" Trevelyan said sadly. "The couple came to Earth on a desperate mission to retrieve the sapphire before the enemy could find it. They have failed. They are lost, trapped within the dolls—and locked in the coach. See! The door is held fast." He turned the handle. "And the key is missing."

"'Ow did it 'appen?" Jim asked. "I mean, them gettin' stuck inside the dolls and shut in the coach?"

"By design of the enemy," Trevelyan replied. "But, we will speak no more of it here. 'Tis better that some things be not uttered in the presence of the image of those of High Faerie, so we will leave them now." Trevelyan made several passes with his hands over the coach and then ushered Emma and Jim out of the hidden chamber, closing the wall behind him.

"Is all well with you, m'dear?" Trevelyan asked Emma as they went back to the sitting room.

---

[1]   These Irish names are pronounced Lady *Neeve* and Lord *KEE-veen*.

"I'm a bit overwhelmed. I had memories, but they came too fast." Emma sat down on the window seat and fell silent.

Trevelyan put his hand upon her arm. "Emma!" She met his eyes. "What troubles you?"

"You said that the enemy trapped Niamh and Caiomhin by design. What did you mean?"

"They needed a physical coach made with the element earth to travel from High Faerie into your realm. An identical copy of the Coach of Air was made by a craftsman called Fergus Cronan from Spanish Point in the West of Ireland.

"At the hour appointed, Niamh and Caiomhin entered the realm of Earth.

"But evil had been tracking them from the shadows. As the faerie coach melded with the physical coach, disaster struck. A thief entered the workshop to steal the physical coach, and in that fateful moment, the essence of the HeartStar was caught in the transfer from one realm to the other." Trevelyan sighed. "The coaches were no longer identical, the door was locked, and the key made of air went missing." He sighed again. "Porcelain's frequency weighs heavy; 'tis slow like the earth whence it came. It drew their hearts down into the angles that separate the worlds and trapped them there."

"What can we do?" Emma said.

"At this moment in time, we can do nothing. Evil set a snare for the House of Air, and the coach is part of the deception. I am its guardian, for if it falls into evil hands and is destroyed, Niamh and Caiomhin will perish. The House of Air is the house of the heart and creates the living green upon your Earth. Niamh and Caiomhin are the HeartStar of all the tree and flower nations, the fourth ray upon the rainbow bridge. The enemy wishes to destroy the Green, the HeartStar. That is why you are in danger, Emma. You are the Air in physical form." Trevelyan paused. "If we do not find a way to free the HeartStar, all that is green and growing on your Earth will die."

Emma's chest contracted and her breath was short. "You mean plants and trees?" she gasped.

"Everything will die, for all is connected within the power of your reality. The death of the Green is the death of all. Now is the time foretold of in Ke-enaan's vision. Emma, whether you know it or not, this is the time of your awakening." Trevelyan leant towards Emma and lowered his voice. "You ask, who is the enemy? The enemy is a gnawing hate that feeds upon itself yet surrounds itself with glamour. 'Tis the life hater, an imposter, a parody of life, working in darkness to destroy the light in all its glory and its forms." He heaved a deep sigh. "Yea, it walks on two legs under the sun of your world yet you know it not."

"You mean like ordinary people?" Emma asked.

"Yes, like ordinary people," Trevelyan said. "But they are not! These dark beings are phasmids, shape-shifters, and they are indistinguishable from the people of Earth. That is, unless you see their auras. That is why those with the sight have been persecuted through the ages; they were destroyed by the servants of the enemy." He paused. "And now the HeartStar has fallen into shadow."

The shockwave hit her. Everything made sense: all the planet's elements, the air, the fire, the water, the very substance of all life, and even space, were under attack from an evil force dwelling on the planet. A cry escaped her lips. Or was it an acknowledgement of a truth well told? The destruction of green and growing things was already underway. Fear seized her like a vice, but she pushed away the darkness.

"What will it take to free my relatives?" Emma's voice was flat and calm.

"We have to find the earthly coach and the sapphire Niamh and Caiomhin sought. Only then can we bring them safely through the angles that imprison them.

"It is only a matter of time before they are found and destroyed, for the radiance of High Faerie waxes bright within the darkness and will betray them." He breathed long and hard. "'Tis yet but a week in your time since Niamh and Caiomhin made their try to find the star-gate stone, and already the green HeartStar of your world is diminishing. Soon the blighted seed of eternal winter will lie upon the Green. Thus the need for haste. In truth! We are in desperate days."

"Do we have any clues to where the mortal coach is?" Emma asked.

"No, we do not. Niamh and Caiomhin have two sons in the fourth density. I have sent the brothers on a desperate errand to track the thief." Trevelyan refilled their glasses. "The enemy has mortals under his sway, and they are, as we speak, searching for the sapphire. I need you to recover the portal stone, and quick! There is no time to lose."

"Any idea where the sapphire is?" Emma picked up her drink.

"'Tis buried in an underground cavern on the summit of Dragon Hill, somewhere on the chalk downs, not far from a town called Brighton."

"I lived in Brighton for a couple of years," Jim said, "and Dragonsbury Ring is the only 'ill with 'dragon' in its name that I know of. But, why do you need us? Why can't you find it yourself?"

"If 'twere only that easy," Trevelyan replied, shaking his head. "Unlike Niamh and Caiomhin, I am freed from Earth's constraints but have no earthly element to convey me underground." He yawned and the black hole of his mouth engulfed the room, and for an instant Emma felt suspended in spiralling galaxies of starry knowledge and silent, shadowy space.

"Nay, would I have gone to all this trouble to contact you if I could have done the job myself?" Trevelyan said. "Evil knows that I am unable to enter their dense domain, but being human, you are able." Looking into their faces, he said solemnly, "Will you help me find the sapphire?"

"Yes," Emma answered without hesitation, knowing now how much was at stake.

"If Em's goin' to 'elp you, so am I," Jim said, stroking Chloe's ears. "It'll be better if we tackle this together."

Trevelyan breathed a sigh of relief. "So it is settled then?"

"Yes," Emma responded. "Jim, we could go to Dragonsbury Ring tomorrow since there's no market."

"Tomorrow! We got a lot of work to do, Em. But I suppose."

"You will have to use your faerie sight to find the cavern," Trevelyan said. "The entrance is buried, but probably not more than twelve inches underground. But take heed! On the summit of Dragon Hill there was once a great temple. In the terrible war that ended in the Separation, it was levelled by our enemy, and a shadow usurped the light and entered into the hilltop. The manner in which you ascend and descend the hill is very important for your spiritual well-being. You must walk up the hill clockwise in a spiral of seven turns, and when you leave, you must walk down anticlockwise on the same path. The Faeries of Place will be able to protect you as long as you stay upon the spiral path."

"Emily didn't tell me about the Faeries of Place. What are they?" Emma asked.

"They are the primordial forces that create the living Earth, and they lie hidden from mortal eyes. When you call upon them, even with faerie sight, you will not see their form, only the geometry that activates them."

"I don't know about this 'ere faerie sight," Jim blurted out. 'Ow do I see it?"

"'Tis the green light of the heart that you see upon the garden, Jim."

"That's what it is?"

"Yes. 'Tis the ability to see beyond the limits of three dimensions, the spell that has been pulled across your eyes," Trevelyan answered. "You have that ability, otherwise you could not see beyond the veil, and I and my realm would be a mystery to you, as it is to most of your contemporaries. Faerie sight was a gift given to mankind by the Faerie realm long ago, but sadly, your race now dwindles. Now," he said, getting up, "'tis time now for us to depart, for you have made the decision to go to Dragonsbury Ring, and the sand in the hourglass is flowing. Come, Chloe!" Trevelyan nodded to Jim and Emma, and he vanished.

The room darkened. The supernal light of Faerie faded, and they were left with the common light of day. There was silence for a moment, and then Jim said, "When I saw Chloe, I thought

I'd died, but obviously, I'm still 'ere. Do you want a drink, Em? I know I do!" He went to the drinks cabinet.

"Yes, I'll have one with you."

Jim put the glasses on the sofa table. Emma picked hers up and, taking a sip, wrinkled her nose and put it down again.

"Tastes a bit rough, don't it, after what we've just 'ad?"

"Yes, it does. It's not like Trevelyan's smooth elixir, that's for sure. I don't think I'll drink it. I'll have a shower instead," she said, getting to her feet.

After Emma had gone, Jim sat in an armchair and stared into the fire. He was totally exhausted. He had convinced himself that Emma had a bit of a mental problem and was hallucinating, but that meant now he was hallucinating too. He felt he was a passenger on an insane ride hurtling into the unknown. He sighed. Seeing Chloe again and knowing she was well had made him happy. That alone made this bizarre experience worthwhile. He downed his drink and set the glass on the table then leaned back, stretching out his legs. With a picture of Chloe in his mind, he drifted off into oblivion.

When Emma came back, Jim was asleep and snoring gently by the fire. Not wanting to wake him, she tiptoed to the kitchen to start breakfast.

A few minutes later, Jim came in. "I must 'ave dropped off," he said, rubbing the sleep out of his eyes.

"I was just going to wake you. Breakfast's ready," Emma said, putting a bowl of porridge on the table in front of him.

"I'm totally knackered." He sat down and stirred cream into his oatmeal. "And look at me. It's a quarter to eight in the mornin' and I'm still in my clothes from last night."

"My mind's so numb I can't think about anything," Emma said as she poured a large dollop of golden syrup on her oats and topped it off with cream. "All I want is something hot, sweet, and comforting."

After a while, Jim pushed his empty bowl away. "Do you know what I can't get over?"

Emma put down her spoon and looked up at him. "What?"

"It's this other world. It's right 'ere where we're sittin', and nobody knows it's there. If I told my mates down the pub that I'd been to Faerie and seen my dead dog, they'd think I'd gone stark ravin' mad." He paused. "Per'aps I am mad. Per'aps we've both gone round the twist. What do you think? 'Ave we lost it? Is this some kind of shared 'allucination?"

Emma put her elbow on the table and rested her head in her hand. "I don't know where it's going to lead us," she said apprehensively. "I feel like I'm taking part in a movie, that none of it's real."

"Or a comic!" Jim replied. "Though there's nothin' funny about this." After a moment, he went on, "You know, when I was a nipper, I always wanted to be like those 'eroes in the comics, savin' the world from little green men in flyin' saucers, stuff like that, and now it looks we've got the starrin' roles in one of 'em."

"Perhaps the comic-book writers were trying to warn us that the world is not the way we're conditioned to believe it is," Emma said thoughtfully. "There must be all kinds of horrific creatures that we can't see hovering around us at all times."

"Yeah, round porno shops and the like," Jim said, getting up. "Don't bear thinkin' about, does it, Em? I'm off 'ome now to change my clothes. I'll only be a bit. Then we'll get to work in the green'ouse."

CHAPTER SIX

A WICKED TURN

Emma watched from the window as Jim drove away. The sky was bruised and a light rain was falling. The melancholy light seemed to exacerbate her unsettled frame of mind, so she turned away and busied herself clearing up the breakfast things. She was preoccupied with the onrush of events as she put the last cup into the dish rack. If there was a secret room in Trevelyan's house, was there a corresponding room in hers? She thought about taking a look at the back of the alcove, but for some obscure reason, she didn't want to go alone. Jim would be back soon, and they could search for the hidden room together and find out if it did indeed exist.

Emma fed the cats and sat down, checking the time. Jim had been gone a good half-hour, though he lived only three miles away. She wondered what was keeping him.

As the seconds ticked by, she grew more impatient, and she dialled Jim's mobile. The phone rang for a long time before he finally picked up. He said he'd had a flat tyre. *That'll make us even more pressed for time*, she thought as she rang off. She made her mind up there and then that she wouldn't wait for Jim; she'd go and see if she could find the hidden room herself.

The first thing that caught Emma's attention when she got to the hallway was the vase of roses on the table. Their blood-red lips seemed to pout and mock, as if affronted by her presence, and she stared at them in horrid fascination, noticing how different they were from the beautiful ones in Faerie. Dragging her eyes away from the sinister blooms, she went behind the table and, putting her palms upon the plaster, tapped gently on the wall, listening intently for any change in sound.

As if in answer to her tapping, something tugged on her solar plexus and a gust of cold air hit her in the back, pinning her against the wall. The surface quivered and then softened, and she had an impression of hands erotically stroking her body. Then a sensuous pair of arms encircled her, and a husky male voice whispered for her to follow. She felt another pull on her solar plexus, drawing her through the wall and into a dank space behind it, heavy with the spicy smell of corruption.

A painful burning sensation stabbed at her throat, and uttering a little cry, Emma staggered back from the wall. Putting her hand to her neck, she found the topaz on her necklace was burning hot, but the moment she touched it, the stone cooled down. She backed away from the wall in fright, dashed around the table, and went to the safety of the kitchen

Her hands were shaking as she sat down at the table. Something awful had tried to take her over. If it hadn't been for the necklace's alert, she would have gone to be one with the voice. The topaz had protected her—but from what?

She thought it best not to tell Jim of her search and what had transpired at the wall. She had to find out for herself what was happening. She was still mulling it over when he walked through the door.

"Nothin' worse than changin' a tyre in the wet," he grumbled, taking off his jacket.

"Jim!" she said before he could sit down. "Umm . . . I was wondering if you'd come with me to the alcove to see if there's another room behind the wall like there was at Trevelyan's."

"Do what?" Jim said, washing his hands in the sink.

"I wondered if you'd come with me to see if there's a room behind the wall."

Jim frowned. "Just because there's an 'idden room there doesn't mean there's one 'ere, does it?"

"But everything else is the same in both houses, so it's quite likely that there is one," Emma argued. "I don't like the thought of there being another room in my house that I don't know about. It bothers me." She dithered for a moment. "Would you help me look, just to put my mind at rest? I'd really appreciate it."

"Can't it wait? We were already behind, and what with the flat, we're even more pushed for time right now. We've got a ton of work to do in the garden to fill the orders, and then a lot of deliveries this evenin' for the restaurant trade tomorrow. We can't neglect the business, especially now it's on the up and up."

"No, it can't wait, Jim. I told you, it's bothering me. I'm well aware that we have a lot of things to do, but we'll have time . . . it'll only take a few minutes, and I won't be able to relax unless I know for sure."

"Oh, all right," he said testily. "But we can't be long."

Emma led him to the hallway and to the wall at the back of the alcove.

"You take the left side and I'll take the right," Jim said, tapping the surface of the wall.

Emma stood back and watched him prod and pat the plaster, but she couldn't bring herself to touch it.

"I thought you were goin' to 'elp me," Jim said without turning his head.

"I came over a bit giddy," Emma lied.

After a few more taps, Jim stepped back from the wall. "I don't think there's anythin' behind 'ere, Em. Let's get to work."

How she wished she could believe him. She knew there was a room there—and she had to find it. Staring at the plaster, she remembered that Trevelyan had pushed on a spot in the upper left-hand corner where the alcove curved into the ceiling, and taking a deep breath, she stepped forwards and pressed on the same place.

With a squeak, the plaster slid back to reveal an arched doorway set in a second wall. Startled, Jim whistled through his teeth. "Well, ain't that a turn-up for the books. Exact same thing we saw at Trevelyan's."

Her fears confirmed, Emma trembled and hung back.

"Come on, Em. Let's see what's in 'ere," Jim said, pushing the door open. He switched on the light, and a dull red luminescence spilt out into the hallway.

"Frickin' 'ell!" He glanced round. "This place is queer; it's creepy. Come and 'ave a look at this."

"I can't go in there, Jim," Emma gasped as she held on to the wall for support. "I'm scared."

"Em, this is your 'ouse. You need to see what's in this room."

"No!" she shook her head and backed away.

"Em!" Jim was stern. "No ifs and buts or wherefores, you 'ave to see this. You're livin' on bloody top of it!" He took Emma's arm and tried to pull her through the door. "Come on!"

Emma struggled for a moment and then, steeling herself, swallowed hard and followed him in.

The space was about twelve feet square with a musty, bitter odour, and Emma started back in fright. Stretched out on the floor before her was a black coffin lying in a reversed pentacle surrounded by half-erased circles bearing strange symbols and designs. Emma shrieked and fled, banging into the rose table and sending the crystal vase crashing to the floor.

She ran out the front door and into the garden. Tears streamed down her cheeks as terrible, deeply buried memories came to the surface. At the wall at the end of the property, she knelt on the damp grass and wrapped her arms around herself, sobbing through a flood of bitter tears.

On the nights that Daddy had bathed her in scented water and then put her to bed with warm milk with honey, she had hideous dreams of lying naked in the coffin—only, she knew now she hadn't been dreaming.

Feeling a hand touch her arm, Emma flinched and curled up on the grass with her arms shielding her face.

Trevelyan bent down and laid his hand on her head. "Emma, 'tis I! Fear not," he said in a strong, resounding tone. Her breath came in short, sharp gasps between the sobs, and finding one of her shaking hands, he pressed his palm to hers.

Slowly, the turmoil in Emma's mind faded, and she let Trevelyan gently raise her to her feet and lead her slowly by the arm back to the house.

Hearing Emma's terrible shriek, Jim looked anxiously behind him. There was no sign of her, but he could see the front door was wide open. Leaving the eerie room, he carefully avoided the broken glass and went out into the garden.

"Em!" he shouted looking wildly around. "Where are you?"

The grounds were quiet, and he heard no reply, so he quickly went to the side of the house and called again, but there was still no answer.

In rising panic, he ran inside hoping to find she'd returned, but the kitchen and the sitting room were empty. Going to the foot of the staircase, he called, "Em! Are you up there?" He heard a thump. Perhaps she was in her bedroom and had fallen down, he thought as he went up. He gave a little knock on the bedroom door. "Em! Are you in there?" Hearing no response, he peered anxiously around the door. There was no sign of Emma, just Lionheart, her ginger cat, coming to greet him.

Jim went back to the kitchen and opened the side door to shout for her again. Silence was his only answer. The house and garden were hushed; not even a bird sang. After closing the door, he sat down at the table in a quandary, trying to collect his wits. He felt sure the coffin was what had frightened her. It had frightened him.

Then he remembered the broken vase in the hallway and thought about the danger to the cats. Getting the dustpan and brush from the cupboard, he went to sweep it up, but when he got to the hallway, he sensed a strange tingling, a hostility that slowly increased as he swept up the broken glass. Turning his attention to the roses that lay scattered on the floor, he found he could barely bring himself to touch them. The dead heads blackened before his eyes, and they exuded a rotten smell that made him want to vomit. Holding his breath, he scooped up the decaying flowers and threw them outside on the grass.

After a couple of deep breaths of wholesome air, he came back inside and closed the door behind him. He stared at the sinister open door to the hidden room. Finally he decided to take another look inside, and he moved behind the table, but a sudden dread made him stop. Fear snaked through his body. *This is ridiculous*, he told himself. *It's just a room.* Trying desperately to keep a grip on his emotions, Jim braced himself and went into the red-lighted chamber.

Behind the coffin, on the wall facing him, was a picture of a priest in red robes holding a skull, and Jim shuddered under the cold stare of those baleful eyes. They seemed to be alive as they glared malignantly at him from the livid, chalk-like face. The painting gave him such an ugly feeling that he grabbed it off its hook and turned it to face the wall.

Jim examined the shelves on two of the walls packed with old dusty manuscripts and tomes, some with Greek and Latin titles, covered in strange symbols and zodiacal signs. A strange compunction drew his eyes downwards to some bizarre metallic objects under the shelves. He looked uneasily upon claws, clamps, and a pear-shaped device with a hinge on top and a crank on the bottom. He choked out a noise as he realised what they were: mediaeval instruments of sexual torture. He'd seen them on a school trip to the Tower of London, and he remembered how much they had frightened and disgusted him.

He turned away to another corner where a squat writing desk sat, its flat, faded leather top piled high with papers and bulging files. Carefully skirting the coffin, he made his way to the desk, picked up one of the folders, and flipped through the contents. He let out a harsh cry. They were photographs of naked, screaming children being lowered into the coffin by a hooded figure. But what was the darkness underneath their pale little bodies? He peered more closely. An ugly thrill of fear froze the back of his neck. Something that was not visible in the photograph was watching him through it. Throwing the folder on the floor, he fled the room.

He was on his way out the kitchen door to search the grounds again when he saw Emma with Trevelyan coming slowly up the garden path towards him.

Jim heaved a sigh of relief and went to meet them. He was grateful Emma hadn't seen what he'd seen, and he hoped she never would. He'd have to burn the photographs.

He tried to calm his mind and push away the images he'd seen as he approached. He didn't want to think about the photographs since Emma had a way of picking up his feelings, and she was frightened enough.

"Thank God you're all right. I was so worried about you." Jim gazed into her pale face. "What made you run away?"

Emma didn't seem to hear him, so he touched her on the arm and asked again, "What made you run off like that?"

"'Tis not the place or time to discuss such dark matters," Trevelyan responded, steering Emma around Jim and into the kitchen. "Suffice to say that Emma has had a shock, and I have woven a spell of peace around her."

"Shock! What 'appened?"

"Come along inside, Jim," Trevelyan said sharply, nodding to the door. "Emma will tell you in her own time, if she so wishes, but now there is no time to lose." Jim followed them inside and shut the door behind him.

"Let's go and sit in the window seat," Trevelyan said, heading into the sitting room.

Sitting down in the window seat, Emma saw the garden shimmer into the soft green light of Faerie. Chloe barked excitedly as she ran up to Jim.

Emma's fears had faded into a calm detachment. She knew now that Trevelyan had known about the secret room all along and had chosen to keep it from her.

"Methinks a glass of my fortifying brandy is in order," Trevelyan said. He poured the drinks and handed them round. "How are you now, m'dear?" he asked, searching her face.

"You knew the room was there," she accused him. "Why didn't you tell me?"

"Yes, Emma, I did know the room was there, for it is the antithesis of mine—and all that walks wholesome in the worlds," he answered. Holding up his eyeglass by its silver stem, he twirled it in front of her. Emma noticed that the lens was now blue.

"In truth! Emma, I could not risk telling you, for consider, were you not upset and overwhelmed by the secrets that I shared with you on our visit to the faerie room? If I had told you of the dark room in your house, of a hidden, evil room, it would have tipped the balance in your mind. Is that not so?"

Emma stared at him but had no answer.

"And there is more," Trevelyan said. "There are lines of power that cross your planet Earth, and where they intersect, the priests of old raised stone circles, round towers, and phallic monoliths. Your house is a power point at the confluence of many of these sacred lines."

"They're called ley lines," Jim said suddenly. "I know a bit about them. Glastonbury Tor is big on that."

Trevelyan smiled. "Your mode of speech is charming," he said. "Ley lines, exactly so! They are the straight tracks that join the major points of power together." His smile faded and his face grew serious again. "Emma, your house is built upon a structure that predates Roman times. Underneath the hidden room is a vault, an ancient temple consecrated to the fertility goddess Agdistis. The blasphemous rituals practiced by her priests opened the forbidden doorway to damnation. Theirs was, and is, a sexual cult of rape and sodomy and bloody sacrifice, and where these abominations are practiced, you will find incubi and succubi waiting in the shadows. When your father followed his lust of the flesh to that forbidden room, he was lost. Forgive his weakness; he stood no chance at all, for over time, the room possessed him and dominated his mind." Trevelyan put his hand on her arm to forestall any further interruption. "We have to drive the evil out of that accursed room, for the lust of your father still exists within the temple's confines and is reaching out for you."

Emma turned pale. *The roses,* she thought. *Daddy was drawing me into the hallway, to the wall, and . . .*

"And there is more." Trevelyan's voice interrupted her thoughts. "From the temple beneath, the enemy has been seeping into my abode and slowly flowing like a black tide into the pink nimbus of the Coach of Air. If the evil continues, it will consume Niamh and Caiomhin. All will be lost.

"But fear not! I have by my arts been able to contain the evil rush, but by the hour the power of its dominion grows, and so I will come with you to your earthly room, and we will go below and clear away the festering evil from dark spaces and send the enemy's slaves back where they belong."

"Yes, but I still don't understand. If you knew the attacks on me were coming from my own house, why didn't you tell me sooner?"

"I couldn't take the risk. If you had known about the cellar, I would not have been able to show you the coach, or even bring you into Faerie," Trevelyan replied. "Your unconscious fear would have forged an energy link from one space to the other, and that would have spelled disaster, for the enemy would have used you to attack the coach and then destroyed you. But now you have seen the Coach of Air, we can proceed."

Looking at Emma's full glass, he said, "Drink up, m'dear. The brandy is charmed and will help settle your feelings and clear from your mind the sorrow that surrounds you."

As Emma drained her glass, Trevelyan rose from the settle. "Now we have to go."

Chloe licked Jim's hand, gave a bark of farewell, and disappeared.

Life and light lowered, and in the next instant, they were back in Emma's sitting room. As she got up, Trevelyan appeared beside her. "When we enter the forbidden room, you will be in peril, Emma," he said grimly.

"Is it absolutely necessary for me to go in there with you?" she asked, hoping fervently that he could do what was required without her.

"Yes, m'dear, it is. If I could spare you the horror, indeed I would, but I cannot, as there is a link between you and the evil influence that dwells beneath your house. Also, I cannot go underground in your dimension without a link to the dense world of under-earth, and you are it, m'dear. So, as dangerous as it may be for both of us, we must proceed together." He patted her arm reassuringly. "For your spiritual protection, I want you to imagine an emerald shape around yourself. Now, close your eyes and look into the darkness."

Emma shut her eyes and saw an emerald turning slowly in front of her.

"Gaze at the octahedron's eight faces with six points each. The geometric figure will protect you against the rising shadow," Trevelyan said in Emma's mind. "This octahedron is a symbol of your lineage in the House of Air. Practice seeing it about you at all times.

"And you, sir," he said aloud to Jim, "will you assist us?"

"Yes, I'll 'elp. But I don't know what good I'll be," Jim replied, nervously pulling on his earlobe.

"You will guard Emma with your life."

Jim looked taken aback and barely nodded.

"'Tis settled, then," Trevelyan said with a grim, set look on his face. "The sands of time are flowing, and we can do no more than flow with them and into shadow tread. Come!"

Emma and Jim followed Trevelyan to the hallway, where he stopped, touched Emma's arm, and pointed to the rose table. Where the red roses had been now sat a crystal vase of fresh white blooms. "Behold!" he said. "White is a symbol of purity and hope, and we will ask the flowers to lift our hearts and strengthen our hands against the enemy."

They stood for a moment by the roses, and then Emma saw a long crystal dagger with an emerald-encrusted handle appear in Trevelyan's hand. She stared at the blade.

"This is Naka, the whirlwind weapon of Gorias, the emerald city, and the bane of foul things. It guards the northern portal of the city and is a symbol of your House of Air. Long and hard was the road to Gorias, which stands still stately amongst the flames. Into great peril I have travelled to bring you the blade of your ancestors. The soul of Naka and yourself, m'dear, share deep memories, and with your permission, I will use the spinning blade against our enemy and then return it to you."

Emma nodded. "I wish I could remember it," she said solemnly.

The hallway grew dark and the air watchful. Trevelyan turned his attention to the doorway in the wall and, holding the glittering dagger before him, advanced into the waiting, blood-red gloom.

Emma gripped Jim's arm tightly with panic.

"'Old up, Em," he whispered, pulling her up beside him.

She took a deep breath and visualised the emerald around her, and then she followed Jim through the doorway.

The room was small and cluttered, and the cold air was tinged with an unpleasant, mouldy smell. "None of us can leave this room until our task is completed," Trevelyan declared grimly, turning the key in the lock on the door behind them.

Anxiety took hold of Emma as she saw the key vanish from his fingers and three rune-shaped seals appear in its place. "What have you done with the key?" she cried out.

"I have taken it, m'dear," he replied, placing a seal on the top and the bottom of the door and the third over the keyhole.

She looked at Trevelyan in dismay. "Why don't we keep the key? I don't like the idea of not being able to go for help if we need it. I mean, what if something happens and we get trapped in here?"

"Trapped!" Trevelyan hissed, his face darkening. "Are we not already in a trap? This house is a trap! And if I gave you the key, it would be to no avail, for the door has been sealed with energy." He gestured at the lock with his finger. "Is it not enough that as every hour passes evil spreads, sending its dark tentacles through the ether to gain access to my hidden room in Faerie to capture the Coach of Air? So you see, Emma, we are already in a trap. Our mission is to spring it!"

Emma bit her lip and nodded. "I know. I just don't like the idea of not being able to get out of here," she answered, looking fearfully at the coffin.

"Don't worry, Em," Jim muttered. "I'll break the bloody door down if I 'ave to. We'll get out of 'ere."

"Brute force will not avail you," Trevelyan retorted, "for the door is sealed with magic. 'Tis true, we cannot escape, but neither can what lies below . . . make entry into the world."

Emma quailed and clung desperately to Jim's arm.

Trevelyan beckoned them forwards to the coffin. "Stand at the bottom of the box. I will take the head."

CHAPTER SEVEN

OLD EVIL

Obeying Trevelyan's order, Emma and Jim stood together at the bottom of the casket, and once they were in position, Trevelyan droned an incantation in a strange and guttural language, interspersed with ugly grunts and clicks.

Emma shivered as the temperature in the damp room fell, and she heard the distant howling of a dog, its frightened cries penetrating the room.

The red lamp above them swayed as if some invisible hand was knocking it, and the bulb exploded with a pop, showering them with glass. For a moment they were in total darkness, and as Emma's eyes adjusted to the sudden lack of light, she saw Trevelyan surrounded by a dim bluish haze, his head slightly tilted to one side and his eyes fixed intently on the coffin.

The howling grew louder and more frantic. The floor quivered and an eerie brown light grew around them. Glancing past the coffin to the end of the room, Emma caught sight of the dim outline of a writing desk and shuddered with fright. The serpentine front seemed to move in a ripple, and the bulging files stacked in piles upon the leather surface held a special kind of dread. Quickly averting her eyes, she stared fixedly at the floor in an effort to control the panic gnawing at her being.

Trevelyan's mantra took on a commanding tone, echoing off the walls and into the nether world, and shadows gathered around them, blacker than the darkness. Then as the ritual reached its climax, something creaked, and Emma stifled a scream as the coffin lid slowly rose. From the widening aperture gushed the brown, filthy light, spilling over the sides and spreading like a stain into the waiting air, and with it rushed the spice of decay. Emma froze as the smell filled her nostrils; it was the smell of the man in the wall who had tried to possess her. Trevelyan barked a string of unintelligible sounds, and Emma looked up to see him jump into the casket brandishing the dagger. The lid slammed shut behind him. A deathly silence fell. Emma gripped Jim's arm even tighter. They were now alone, imprisoned in the cramped and evil room.

Jim took a flashlight from his pocket and shone it around. "'E jumped in the coffin, Em. Did you see that?" he whispered shakily.

"All I know is, he's gone, and we're stuck in here," Emma said anxiously.

Her fear had presented itself in just the way she had imagined it would. Taking a couple of shallow breaths of the fetid air, she tried to stand outside herself and observe the fear without being part of the emotion.

Jim's small flashlight cast a narrow beam that illuminated nothing in the cloying darkness, and they stood motionless, not knowing what to do. "There's no point in us stayin' up 'ere," he said. "I don't like to think of standin' 'ere waitin' like sittin' ducks for somethin' from . . . underneath to pick us off."

There was a tense moment of silence. "'Old the torch steady on the coffin," he whispered, giving Emma the flashlight. "I'll open the lid. The only way we're gettin' out of 'ere is to follow Trevelyan."

Jim swallowed and clenched his teeth, and then he slowly raised the coffin lid.

"Ugh!" He staggered back as more fetid air rushed out to meet them. Emma coughed and dropped the flashlight.

"Em, we 'ave to do somethin'. 'E may need us." Jim picked up the torch and shone the light into the coffin. "Look! There's no bottom to the box," he said, putting his hand where the retaining board should have been. "There must be some kind of mechanism that makes it slide or somethin'. It's just a big black 'ole."

Angling the beam into the yawning darkness, he searched from side to side. On the right, the light caught the faint outline of a step, and brushing away faded black silk hangings, he trained the beam onto the step.

"There's a flight of steps leadin' to a cellar," he said, climbing over the edge of the coffin. "I'm goin' down." He hung on to the side boards for support and lowered himself in.

"No!" Emma cried in panic. "Don't go down there!"

"Come on. It's the only way, and its best we stay together," he called, climbing down the steps.

Cold perspiration broke out on Emma's forehead. She didn't want to stay or leave; she just wanted to get out. *You have to go,* she thought. *Trevelyan needs your help.*

The sensation of a cold hand stroking her neck propelled her to action, and with a tiny cry, she followed Jim into the coffin.

The staircase was steep and greasy. On one side of the steps was nothing but darkness, and on the other, a mouldering, dripping wall. Emma found it easier to go down backwards on her hands and knees.

This is a nightmare, nothing more than a nightmare, she repeated to herself as the horror of her experience deepened with every step. She remembered Emily telling her that she had to confront whatever it was in a bad dream that she was afraid of, and the notion helped harden her resolve. After a twist to the left and a few more steps, she found herself on the damp earthen floor of the cellar.

Getting to her feet, she could see nothing but interminable shadow. Jim swung the torch around over countless bones and broken skulls littered on the ground. Emma gasped and grabbed his arm. It was the nightmare. She was in the catacombs, only this time she was awake.

Letting go of Jim, she shrank back. Orange vapours weaved and danced in front of her, but she thought she saw a faint blue radiance at the end of the room. Straining her eyes, she saw Trevelyan with his arms raised, both hands on the dagger hilt. A charge spiralled out of the blade into a seething ball of putrid outer-spectrum colours that rotated anticlockwise in the air above his head. It seemed that he turned and called her name and then tossed the dagger through the air towards her.

Then everything was cut off by a leaden orange light. Emma's energy was immediately consumed, and she saw the emerald around herself contract and disappear.

"Jim!" she shouted hysterically. "Where are you?"

There was no answer, just echoes of shrieks, moans, whimpers, and carnal sighs and groans.

She had to get away, get back upstairs, get out. Emma made a desperate charge at the staircase and got to the bottom step when a pair of strong arms encircled her. "Jim!" she cried out in relief, turning her head towards him.

A soft, cold hand gently tilted her chin up, and an animal aroma flooded her nose. Emma let out a choking sound and froze. A well-endowed naked man was gazing into her face, his short blue-black hair slicked back from his forehead and his amber, cat-like eyes studying her sensually, hungrily. His soft lips touched hers, and he whispered, "It's been a long time since we've been together." The kiss deepened and then his lips withdrew. "I knew that eventually you would find me," he purred, and he licked her face.

Emma gazed at him. Small oak leaves dotted with tiny acorns bloomed, faded, and then bloomed again on his smooth, golden skin, and she swooned as his long delicate fingers caressed her breasts and then travelled down her body. Her pulse quickened. Breathing in his musky perfume, she trembled with an irresistible urge to be a part of him.

"Lovely Emmy," he crooned, pulling down the zipper on her jeans and easing them gently off her hips. Emma tensed. Only Daddy called her Emmy.

A vague memory surfaced. She was in the cellar with hooded figures in red robes. A fire burned in a brazier, and above the awful chanting, she heard the screams of children. But it was the smell she remembered most, the stench of animal musk mixed with decay as long slim fingers probed her body.

Trevelyan's words came back to her: "It was, and is, a sexual cult of rape and sodomy and bloody sacrifice, and where these abominations are practiced, you will find incubi and succubi waiting in the shadows."

In a flash of insight, Emma knew what had control of her. Baring her teeth in atavistic fury, she shrieked, "You possessed Daddy and you made him hurt me! I know what you are. You're an incubus." She twisted out of his embrace and savagely raked his face with her fingernails.

"No, Emmy! You loved me once," he purred, forcing her hands away and fastening his lips on her mouth.

Her will was overpowered by her baser instincts. She was naked now, and sinking down onto the bone-strewn earth, she pulled his body down on top of her, passionately returning his caresses. She could feel his member hard against her thigh.

An agonising pain burst in her back and shot to her throat like a knife cut. With a scream, Emma rolled out from under him and away from what had hurt her. Looking at where she had lain, she saw Naka. She rolled over to pick up the blade, but the incubus was on top of her again, forcing his knee between her legs.

"It was you!" she screamed. She headbutted him in the face in a desperate attempt to distract him while her fingers felt for the dagger. "You made Daddy forget I was his daughter!"

Finding the hilt, she grabbed it and stabbed at his back, but the incubus was too quick for her. His hand on her wrist, he tried to wrestle the blade away from her.

"Makanisha nigaka nahesh." The unknown words exploded from Emma's lips, and the syllables echoed round the chamber, gaining power and momentum with each reverberation. The air grew hot, Emma's breath was failing, and she gasped for oxygen in the conflagration of the whirling sound. Her will almost failed her again. "It's not too late," he whispered. All she had to do was give in to him and all her cravings would be satisfied. Emma desperately tried to build the octahedron around herself, to purge him from her mind, but the desire in her body only grew, and she slipped away into desire, unable to resist him.

A deafening crack assaulted her eardrums, and a hideous red-orange glare erupted in every nook and cranny. For an instant she felt his grip on her wrist relax, and wrenching her hand away, Emma raised the knife and stabbed the incubus in the back. The blade bored into his flesh like a screw and then spiralled back upwards. A roaring came to her ear as streaks of emerald and ruby light whirled about her. Every atom in her body shook in the spiralling vortex. She felt herself separate from her body—and then she was falling, tumbling down lightless corridors of infinity into merciful oblivion.

When Emma came to her senses, she was lying on the sofa in the sitting room, covered with a blanket. Blinking, she struggled to remove the cover and noticed she was naked. Finding her dressing gown on the arm of the settee, she quickly put it on and went in search of Jim. He was in the kitchen making a cup of tea.

"Em! You're awake!" he cried. "I was so worried."

"Where are my clothes?" she asked, embarrassed that Jim had seen her naked.

"Umm . . . I don't know. Trevelyan found you lyin' at the bottom of the steps leadin' up from the cellar. You didn't 'ave no clothes on. I don't know where they went, because you were dressed when we went . . . below."

"Why did you leave me down in the cellar on my own? I could have died down there!"

Jim looked at her anxiously. "We didn't go anywhere. It was you who disappeared. It 'appened almost immediately when we got down there."

"What do you mean?"

"You vanished, Em."

"Did you see Trevelyan in the cellar?" she asked nervously.

"Not straight away. I saw 'im after a bit trainin' that crystal knife on an 'orrible thing. It was then that I noticed you'd gone; I didn't know what to do. Then there was a noise like an explosion, everythin' was judderin' and orange, and then it got black as pitch. I saw a little beam of light on the floor. It was my flashlight, and I was all 'appy it was workin'. Next thing, Trevelyan's at my arm with a blue light around him. 'Jim,' he says, 'take Emma upstairs. I will join you later.' He pointed to the wall at the bottom of the staircase, and I could see you all crumpled up like you'd been thrown down. 'The door into the hallway is open,' he said as I started up the stairs. Good job you don't weigh much, Em. It was 'ard goin' up them slippery steps with you over my shoulder. You should've seen that little room. Everythin' was shredded and the coffin was in bits. It looked like a bomb'd exploded in there."

"What happened to Trevelyan?"

"I don't know. He stayed down in the cellar after I took you out. 'E was gone for quite a while, and when 'e came back, 'e seemed better, more cheerful like. Then 'e mumbled stuff over your body while you was sleepin' and waved his 'ands a couple of times and that was it."

Emma fell silent as she tried to add two and two together. Trevelyan had told her that after Emily's death she no longer had protection, and thinking back, she realised that her problems had started within three weeks of the funeral, and so had her preoccupation with the roses. She had been subtly and insidiously lured to the roses in the hallway, and she realised now that they acted as a conduit for the desire that lay hidden behind the wall. Emma sighed and rubbed her fingers across her brow. She was so mentally exhausted that fear had been replaced with pity, pity for the everyday man and woman in the street. They didn't know that all the monsters of myth and legend were hiding in 'the shadow out of light' and that humans were their prey.

She wondered about Trevelyan and hoped he'd soon return. She had so many questions she needed to ask him.

"Did you go back in?" Emma asked, breaking the silence. "Is the room . . . still there?"

"Yes. While you were sleepin' I did go and 'ave a look. I pressed on the wall at the top, like you did, but nothin' 'appened.

Whatever Trevelyan did, I 'ope that room's been sealed forever." Jim paused and looked at her thoughtfully. "At one point, I doubted if we'd get out of there alive."

The ring of the telephone broke the tension in the atmosphere. "I'd better get that," Jim said, getting up.

"It was the Red Lion 'Otel," he said as he hung up. "They're wonderin' where their veggies are. As much as I'm shook up, I 'ave to go and make the deliveries." He took a deep breath and exhaled sharply. "We can't let the business go, especially now it's takin' off."

"I'll get dressed and come with you," Emma said. "I don't feel like being here on my own."

"Okay, I'll go and get started."

After Jim had gone outside, Emma had a shower, got dressed, and then went out to the garden. She found him in the greenhouse bunching up the radishes, and she mechanically helped him with the vegetable orders. In a couple hours they were finished packing their produce into bags and were ready to deliver them.

Emma sat in the van as Jim made the deliveries. Her father came to mind. *Poor Daddy,* she thought, without a hint of anger or vengeance. He had fallen prey to old evil. She, too, had almost become the victim of the same sexual force and realised how easily one could fall.

It was almost ten o'clock when Jim pulled the van up in Emma's driveway. As soon as they went inside, Emma got the brandy bottle and glasses and brought them to the table. "Would you stay?" she asked, pouring out the drinks. "The bed's made in the spare room, and I'll sleep better knowing you're in the house."

Jim took a gulp of brandy. "Okay, Em," he said as he put his arm around her shoulders. "If you feel like talkin' about what 'appened and why you disappeared, I'd like to 'ear it, but only if you want to tell me."

Emma gazed at him. "Not now. I have to think things through, and I'm not really sure myself what happened." She paused. "All of this shit that's going on is a bit too much for me to handle, and I'm so beaten down that I don't want to go to Dragonsbury Ring in the morning. But I promised Trevelyan I'd go." She sighed. "Now I know what's at stake, I have no choice."

Jim nodded in agreement. "I don't want to go either, especially after what we've been through today."

"I wish Trevelyan were here. I need some explanations." Emma sent her thoughts out to him on the air, but all was still and she found no resonant response.

"'E probably had a lot to do . . . downstairs."

Emma suddenly remembered Naka. "The dagger! Where is it?" she asked in alarm.

"To tell you the truth, I don't know what 'appened to it. The last time I saw it, Trevelyan was pointin' it at that 'orrible thing in the wall. I was mesmerised by that awful spinnin' light, and when I tried to look away, I couldn't. Then all 'ell broke loose, so to speak. I must've gone out of time or somethin' because I don't remember anythin' that 'appened next, not clearly. But I know that when I saw Trevelyan again, 'e didn't 'ave no dagger."

"I've lost Naka," Emma said miserably.

"P'raps it'll make its way back to Trevelyan," Jim said, trying to raise her spirits.

Emma put the thought aside and yawned. "I think I'll go to bed and hope I get some rest. I've had enough of today."

Emma went upstairs, and Jim followed her shortly afterwards.

Emma tossed and turned. It didn't matter how she lay, she couldn't get comfortable. First she was hot and then cold. She was overtired and sleep wouldn't come, so she stared at the ceiling, hoping for the dawn.

CHAPTER EIGHT

DRAGONSBURY RING

The night passed slowly, and when Emma did drop off to sleep, she plodded from one fitful nightmare to the next. She awoke early, stiff as a board. She crawled from the covers, sat on the edge of the bed, and stared at the luminous hands of the clock on the bedside table. It was four in the morning. She yawned, still totally exhausted from the terrible traumas she'd endured, and she knew that going to Dragonsbury Ring would just extend the hideous waking nightmare. But the Green was at stake, and she had no choice. Downstairs, the cats were crying to be fed, and after she had tended to them, she made a pot of tea. It had just gone five when she called Jim down for breakfast, and in half an hour, they were ready to leave for Dragonsbury Ring.

"We'll take this with us," she said, filling a thermal flask with hot tea. "It's going to be cold up on that hill."

"I'll go and get a shovel from the toolshed. Just in case we find somethin'. Don't forget to bring some extra clothes in case we decide to stay in Brighton for the night. We'll take my Escort; it's better on petrol than your Audi. I'll meet you in the car."

Putting on her wellingtons and windcheater, Emma took her pendulum from the kitchen drawer. The diviner had been a gift from Emily for her eighteenth birthday. After grabbing a few clothes and making sure she had turned the stove off, she went out to the car.

They drove east and got the first glimpse of the hill as the sun rose, casting the ring of budding beech trees on the crown in a sinister silhouette. Emma shuddered with apprehension at the dark outline of the mount, wondering what lay in store for them.

By the time they parked the car in the lay-by, the sun had cleared the horizon and the eerie light had vanished with the stars. They climbed over a stile and walked along a narrow track hemmed in by dripping, stunted trees. Emma shivered and put her cold hands in her pockets, wishing she'd brought her gloves.

Following the damp and uneven footpath, they finally came to the foot of the hill. "The hill is posted," Emma said pointing to a "No Trespassing" sign nailed to a fence post. "But private property or not, we are going to the summit." Standing quietly for a moment, Emma bowed her head and in a low voice asked the Faeries of Place for permission to ascend. A slight breeze ruffled her hair. She took that as a sign and nodded to Jim, and they began their climb up Dragonsbury Ring in a clockwise spiral.

The climb was steep, and halfway up the hill, they stopped for a breather and looked around. The downs were gloomy with patches of fog, and the lowland vale beneath the hill was filled with heavy mist creeping inland from the sea. By the time they reached the summit, grey clouds had blotted out the promise of the morning, and a misty rain began to fall. Emma took the pendulum from her pocket, held it over her palm, and focussed her attention on the whereabouts of the cavern. First she asked about the west side of the hill, and the pointer swung anticlockwise to give a negative response. She asked about the north and got the same answer. When she asked about the east, the pendulum reacted by swinging quickly clockwise.

"The pendulum says the entrance to the cavern's on the east side. Let's see if we can find it."

"What's that lyin' on the grass?" Jim asked, pointing ahead.

A few yards in front of them was the crumpled shape of a big white bird, its wings spread out limply on the ground.

"Poor thing," Emma said, hastening to the body. "Oh God! It's a gannet and some bastard has stuck something through its eye!"

"What?" Jim exclaimed, getting down on his hands and knees beside her. "It's pinned to the ground with a bone . . . and some'ow it's still alive. 'Old on to the bird for a minute while I try and free it."

As soon as Emma's hands were on its body, Jim carefully pulled the bone out of the ground, and then he gently drew the sliver down through the gannet's ruined eye.

"Ugh!" he shouted, dropping the bone in surprise. "That sucker was squirmin' about in my 'and!"

Emma looked at the four-inch needle of bone lying on the grass. It was ugly, but it certainly wasn't moving.

"Sure you didn't imagine it?" she asked, glancing at Jim nervously.

Jim shook his head and stared in confusion at the horrid thing. "No, Em, I don't think so. Come on, let's get this over with. This place gives me the creeps."

Emma put the gannet gently inside her jacket to keep it warm and carefully pulled up the zipper.

"Em, look at the grass. It's all bruised," Jim said, pointing to the ground beneath their feet. "Considerin' this is private property, there's been a lot of people trampin' around up 'ere. Recently, too, by the looks of it."

On further inspection, they realised they were standing in a circle about twelve feet wide, delineated by a reddish brown powder that glistened on the grass. Moving to the centre of the ring, they saw three curved indentations forming a triangle. Around the indentations was a sticky patch of reddish brown stuff. Jim bent down to get a better look and suddenly jerked back.

"What is it?" Emma asked.

"Looks like dried blood. There's a lot more 'ere than the gannet would 'ave in its entire body. And it stinks. What is that smell?"

"Smells like bitter incense." Emma wrinkled her nose. *Incense,* she thought, *and a bird pinned to the ground and a blood circle.* The realisation floored her: the enemy had got there before them.

Closing her eyes, she switched to faerie sight and looked around the summit but saw nothing but evil radiations emanating from the hill and a faint residue letting her know the sapphire had rested there.

"Someone's beat us," she choked out. She held the pendulum over her palm and, concentrating on the sapphire, asked if it was still up on the hill. The pendulum swung to the left, answering no. Despair swept through her. "Jim," she said dejectedly, "the sapphire's gone."

"You put an awful lot of trust in the pendulum," Jim responded. "You might be mistaken. Maybe you subconsciously influenced the answer."

"No, Jim. The devil worshippers Trevelyan warned us about have been here already and taken the sapphire." Trying the pendulum again, she got the same answer. "There's no point in hanging around here. I'm going to take the gannet to the car."

"But what are we goin' to do about the sapphire?" Jim protested.

"We're dealing with black magic, Jim. That's what this shit is all about." She pointed to the blood circle. "I'm telling you, the sapphire's gone. We're too late!"

"Okay, Em, you go on down. I'm goin' to look for the cavern, and if I find a disturbed area, then we'll know for sure."

Emma walked off into the fog. She had failed. The sapphire was gone and they had no clue who had taken it. Confronted with the hopelessness of her situation, she started to cry.

On the third circuit down the hill, a nameless panic seized her. She wanted to run back to the car by the shortest way, straight down, but although she broke out in a cold sweat, she continued step by step to keep her feet on the spiral path.

Soon the urge to run came again, only stronger this time. Emma stopped in her tracks, closed her eyes, and tried to steady herself.

At the back of her eyes, little emerald polyhedrons appeared. She realised what they were, and she asked the Faeries of Place to help her.

Almost instantly, her plea was answered. The fog thinned out around her, and she saw the dim outline of a path alight with faerie glow below her. She uttered a heartfelt thanks for her salvation and continued down the hill, making it safely back to the car.

Jim watched Emma disappear into the mist. *Better get on with it,* he told himself. *The fog is gettin' thicker and soon I won't be able to see nothin'.*

Staring apprehensively up at the beeches, he wished they could talk. Those silent sentinels that for centuries had borne witness to men's madness could have told him a lot.

On his way to the east side of the trees, a dark patch of broken and uneven ground came into view, and as he got closer, he realised that it was a patch of dug-up earth. *It has to have been done earlier this morning,* he thought as he examined damp clods of chalk piled up around a six-foot square. Emma was right, someone had got there before them, and now he had the proof. He thrust his spade into the loose ground and pressed on it with his foot. It clanged on metal, and he jumped.

Fear seeped into his body in a long, slow crawl as he looked nervously around the clearing. The fog was thickening; he should be starting back. Taking a last look at the site, the clods of chalk morphed into dreadful dead faces. He stifled a cry and tried to turn away, but a strange fluidity propelled him towards the heads. Jim pitched forwards and fell, hitting his head on a clump of dirt. Stunned, he lay there for a few moments to collect his wits before he struggled to get up. His fingers closed around a damp piece of cardboard about two inches wide. As he touched it, a shock ran up his arm, and he dropped it. Realising that the piece of card might be a clue to the identity of the people who had taken the sapphire, he bent down to pick it up again, but an icy draught wrested it from his fingers and blew it into the fog. "You could 'ave got it," he muttered to himself. "Shock or no shock, now it's gone."

The fog was so thick that Jim lost all sense of direction as he wandered across the summit. Tall, dark shapes appeared out of the fog and loomed over him. He realised he was in the ring of trees and tried to get his bearings.

The surge of adrenaline that had powered him was gone, and the vague sense of malice he had felt was now real. A presence sapped his energy, and his eyelids felt so heavy he could hardly keep them open. His feet felt like lead weights as he staggered forwards like a drunkard through the trees. Losing his footing, he lurched and fell, banging his head again and scraping his chin on a tree root. Opening his eyes, he saw the piece of cardboard trapped at the base of the tree trunk before him. He snatched it up; it was a matchbook. He stuffed it in his pocket.

Icy, vaporous hands raked at his clothes, and he watched as ghostly arms stretched out to smother him. He cried out, but his scream was cut short by a purring whisper.

"Run! Run!" It urged, and he felt warm lips brush his ear.

Electricity surged through him, and without thinking, he bolted headlong into the fog, slipping and sliding down the slope to the bottom of the hill. From out of the murk, he felt something stab his hand and knees, ripping at his jacket and his trousers. Uttering a shriek, he fell heavily on the rain-soaked grass. The shock of the pain was suddenly blotted out by burning sexual desire. The husky, purring voice came again, urging him to touch himself, and just before he passed out, Jim saw himself as a stag in rut surrounded by waiting females. With a long, low carnal bellow, he slid his hand down his pants.

When he came to his senses, he was lying in the ditch by the road at the bottom of the hill, entangled in a barbed wire fence. His hands hurt like hell, and blood trickled down his fingers. After freeing himself from the fence, he pressed down on the bottom wire and slid through, ripping the back of his jacket on the way. His legs were weak and his genitals felt horribly swollen and sore, and there was a sticky patch in his pants. *What the hell?* he thought. What had made him do that? He had been so badly frightened that sex was the last thing on his mind. He staggered out into the road, but the fog was so thick he couldn't see a thing. He turned to the left and walked on slowly, keeping his foot against the grassy edge. Knowing Emma would be worried about him, he got out his cell phone to call her, only to find that the battery was dead.

Emma waited nervously in the car with the window rolled partly down and the doors locked. The fog had swallowed up the car and it was now so thick that the road had disappeared. She wished Jim would hurry up. It seemed that he'd been gone for hours. She looked over her shoulder at the gannet lying very still on the back seat. She leaned between the seats and gently touched it. It was warm, and she knew it was still alive. She heard a muffled cry and, turning in her seat, switched on the headlights. "Jim! Is that you? Where are you?" she shouted out the window. There was silence, and then she heard him shout.

"I'm over 'ere!" A few seconds later, he stumbled towards the car.

"Jim! Are you all right? What happened? You're bleeding."

"Yes. Just a bit shook up," he said breathlessly, leaning on the car. "Barbed wire. I ran straight into it. Do you think you could drive, Em?" he asked, holding up his bloodied hands. "I'm pretty shaky."

Emma started up the engine, and Jim got in beside her and turned up the heat. "Where's the flask of tea, Em? I'm freezin'."

"On the seat next to the gannet. Let me get it for you." She reached back and then handed the flask to him.

"Mmm, just what I needed," he said, pouring himself a cup.

"Which way do I go? I can't see a thing," Emma said, peering into the fog.

"Right and right again at the crossroads. One of my old friends, Sue, has an animal sanctuary not far from 'ere. She used to be a veterinary nurse and she'll know what to do with the gannet. We'll take it there. You'll like her. She's into a lot of spiritual stuff, 'ealin' and the like."

Emma pulled blindly onto the road and crawled along, expecting any minute to run into something. After a mile or so, the fog began to thin, and by the time they reached the crossroads, the road was clear. She was about to turn right when a green

Mercedes hurtled straight through the halt sign. The driver's head was thrust forwards, and his hands clenched the steering wheel.

"Jim! That sucker almost hit us," she said in alarm.

"What you on about?" Jim said with a yawn. "I must 'ave dropped off."

"We nearly got hit by a green Mercedes that ran the halt sign. It was going towards Dragonsbury Ring." There was a long silence, and then she said nervously, "I have a feeling whoever was driving the Merc was looking for us."

"Lookin' for us! Why? I mean, 'ow would anyone know we were up there?"

"I don't know," she said uneasily, "but . . . whoever the man was, he is insane. A madman. It's given me a bad feeling."

"I found the site of the sapphire east of the trees, just like the pendulum said," Jim said, looking at Emma nervously. "Damn! I left the shovel up there."

"Well, we are not turning round for love or money. We'll just buy another one."

"Somethin' 'appened to me up there," he said slowly. "After you'd gone down with the gannet and I was on my own, I could feel somethin' doggin' me. In the end, what with the fog closin' in, I panicked and ran straight down the 'ill and 'urt myself on the fence." He paused for a moment. "I didn't retrace my steps . . . it's worryin' me a bit, Em. I 'ope I 'aven't 'urt myself . . . other than physically, I mean."

An ominous feeling swept over Emma as she listened to Jim. "Something was following me too, trying to make me run," she said.

"I wonder what it was," Jim muttered. "Well, I didn't come away empty 'anded. I found this by the pit." He sniffed and gingerly pulled the matchbook from his pocket. "It's from a nightclub called the Blue Lagoon, in Baxter Street, Brighton," he said, reading the advert on the front. "Specialty exotic dancers."

Emma glanced at him and thought she saw a strange glow in his eyes, but it vanished in an instant.

"Gosh, I'm really tired all of a sudden." He yawned

"You probably caught a chill. It was bloody cold up there."

"I thought that after we've left the gannet with Sue, we would go on to Brighton and check out the Blue Lagoon. The matchbook is the only clue we 'ave to whatever was 'appening up there. You never know; it might lead us to the sapphire."

CHAPTER NINE

HIDDEN POWER

Greenfern Animal Sanctuary was about five miles along the Eastbourne Road outside of a little village called Appleton. "Turn left at the fork," Jim said as they left the village. "We're nearly there."

Emma turned into a narrow, sunken lane. The high, shaded banks on either side were full of dark ferns and great tree roots that stretched like giant spiders crawling to the road.

"Greenfern is just up 'ere," Jim said, pointing to the right. "Pull over by the sign and I'll open the gate."

"What about your hands?"

"They're not that bad. I can still use them."

Once they were through and the gate was closed behind them, they drove down a steep lane bordered by a low moss-covered wall. At the bottom of the hill was a two-storey grey-stone house and outbuildings with a gravelled parking area.

Emma switched off the engine, and they both got out. Opening the back door, Emma picked up the gannet and cradled it in her arms as she followed Jim to the side door.

A short, rather dumpy woman with unkempt ash-blonde hair stood at the entrance. She looked to be in her early thirties, and her smile radiated warmth and a sunny disposition. "Hello, mate!" she called when she saw Jim. "I must have known you were coming. I've just put the kettle on for tea. Though, you look like you might need something a little stronger." She eyed Jim critically. "You're all muddy."

"I fell down and 'ad a run-in with a barbed wire fence."

"Well, come on in," Sue said, waving them inside.

Emma followed Jim into a big, warm, and cheerful kitchen. A wood-fired Aga stove stretched along the left wall, and in the centre of the room sat a round table spread with a bright red-and-white tablecloth that matched the curtains.

"Sue Browne, this is my friend Emma Cameron. She's my partner in the market business," Jim said.

"Pleased to meet you," Sue said with a friendly smile. "Welcome to Greenfern Sanctuary."

"I'll wash the dirt off my 'ands." Jim went to the sink.

"See if you can get the puncture wounds to bleed," Sue said. Turning to Emma, she asked, "What have you got there?"

"We found a gannet on Dragonsbury Ring, and Jim suggested that we bring it here to see what you can do for it."

"Take a seat." Sue gestured to the oak chairs set around the table. Carefully taking the bird from Emma, she sat down beside her and set the gannet in her lap. "What were you two doing up on Dragonsbury Ring so early in the morning?" she asked, examining the bird's limp body.

"We were out for a walk," Emma said quickly.

"A walk!" Sue exclaimed, "I bet it was bloody cold up there." Her face grew hard. "Some bastard deliberately blinded its right eye. I'm surprised it's still alive."

Emma felt guilty about deceiving her, but what else could she have done? The truth was so fantastic that she could hardly believe it herself, and she didn't want to burden Sue with the reality of things.

Taking a bottle of Rescue Remedy from a cabinet by the door, Sue put a few drops in the gannet's mouth. She wrapped the bird in a clean towel and laid it in a box by the Aga to keep warm. "Do you want some Rescue Remedy, Jim?" She waved the bottle at him. "You look like you could use some."

Jim nodded and took the bottle and then put a few drops under his tongue. "I'm surprised the bird's alive," he said. "There was a piece of bone through its eye that staked it to the ground. You'd've thought that so much damage to its 'ead would've finished it off."

Sue looked at him uneasily. "What kind of bone?"

"I don't know. It was long and narrow like a skewer. It looked like it'd been sharpened and made especially for the purpose." Jim shivered. "I think I caught a chill up on the 'ill. I'll take a shower, if you don't mind. I've got a change of clothes out in the car."

"Wait a minute, Jim," Sue said. "Of course you can have a shower, but first, what happened to the bone?"

"I left it up there. It gave me a bad feelin', and I threw it on the ground. Did I do somethin' wrong?" he added hesitantly, sitting down.

"No, but I think you know a lot more about this gannet business than you're telling me. First off, I don't believe that crap about you two being out for a walk on Dragonsbury Ring so early. I mean, it's not like you live just round the corner or it's summertime, is it? In view of the circumstances, I think you'd better tell me the truth." She paused momentarily. "The gannet you brought here was used in a black magic ritual. It was blinded in the right eye so that when it died, its soul would fly left towards the devil. Now the bird's at my sanctuary, I'm likely to be psychically attacked."

Jim jerked forwards. "Oh, Sue! I . . . I wouldn't've . . ."

"It's all right, Jim. I know you did what you thought was right."

"We'll take the gannet to a vet if you don't want it 'ere," Jim said hastily. "Don't want to bring any trouble to you and the sanctuary."

"It's better if the bird stays here," she answered. "Trouble will follow it wherever it goes, and I'm better equipped to deal with the evil attached to it than Joe Public. But we have to find the bone that pierced its eye, otherwise I'm at risk and so are my animals. So tell me the bloody truth."

Emma met Jim's eyes, and the glance said a thousand words.

"Better 'ot the tea up," he said. "My shower's goin' to 'ave to wait."

Sue reached for a pouch of tobacco lying on the table. There was a long silence while she nervously rolled herself a cigarette. "Anyone else want one?"

"I do," Emma said. "One won't hurt."

"Make it three," Jim said. "I might as well get first-'and smoke!"

Sue lit her cigarette and passed the lighter to Emma. "Well," she said, "I'm waiting . . ."

"Go and have a shower," Emma said to Jim. "I'll tell Sue what's happening."

Emma told Sue her story, starting with the nightmare and ending with the gruesome find on Dragonsbury Ring. "That's why I didn't tell you the truth in the first place," she said. "I didn't really want you to get tangled up in . . . whatever we're in."

Sue stared at the flagstones on the floor and then slowly raised her head. "I don't know what to say. It's not that I don't believe you, I do . . . but it's too horrible to think about." She refilled Emma's teacup and rolled another cigarette. "I hope you know how to pray, Emma, because we are going back to Dragonsbury Ring. We need to find that bone," she said with a determined look in her eyes.

Their talk turned to lighter matters. Sue chattered about the sanctuary and the earth-healing ceremonies she conducted at the quarters of the year. Emma talked about Emily and the rituals they had practiced together. They found they had a lot in common and enjoyed each other's conversation. After Sue had asked a few questions about Trevelyan and Faerie, the conversation turned to Jim.

"I've known Jim for years," Sue said. "He was part of our animal-rights group when he lived in Brighton. I haven't seen him since last summer, and he's changed an awful lot. He's much thinner and rather pale. Has he been sick?"

"Not that I know of," Emma replied, "but . . . actually, I'm a bit worried about him myself. Trevelyan gave us special instructions about Dragonsbury Ring, as I told you, but Jim got frightened and came running straight back down the hill in the fog. That's how he ran into the fence. He seemed different when he came back." Emma paused and nervously bit her bottom lip. "I didn't notice the change in him straight away. The fog was so thick, and I was busy concentrating on the road, but when we got to the crossroads, the fog lifted, and he complained of being tired. It's true, we haven't had a lot of sleep, but when I glanced at him, his eyes were all bright and shiny . . . it's hard to put into words, but somehow it was spiritually horrible, if you know what I mean."

Sue nodded. "We'll have to keep a close eye on him. Meanwhile, I have some protective herbs that may help him. I'll go and get them."

She took down a glass jar of white angelica and another of juniper berries from a shelf.

At that moment, Jim came into the room rubbing his wet hair with a towel. "I found somethin' at the dig site," he said, sitting down and putting the matchbook on the table. Sue picked it up and examined the cover and then held it to her nose. "It smells like spikenard, mixed with something nasty."

"Spikenard! What's that?" Emma enquired.

"It's the oil that Jesus was anointed with before he was crucified," Sue said, getting up and filling a large bowl with warm water. She added a few drops of tea tree oil and brought it to the table. "Jim, let me take a look at your hands."

Jim winced as she straightened out his fingers. "Ouch!"

"There. That only took a couple of minutes," Sue said as she lifted his fingers from the water. "They looked a lot worse than they do now." Sue took the bowl to the sink and tipped out the water. "Before we go to Dragonsbury Ring, I'll take the gannet to my ceremony room. It'll be safer there." She cast an uneasy glance at the bird before picking up the box and hurrying through the sitting room door.

"I wish we brought the bone back with us," Jim said regretfully. "Now we've got to go back there again, and I don't want to go."

"Neither do I, but it wasn't our fault. We couldn't have known."

Sue returned to the kitchen with two small paper bags. "I thought you'd need a little extra protection for when we go up there," she said, handing the bags round. "I want you to put the berries in the right pocket of your trousers and the dried root and flowers in the left."

"Why?" Jim looked at her moodily.

"Just to be on the safe side."

"The safe side of what?" he answered, fidgeting in the chair.

"Emma told me that you ran straight back down the hill."

"Yeah! Yeah! But what's that got to do with berries and flowers?"

"They're plant allies, Jim. They vibrate much faster than we do, and that helps us keep our balance when we're frightened."

"Okay," he said reluctantly, and he put the herbs in his pockets.

Sue glanced out the window. "Looks like rain. Better wear my wellies. We'd better get a move on. I want to get there by noon. Even though the sky's cloudy, the sun will be directly overhead."

Five minutes later they were ready to leave. Locking the kitchen door behind her, Sue followed Emma and Jim to the car park. "We'll take my car," she said. "It won't draw attention. You'd be surprised how nosy the village people are when they see a strange car driving around. They report the registration numbers to the police."

"What do you mean by drawin' attention? Do you think we're in any immediate danger?" Jim asked as Sue pulled up the track.

"Possibly," Sue answered.

"What's that supposed to mean?" Jim shot back.

"My experience with satanists is limited, but what I do know is that they're all psychotic and that means they're dangerous . . . and unpredictable."

Emma laid her head back on the rest. The last thing she wanted was to go back to the hill. She couldn't see the point. Bone or no bone, the sapphire was gone and would soon be used against the Green. The thought depressed her, and she gazed miserably at the rolling downs and quiet country lanes they passed, wondering how much longer the peaceful Green would last.

"The idea of a cavern under the summit really creeps me out," Sue said as they turned onto the Spelborough Road.

"I think it creeps all of us out," Emma said quietly. "I wonder what's under there."

"We may have to take a look and find out," Sue said. "Whatever went on down there has everything to do with the sapphire, the gannet—and us."

"What if we can't find the bone?"

"I don't know. We'll just have to hope for the best," Sue replied. "And take things as they come."

"What kind of fuckin' answer is that?"

"The best I can bloody do!" she said sharply.

What's got into Jim? Emma wondered uneasily.

Sue pulled into the lay-by at the bottom of the Dragonsbury Ring. "We'll park here behind the bushes," she said, cutting the engine. "Then no one will be able to see the car from the road."

Sue got a spade out of the boot and locked the car.

"I'll carry the spade," Jim said. "My 'ands feel a lot better."

They stood on the verge for a moment and listened for any sound of vehicles or voices. All Emma heard was the drip, drip of raindrops on the tarmac.

Satisfied that all was clear, they climbed over the stile and walked in single file along the chalk footpath to the base of the mount. "We're going to have to be careful we're not seen," Sue said, glancing at the "No Trespassing" sign. "We don't want to get done for criminal trespass."

Stopping at the foot of the hill, Emma bowed her head and petitioned the Faeries of Place for permission to ascend. She took a bird call as an answer that all was well. "We can go now," she said, and they set off up the hill.

The rain came down steadily, and the ground was slippery underfoot. Emma kept her head down, watching her footing, trying not to think, existing only in the moment.

After what seemed an age of toiling upwards, they reached the top and took shelter under the beech trees to catch their breath. The wind had picked up and was pelting them with rain and flying twigs.

"Jim, where did you find the gannet?" Sue yelled over the wind.

"Over there." Jim pointed to the centre of the ring. "Come on, I'll show you."

Moving swiftly, they walked across the hilltop.

"It was about 'ere, wasn't it, Em?" Jim asked as he stopped and looked at the grass.

"Yes, the bone should be somewhere around here."

Putting down the spade, Jim got down on his hands and knees. "It should've been lyin' right 'ere," he said anxiously. "I can't see it."

"Did you throw it somewhere?" Emma asked.

"No, I dropped it. I didn't bung it anywhere, if that's what you're gettin' at."

"It should be here, then," she said, continuing to look.

Sue joined in the search, but after a few minutes, they gave up.

"It's gone," Jim groaned. "Somethin's taken it. What do we do now?"

"Not something, some*one*," Sue muttered. "The bone is cursed and no animal would go near it; they know better. The satanists knew that whoever was coming to get the sapphire was a caretaker and would have helped the bird. They bet on your compassion and got lucky. Anyway, we'd better not hang around in the open." She took a worried look at the road below. "Let's get going. This place gives me the creeps. Jim, where's the pit?"

"On the east side of the ring, about twenty yards from the trees," he replied hoarsely, picking up his shovel and then dropping it. "This way."

Jim just left the spade where it lay. Emma glanced at him apprehensively. He seemed to be unaware he dropped it. She picked it up and, with Sue by her side, followed him through the beeches to the east side of the rise.

"'Ere's the excavation," he said nervously, pointing to a square of slushy chalk.

"Somebody's been up here since we left." Emma pointed to a fresh cigarette butt on the ground.

"There's nobody about now," Sue said taking another look around. "But they could come back at any time. We'd better get a move on."

Putting the spade into the loose earth, Jim cleared away the chalk.

"The main ceremony for the sapphire would have been held in the cavern," Emma said. "I wonder if the gannet was a secondary spell."

"If it was," Sue said, "the bird's energy will have an association with the satanic ceremony. It's what is called a 'sending'. We have to go down there," she pointed to the cavern, "and find out what the connection is. Our lives may depend upon it."

The covering of earth was only a foot deep, so in a matter of minutes, Jim had exposed a shiny metal door. In the centre was a large ring.

"This sucker's brand new," Jim said, heaving upwards on the handle. The door pivoted open, revealing a flight of stone stairs leading down into darker shadows.

The air that rushed out to meet them was cold and heavy with the stink of bitter incense. Sue took out her pocket flashlight and switched it on. "Here goes," she said apprehensively, starting down the steps.

"Come on, Jim," Emma said, seeing he was hanging back. "Or would you rather stay here and keep guard?"

"No! I'm comin'."

The stairs led down to a space that daylight couldn't penetrate, and here they stopped. Sue shone her torch into the darkness. From the little they could see, it seemed they were in a fairly wide cave. "I wonder how far back it goes," Sue murmured, walking a few steps forwards and shining the light around.

As the outermost beams of the torch breached the blackness, Emma thought she saw two red points of light glowing on the floor. "Sue! Shine the torch on the ground ahead."

The earthen floor beneath them had been cleared of rocks and was firm and smooth. The light revealed an inverted pentagram enclosed in a double circle with two red gemstones set at the base of the upright points.

"The two rubies represent the blood-filled eyes of Baphomet, the satanic goat," Sue said grimly. She shone the light directly onto the pentacle, but the darkness swallowed up the beam.

Closing her eyes, Emma summoned her faerie sight, and when she looked into the pentacle again, she saw a bone and a white feather tied to a small bundle in the centre of the star. She pointed it out to Jim and Sue. "I'm going to get it," she whispered.

As Emma moved forwards, the torchlight dimmed, flickered, and went out, leaving them in shadow. A loud clang came from behind them, and the meagre daylight shining down the stairwell was suddenly cut off.

"Someone's slammed the door! We're shut in!" Jim cried in panic.

They were trapped in the rotten-sweet effluvium of evil.

That odour was terrible enough, but Emma detected another, the faint, indescribable stench of dead flesh. To her dismay, the rubies in the pentacle began to glow.

A mephitic red fog streamed upwards, twisting with incredible swiftness into a huge, hunched, hooded shape. Lowering her eyes, Emma stared at the ragged hem of a heavy red cloak hovering about three feet above the circle.

Behind her, a high-pitched keening escaped from Jim's throat, and Sue prayed in a shaking voice for their deliverance from the glowing apparition.

Emma shuddered. Terror banged at the doorway of her mind, and turning inward, she desperately called upon her faerie power for help. Then Trevelyan's words catapulted into her mind: *"Withdraw from thought, for thought is the root of fear. And if you do not fear, the enemy is impotent."*

Reinforcing the emerald shield around her, Emma slowly looked up. The soul-destroying hate that looked back at her below the hood blasted her psyche. She cried out and staggered backwards.

In the churning hate, she forced herself not to think, not to let the fear hold sway, not to give away her power. Choking against the noxious fumes that flooded into every pore, she took a shallow breath and then reached up to grasp her topaz necklace.

"Eh-hon-na-he-*ssh*!" she cried, accentuating every syllable and sending the sibilant down into the earth.

An electric shock shot up her spine, momentarily paralyzing her, and then a majestic power swept through her body. Lifting her eyes defiantly, she pulled the topaz from its chain. The jewel drew across her fingers and then morphed into a long, glittering knife.

Standing strong in the emerald light, Emma raised her arm and hurled the knife at the burning ruby orbs that she knew instinctively looked not only out but in into misery and death.

There were blasts and rumblings, and small rocks tumbled from the ceiling. The emerald light flooded the pentacle, and the demon responded with a dreadful neighing scream. The churning grey vapours shrank back, spiralling into the lustreless ruby stones, and the awful light around the pentacle slowly faded.

Diving forwards, Emma grasped the bundle and put it in her jacket pocket. The blackness in the vault was thick and suffocating. Emma lost all sense of direction and wandered in the dark. She had no idea of where she had stood or how many steps she'd taken, and in that moment, she wasn't even sure who and where she was. All she knew with any certainty was that she had got what she was looking for.

The rays of a torch suddenly blinded her.

"'Ere, Em!" Jim cried, grabbing her arm and pulling her body to him.

"I've got the bundle," Emma whispered into his neck. "It's in my pocket. We've got to get out of here." Her body was stiff and her words came in a monotone.

Releasing his grip on her slight frame, Jim swung the light into her face again. Her eyes had shrunk back into their sockets, and the black holes of her pupils had swallowed up the green.

Leaving Emma with Sue on the bottom step, Jim raced up the stairs and pushed and pounded with all his might against the metal door. Sue joined him on the top step, and together they heaved, but the iron slab wouldn't budge an inch. They were entombed.

"'Elp! 'Elp!" Jim screamed at the top of his lungs, but the sound of his voice was thrown backwards by the iron sheet. Sue took a step down, drew in a breath, and released a piercing, metallic holler, quickly followed by a more harmonic note. The sound electrified the air and woke Emma from her stupor.

She grabbed Sue's arm. "Let's shout for help together."

Synchronising their breathing, they gave a mighty shout. "Again, Sue, let's do it again!" Emma shouted, fully in her senses and determined to get out.

"This ain't gonna work," Jim said. "Let's see if we can find anythin' to 'ammer at the door with. That's our only 'ope of someone 'earin' us." He shined the torch ahead and went back into the cavern. Emma followed him down to the bottom step and then watched the beam as it played around the walls and floor.

"This will do," he said, grabbing a small brass brazier and carrying it up the stairs. When he got to the top step, he turned the brazier upside down and swung the base at the door. The clang was deafening. Jim hammered away until his arms were tired. "It's no good. I'm exhausted," he said dejectedly.

Standing in the dark on the cold stone steps, Emma listened. Fearful seconds ticked by, and the deathly silence was broken only by the blood pounding in her temples.

From above, she thought she heard a muffled response. Jim hit the door again, and after the reverberations had died away, they were left in silence.

Slowly, as if in answer to their prayers, the iron door creaked on its hinges. A crack of light showed at the edges, and then sunlight flooded the shaft. They bolted up the steps and out into the sunshine. Jim went last, and he threw the brazier down the steps and slammed the trapdoor shut behind him.

Standing in front of them looking totally bewildered was a tall, gangly, sandy-haired teenager in a red anorak and hiking boots. "I was walking the footpath," he said. "Got to do it these days. These landowners like to block them off. Don't like public rights of way across their land. Anyway, I heard all this booming underground, and at the risk of getting caught for trespassing, I thought I'd take a look. It took me a couple of minutes to find out where the sound was coming from," he said, looking at the door. "Excuse my curiosity, but how did you get shut in? And, what is that—"

The ground shuddered beneath them, almost knocking them off their feet, and the air popped and crackled with electricity. Alarmed, the hiker backed away and broke into a run, quickly disappearing down the hill.

"We'd better get out of 'ere," Jim yelled, picking up the shovel.

A bitterly cold blast of air hit Emma in the face as she turned to cross the clearing, and a powerful magnetic force sucked them all back towards the iron door.

"Hold hands!" Sue screamed, trying to keep her footing. Linking their hands, they inched away from the cavern, forcing their feet forwards, one step and then the other.

After an eternity of pushing through the cold, smothering force, the pressure slowly eased, and they stumbled forwards. Down one side of the hill the road was clearly visible, and Emma anxiously kept watch upon the narrow, twisty lane.

Halfway down the spiral, the sound of a vehicle on the road below reached them.

"Get down!" Sue hissed, "We don't want to get caught up here."

They hit the soggy ground. Emma hoped their green macs and wellies would act as camouflage. Raising her head, Sue peered through the hedgerow. "Looks like a Range Rover," she whispered.

The vehicle went past and then turned into the lay-by. A moment later, a door slammed.

"The bastards are checking on my car," Sue said worriedly.

After a little while, the Range Rover reappeared and drove slowly back towards them.

"Keep your heads down," Sue whispered. "I think they're looking for the owner of the car. I don't fancy meeting up with them."

The vehicle slowed to a crawl along the road, but then it went round a bend and out of sight.

"Come on!" Sue said, setting off at a run. "Let's complete the spiral and get the hell out of here."

At the bottom of the path, they heard the sound of another vehicle in the lane and hid behind the hedgerow. Through the bushes, they saw the same Range Rover coming along the road.

"They're driving up and down until the owner of the parked car comes back," Sue said, putting her hand into her pocket and pulling out her car key. "We can't hide all day, so I'm going to try and think up a cover story. I want you and Jim to sneak away along the footpath and get to my car. Here are the keys. Don't get involved. Just get clear, and call Chief Inspector Farran at the police station in Market Thorpe if I don't return."

"But—"

"No buts, Emma. We're dealing with psychotics and we can't take any chances."

The vehicle drew nearer.

"Quick! Go!" Sue hissed and took off.

Emma and Jim crouched behind the thickest part of the hedge, and as soon as the Range Rover had passed, they made their way along the inside of the hedgerow to the car.

As the vehicle came around the corner, Sue stepped into the road and waved for it to stop. The window of the Range Rover slid down, and a hawk-faced man stuck his head out. "Yeah!" The tone was surly.

"My beagle bolted after a rabbit, and I've lost him. You haven't seen him, have you?"

"Lost your doggie?" The voice was mocking, and the man's beady eyes bored suspiciously into hers. "What were you doin' on the hill?"

"I lost my dog and I was looking for him. Have you seen him? He's only so big." She measured with her hand.

"How did you come to lose your dog? Don't you know you have to keep dogs on a lead? This is all private property." The man waved a nicotine-stained hand out the window towards the hill.

"I was on a public footpath, and as I said, a rabbit ran out of the hedge. My dog pulled the lead out of my hand and ran off."

The man gave a harsh laugh. "It's probably been caught in a snare somewhere." He leered at her.

The stress of the last hour suddenly took its toll, and Sue burst into sobs. "I'm just looking for my dog, all right?"

"Plump and pretty is boo-hooing," the driver said to his mate, a rat-faced man who made rude gestures at her with his fingers.

Sue suddenly realised that the driver was taking a photo of her with his phone, and she quickly looked away.

"Something's probably eaten it already." The driver laughed and put the phone down. "Now, tell me again. What was you doing on the hill? You don't come from around here, and I think you should come with us so the boss can ask you a few questions."

Alarm bells rang in Sue's mind as she saw the passenger door open.

She ran along the verge towards the lay-by and gave a distinct holler. She knew Jim would recognise the distress call from their anti-hunting days.

"Wait!" Both men were out of the vehicle and sprinting after her.

Emma sat tensely in the car with the engine running and the window rolled down, ready for action.

Sue's call reached them, and Jim cried, "Sue's in trouble! Quick!"

Emma accelerated in the direction of the sound. Rounding the corner, she saw Sue running towards her with two men in hot pursuit only yards behind. Switching on the headlights, she screeched to a halt beside her beleaguered friend. Sue jumped into the back seat, and Emma put her foot down. In her rear-view mirror, she saw the men running back to the Range Rover.

"That was close," Sue said between pants. "They didn't buy my story and tried to kidnap me."

"Kidnap you! Are you sure?" Emma exclaimed.

"Of course I'm bloody sure."

The sky drew dark as Emma drove towards the coast. Thunder rumbled ominously in the distance.

"Come on, Emma, drive faster," Sue said. "The whole set-up on Dragonsbury Ring has made me fear for the safety of the gannet."

The horror of the last hour had entirely exhausted Emma. Her head ached and her chest was tight, making it difficult to breathe. In an effort to calm her nerves, she concentrated all her energy on driving.

Rain started to fall as they turned onto Appleton Road. The motion of the car suddenly made Emma feel queasy, and she opened the window.

"Are you all right?" Sue asked with alarm. "You look very pale."

"No. I feel sick. Have to stop."

Emma pulled over on the verge, opened the door, and retched in the ditch.

"I'll drive," Sue said when Emma came back to the car. "Why don't you lie down in the back and have a rest."

CHAPTER TEN

THE SENDING

Closing her eyes, Emma laid her head on the seat. Her mind was fractured, and she felt nauseous and physically exhausted. She'd been hijacked and thrown head first into nightmare of unimaginable proportions. Her normal life, whatever normal was, had been totally screwed, and there was no way out. Trevelyan had said that she had agreed in another space and time to save the Green, but the knowledge did nothing to appease the resentment she felt now.

"The dogs are loose," Sue cried, stopping the car.

Emma opened her eyes. "What's going on?"

"Someone's been here and left the gate open," Sue answered anxiously. "I'm going straight to the house. If I drop you off here, Jim, can you close the gate behind me?"

Jim nodded. "Sure." He got out.

Sue drove through the gate and down the track to the car park. After a quick look at the stables to make sure the doors were shut, she hurried to the house.

"Be careful, Emma, the window's been smashed and there's glass all over the floor," Sue said as Emma came in the door. Cautiously stepping around the glass, Emma saw two sets of muddy footprints leading to the lounge and back again.

"I'm off to check on the gannet and then have a look upstairs," Sue said, and she disappeared through the door.

"I'd like to get my 'ands on the bastards that did this," Jim said angrily, looking through the kitchen door at the glass. "Where's Sue?"

"She's gone to check on the gannet. I hope it's all right."

"Me too. I'd better get this glass off the floor," Jim said, "before one of the animals steps on it." He took the broom and dustpan from the cupboard and started sweeping up the mess.

"Whoever broke in here didn't harm the gannet, but this was definitely planned," Sue said, coming back into the kitchen.

"Planned!" Emma exclaimed. "How do you know?"

"They emptied my dirty-washing basket on the floor and took my soiled underwear and my hairbrush," she replied, putting a bicycle pump and an incense burner on the table. "No doubt they're going to try to curse me with my hair and body fluids. I can take care of the sending myself, but it's my animals I'm afraid for. These types of people hurt things just to get their rocks off, and I don't want any of my critters nailed to the door."

Emma felt dreadful. Unwittingly she had put Sue and all her animals at risk. "Sue, I feel awful," she said apologetically. "I'm sorry to have dragged you into this—"

"Like the bleedin' rest of us," Jim mumbled. "But don't be blamin' yourself, Emma. It's that Trevelyan creature that's be'ind all this. I'm tellin' you, if I'd've known what we was gettin' ourselves in for, I would never've agreed to go to Dragonsbury Ring. 'E's no good."

"He saved my life and yours too," she retorted sharply, noticing uneasily that he had called her Emma.

"We've only got 'is word for that. 'E put a spell on us, and now we're payin' for it. 'E's probably watchin' us now and 'avin a damn good laugh at our expense. 'E really saw you comin', Emma."

Emma glanced at him in dismay. He sneered, oddly confidant, and using her sight, she saw a definite tainted-orange glow around him. She quickly looked away. A shudder ran through her. It was the same colour she had seen in the crypt when the incubus attacked her.

She bent her thoughts to Trevelyan but could find no resonance in the ether. And that made her even more fearful. Building an octahedron around herself, she tried to push the fear away. *Don't think*, she repeated to herself over and over. *Just be present*. That was easier said than done.

"Did you make the tea, Emma?" Sue asked, "If not, I'll put the kettle on."

"Yes. Oh!" Emma jumped up. "I forgot; it's stewing in the pot."

"Stewed enough to stand a spoon upright in," Jim commented. "I like the sound of that." He leered at Emma as she handed him his cup.

"What's the bicycle pump for?" he snorted.

"Just a little added protection," Sue replied, eyeing him coldly. "It's filled with holy water, and it doubles as a cosh."

"A cosh and 'oly water!" Jim exclaimed. "What, we 'avin a bloody exorcism?"

"Yes, Jim, and you don't have to join us if you'd rather not," Sue answered solemnly, shooting an uneasy glance at Emma.

Jim grunted. "I'm off to 'ave a shit," he said, going towards the bathroom.

Emma waited until she heard the door close behind him, and then she said anxiously, "I wonder what's got into him. He's rough but he's not crude, and his sexual innuendos are making me uncomfortable. And I've seen an ugly orange glow in his aura. There's something I haven't told you, haven't told anybody." Emma paused and then went on to tell Sue what she had experienced in the cellar.

"And you're seeing the same colour around Jim?"

"Yes," Emma replied. "I think he's being attacked by a succubus. I found the herbs you gave him for protection on the floor of the car. He must have thrown them down. And he keeps on calling me Emma. In all the time I've known him, he's never called me that."

"Hmm. He is acting very odd, not like him at all," Sue said. "There's a lot more going on here than meets the eye. I'll check out his energy when he comes back." Leaning forwards, she put her hand on Emma's arm. "I've got a bad feeling about the gannet. By rights, the bird should be dead, Emma, dead. There's a hole right through its skull. I think the bird's body is possessed, and that means we're up against a very powerful black-magic spell, maybe cast by more than one sorcerer. My guess is there are two of them, the god and mother goddess. Oh!" She dropped her voice. "Here he comes."

Jim came slouching back into the kitchen.

"Could you light the incense burner, Jim?" Sue asked before he could sit down. "You'll find charcoals and frankincense resin over there." She pointed. "And then come join us in the ceremony room. Come on, Emma, let's go and make our preparations."

Leaving Jim in the kitchen, they went through the sitting room to a side door. "I saw the orange glow in his aura," Sue said as they walked through the conservatory. "That's why I asked him to light the incense. It should see the succubus off, at least for the time being."

At the end of the walkway, they arrived at a stout oak door with a dainty silver horseshoe nailed to it with the arch pointing upwards as protection against evil faeries. It reminded Emma of Emily's little saying: "Up for luck and down for Puck."

The ceremony room was big and painted in a muted shade of green. On two sides were padded benches and opposite the door, a bookcase. A large pentacle surrounded by two circles had been drawn on the floor in yellow chalk, and the gannet lay in the centre of the star.

"I put the gannet's head facing the south," Sue explained. "That's the direction of fire, and we want the bird to live until the curse can be removed."

Looking around the circle, Emma noticed that Sue had addressed the other cardinal points as well. A bowl of dirt guarded the north, incense burned to the east, a yellow candle had been lit to the south, and a bowl of crystal water sat to the west.

Jim arrived in a haze of smoke carrying the smudge pot, and Emma noticed that the orange taint was gone.

"We'd better take a look inside the sending," Sue said. "Emma, bring the bundle over here to the table, and Jim, keep us wreathed in the incense while I open it. That'll protect us from what's inside."

The packet had been wrapped in black cloth and then sealed in a thin plastic bag. Attached to the top of the bag was a small gold feather tied on with a piece of sinew. Holding the sending in the smudge smoke, Sue slipped off the plastic cover. As she pulled away the black fabric, a rotten smell flooded the room. "Phew! Stinkhorn," she said, pinching her nostrils.

"What a pong!" Jim said, wrinkling his nose. "Smells like a sewer."

"It's called *Phallus impudicus*, the witch's egg. Looks like there's blood in the slime." Sue peered at the fungus. "I bet you a penny to a pound that's menstrual blood."

"Seems everything these sickos do is sexual," Emma said with a cough.

"That's because sexual energy is the most powerful force on earth. Degenerate sex is a magnet for demons." Sue took a tin can and a small crystal knife from the shelf. She put the fungus in the can and pushed the lid on tightly. "Now this is what we're going to do." She passed the knife through the smudge smoke and gave it and the feather and bone to Emma. "I want you to go in the pentacle, put the feather and the bone next to the bird, and when I've finished calling the directions, stab the gannet through the heart."

Emma balked at the idea. "Me! Why don't you do it?"

"Because this gannet business is all about you, and you have to bring it to a conclusion."

"I'll do it," Jim offered.

"No!" Emma interjected, suddenly loath to let Jim touch the gannet or the knife. "I just don't like the idea of taking anything's life, cursed or not, but I'll do what's necessary."

Sue looked at the clock. "It's ten minutes to three. Let's get this show on the road. As long as the gannet lives, all of us are in danger." She fanned incense over Emma's head and then around herself. "There's an opening in the pentacle on the east side. We'll stand over there."

They congregated behind the brazier of burning incense. Emma saw an opening in the pentacle in front of where she stood.

"In you go, Emma," Sue whispered, giving her a nudge. Emma hesitated for a moment, and then, swallowing hard, she stepped in.

Sue closed the circle behind her and said a prayer petitioning lords of Falias, Murias, and Finias to guard their respective compass points. As she called upon the Lord of Gorias, the emerald city in the sky, Emma felt a subtle stirring in the air above her head. An ice-cold dampness seeped through the floor, and the candle flame on the south side of the pentacle turned a vivid orange red, flickered wildly, and then went out. The temperature dropped, and a sickly sweet odour penetrated the room.

A chill wind began blew around the circle, and leaden light descended over the room. "Emma!" Sue shouted in alarm. "Something's wrong. Quick, stab the gannet through the heart!"

The wind blew stronger as Emma raised the knife, but before she could strike the gannet, a blow from above knocked her off her feet. A heavy body sat astride her, and she felt hot breath upon her face.

"Jim! Get off me! Get off me!" she screamed as he viciously gripped her wrist and tried to take the knife.

Adrenaline surged through Emma's body as they struggled on the floor, and she kicked him with both feet and crawled towards the gannet. Raising the knife a second time, she could feel Jim's sweaty hands groping her bare legs under her skirt and pulling her body back towards him.

In a final desperate effort, Emma lunged at the bird. There was a crack as her head hit the floor and the knife flew from her fingers.

When Emma came to, she was lying on the floor.

"You all right, mate?" Sue asked, standing over her. "Come on, let me help you up."

Emma shakily looked around and saw Jim stretched out in the pentacle. There was blood on his face and a broken flowerpot beside him.

"I had to clock him one," Sue said grimly. "He tried to rape you."

"Oh my God!" Emma exclaimed weakly. "What happened?"

"I don't really know, it happened so fast," Sue said, helping Emma to a seat. "A dirty neon-orange glow appeared over your head, and a bolt of light shot out of it and hit you in the face. Then Jim dropped the smudge pot and it rolled into the pentacle. That broke the circle and left you spiritually defenceless. That's when he attacked you. As he flung you onto the floor, the knife flew out of your hand and went straight through the gannet's heart. Then there was a flash of orange light. It blinded me for a minute and I couldn't see a thing. When my sight cleared, I saw him trying to drag you underneath him, so I picked up the nearest thing I could find and hit him with it."

"The knife must have been guided by Faerie," Emma said. "Or we just got lucky."

"Well, the bird's gone on, and that's a blessing," Sue said. She went to Jim's body and checked his vital signs. "Don't want him choking," she said, turning him on his side. "We'll check on him later, but I think he'll be round in a few minutes. Come on. Let's go to the kitchen. I'll clean up in here later."

Emma tried to find Trevelyan, but there was still no sign of his presence on the air, and she wondered anxiously if something had happened to him.

She was in a daze as she stepped into the conservatory, and she barely felt Sue's hand on her arm, guiding her to the kitchen. Sue grabbed a bottle of whisky and glasses from a cabinet in the sitting room, and once they were in the kitchen, she poured out two good measures and sat heavily in a chair beside Emma at the table.

"What am I going to do? Jim's being attacked by a succubus." Emma flexed her wrist and winced in pain. "We came in his car, so I've got to go home with him. What if he gets taken over and attacks me again?"

Sue regarded her gravely. "I don't know. He probably doesn't even know what happened to him."

Emma sipped her drink. "I know exactly what Jim's going through thanks to my brush with the incubus, but he's a danger to me. He can't help himself, just as I couldn't. I was lucky." She sighed long and hard. "Why is all this sexual shit happening? I've tried to contact Trevelyan, but I can't find any trace of him, and I don't know what to do for Jim."

At that moment, Jim stumbled through the door holding his head. "What 'appened to me?" he asked miserably

"You were possessed by a succubus, and you attacked me and then you tried to rape me," Emma shouted.

"What!" Jim swayed on his feet and then lurched into a chair. "This isn't true! Tell me it isn't true."

"You attacked her, all right, and I cracked you on the head with a flowerpot," Sue said.

Gingerly touching his head, he looked at Emma in confusion and defeat. He put his head in his hands and sobbed piteously. "Em! I'm so sorry," he cried wretchedly through his tears. "I'd never 'urt you . . . you know that. The last thing I remember is sweepin' up the glass. Please believe me, Em. I 'onestly don't remember." He stretched out his hand to touch her.

"Keep away from me!"

Sue got up and took another glass from the cupboard, poured a drink, and put it on the table in front of Jim. "Have a drop of whisky. It'll help steady you. Then perhaps you should take a shower and clean yourself up a bit," she said kindly. "Get that blood off your face."

"I'll do that," Jim said, his voice shaky. He downed the drink in one, and with a last pleading look at Emma, rose from the table.

Sue went into the sitting room and returned with a book and a small can. "This is pepper spray," she said. "Put it in your handbag. If he's attacked again, at least you'll have a fighting chance." She flicked through the pages of the book and then showed a page to Emma.

"Succubus," Emma read, "from the Latin *succubare*: to lie under. A succubus is a female demon, a sexual vampire that sustains itself on the sperm of mortal men, draining them of their fluids until they waste away and die."

"John Keats wrote about succubi in his poem 'La Belle Dame Sans Merci'," Sue said. "'O what can ail thee, knight-at-arms, alone and palely loitering? The sedge has wither'd from the lake, and no birds sing.' Not a pleasant prognosis." She stood up again. "I've got a lot of chores to do in the yard. Want to come with me?"

"No, I'll stay here," Emma said distantly. She was preoccupied with thoughts of going home with Jim alone. She decided she would drive back to Basingstoke. That way, if he did intend to attack her, at least he couldn't turn off along some lonely country road.

Her mind wandered to the matchbook he'd found. It was their only clue to whoever had beaten them to the sapphire. She had to go to the Blue Lagoon and check it out, and Jim would have to take her. Again she sent her thoughts out for Trevelyan, but all was still and silent. Where was he when she needed him?

Jim came back soon and hesitantly sat down. "Em," he said, "if we're goin' to Brighton to check the Blue Lagoon, we'd better think about goin'"

She looked at him warily. "I'm frightened to be on my own with you. The succubus used you to attack me. What's going to stop her doing it again?"

"I'm just as scared as you are that it'll 'appen again. She takes over my body and I'm 'elpless." He nervously pulled on his earlobe. Then he said miserably, "You'll never understand."

"I do understand. I never told you this, but the reason I didn't have any clothes on when you found me in the cellar was because I was taken over by an incubus."

"What?" He stared at her in horror.

"We're victims of sexual demons, Jim."

"There's somethin' I should 'ave told you too, Em. After I ran down from Dragonsbury Ring, I was attacked. She 'ad sex with me at the bottom of the 'ill. I couldn't do nothin' about it. I wish Trevelyan were 'ere. 'E'd know 'ow to 'elp," he said, swallowing hard.

Emma checked his aura for orange, but there was no trace of the unclean spirit in his energy. He was Jim again, but for how long?

The grandfather clock in the hallway chimed five. "If we're goin', we'd better get off."

Emma shivered. She was taking a risk just being around him. Before she could give him an answer, Sue came in carrying a bucket. "Are you coming with us to the Blue Lagoon?" Emma asked, fervently hoping she would go.

"No, those thugs in the Rover took my picture, and they're the type to frequent a stripper joint like that. Anyway, I've got to go into town and get a piece of glass cut. I can't leave the window like this. I'm going to have to get a move on."

"Are you goin' to report those men in the Range Rover?" Jim asked, stretching his legs.

"I don't know. I'll see if Tony, that's Chief Inspector Farran, is on duty. If those thugs got my address through the national police database, I'm going to have to be careful who I talk to." Sue put on her jacket.

"Well, Em," Jim said, "shall we go?"

"Yes." On the way out, Emma caught Sue's eye, and patting her handbag, gave her a knowing smile.

CHAPTER ELEVEN

THE READING

Leaving Greenfern shortly after five o'clock, Emma and Jim made their way to Brighton. The rain had cleared, but the sky was still leaden and threatening, reflecting their sombre mood.

"You all right?" Jim asked as he parked in the multi-storey car park by the seafront.

"Yes," came her curt reply. But she wasn't all right; she was frightened and still disorientated from his attack.

As they walked along the promenade past the rows of brightly painted shops, Emma relaxed a little. If Jim was taken over again, there were plenty of people around to subdue him.

A police car pulled up a few yards ahead of them, and Jim hurried towards it. "Cops! They're sure to know where Baxter Street is."

Emma watched as the sergeant gave directions, and as Jim came back, the officer eyed her up and down. She felt he was looking right through her, strip-searching her with his eyes, and quickly looked away.

Turning right, they walked along the busy street to the traffic lights. "Left at the lights, right by the off-licence, and then left again," he repeated the directions.

"That copper gave me the creeps," Emma said as they crossed the road. "There was something weird about him."

"Yeah! There was somethin' shifty about 'im. After 'e'd given me directions, 'e asked if I was lookin' for any place in particular. I was goin' to ask 'im about the Blue Lagoon, but I thought better of it."

"So what did you tell him?"

"That I was doin' some market research and needed to interview shopkeepers in a not-so-well-off part of town, and someone'd suggested Baxter Street."

"Impressive," Emma murmured.

It was a good ten-minute walk before they found Baxter Street. It was a drab road lined with buildings originally built in the eighteen hundreds to house railway workers and their families. The mean, narrow buildings seemed to lean forwards, and the street was quiet but for the clicking of their boots upon the pavement.

The nightclub was situated in the middle of a block of dingy, dark terraced buildings that stood shuttered against the street. The club was a black windowless cube with an iron-bolted front door. Above the entrance was a single caged light bulb that flickered yellow in the gloom, and on the door a hand-lettered sign read, "Open at seven."

Jim looked at his watch. "We've got over an 'our before it's open. Let's walk to the end of the road. Maybe we can make some discreet enquiries."

Several doors down from the club was a fish-and-chip shop, and the air coming from the open door was stale and stank of rancid fat. Several pimply kids were leaning on their bicycles outside eating crackling from greaseproof paper bags, and to Emma's disgust, one hawked on the pavement as she and Jim passed. She averted her eyes across the road to a business with a colourful green door and windowsills. The brightness of the paint in contrast to its shabby neighbours had an almost hypnotic effect on her. Grabbing Jim's arm, she pointed at it. "Let's go and see what that shop's all about."

They crossed the road and saw a snappy sign hanging on the freshly painted door:

I an' I, Inc.
Psychic readings, tarot cards, crystals, candles, love potions, and
good luck charms.
Prop. Omar St Louis

Underneath, a smaller sign said, "Closed. Open again at six."

Emma decided there and then that she wanted a reading. If this person wasn't a fake, he might be able to shed some light on who was attacking her.

Jim's stomach rumbled. "What do you say we get a bite to eat? I'm starvin'."

"All right, but I'd like to stop here on our way back to the Blue Lagoon." She pointed to the psychic's shop. "I'm going to have a reading. And maybe you could find answers to your . . . problem."

"Okay, Em, but first we'll see 'ow your readin' goes. Right now all I can think about is food. Even the smell of the fat from the chip shop's beginnin' to smell good."

Rounding the corner into Waldorf Street, Jim pointed to an Indian restaurant. "Let's try this," he said eagerly, steering Emma across the street. "Looks like a clean place, from the front, anyway," he added.

The Taj Mahal was empty, but as soon as they entered, a waiter appeared from the back to greet them and take them to a table. Sitar music played softly and the air was full of delicious aromas coming from the kitchen.

"This is a nice place," Jim said, looking round. "I'm glad we came in 'ere."

After placing their order, they sat in strained silence and waited for their food. Emma nervously watched Jim for any sign of a change in personality, but so far he was normal. The waiter returned with a trolley and served two plates of dhal and rice and two halves of lager.

"There's a club round the corner in Baxter Street called the Blue Lagoon. Do you know it?" Jim asked him.

The Indian man's dark eyes shifted uneasily from side to side, and his face turned a paler shade of brown. He shook his head and quickly turned away to wait on new customers coming through the door.

"Did you see the look on 'is face when I mentioned the club?" Jim hissed.

Emma nodded.

They finished their meal, and as they paid the bill, the waiter whispered to Jim, "The Blue Lagoon, very bad place."

Back outside, a light rain had begun to fall, and as they turned the corner into Baxter Street, a cold wind whistled along the narrow road towards them. Reaching the fortune teller's brightly painted door, Emma pushed it open. Little bells tinkled above her head, and the warm smell of amber flooded into the street. The shop was dimly lit, and reggae music played softly in the background. As there was no one in attendance, they hovered by the counter and looked around. Behind the front desk were rows of shelves packed with candles, herbs, resins, incense holders, and myriad other things all piled on top of one another. The counter itself was glass and was almost completely covered by bowls of beads, feathers, trinkets, and good luck charms of one sort or another.

"Can I help you, mon?" The voice was West Indian, deep, rich, and sonorous. From the shadows at the far end of the room emerged a thin man about six feet tall dressed in a purple kaftan. Long dreadlocks streaked with grey hung about his shoulders, and a heavy chain of amethysts glittered on his neck. "I am Omar St Louis," he said, looking at them with dark and serious eyes.

"I see from your sign that you do tarot readings. Is it possible to have a reading?" Emma asked hesitantly, taken aback at the sight of him. He was so tall, so imposing, and so black.

Omar nodded. "For the straight five cards, I charge a tenner, or a half-hour reading for thirty quid, mon."

Reaching in his pocket for his wallet, Jim said, "I'll pay for the readin'."

"My name is Emma, and this is my friend Jim," she said, hoping that Omar wasn't a bullshitter that had moved up from the pier.

"Come this way, mon, to my reading room," he said, leading them down a narrow hall. The tilted floor creaked with age, and the walls were plastered with bright posters of Jamaica, healing plants, and one of a flying saucer hovering over Stonehenge.

They followed Omar through a screen of thin bamboo canes into a comfortable studio. The lighting was dim, and the warm air hung heavy with the sweet scent of amber. The walls were decorated in shades of red, green, and gold, and on the wall facing them was the Jamaican flag and a poster of Bob Marley. In one corner was an altar, partially covered with red silk and set up with candles, statues, and photographs. In the centre of the room was a round table with two chairs opposite each other. Resting on the tabletop were a pack of tarot cards and a bell.

"Please sit, sit down," Omar said, bringing up another chair for Jim. They settled down, and the Jamaican man took his seat directly opposite. Next to him on a small, low-legged table were a ball covered in a blue velvet cloth and a bowl of small stones with several copper-wire pyramids beside it. Placing the tenner Jim had given him on the low table, Omar flicked back his dreads, picked up the bell, and rang it three times each in the four directions. He handed the deck of tarot cards to Emma. The deck felt like a lead weight in her hands. Now that it came down to it, she didn't really want to know about the nightmare that had become her waking life after all. She sat motionless, fighting back an urge to throw down the cards and run. Emma felt Omar's eyes upon her.

"Concentrate on the question you want the cards to answer. Then shuffle the pack, cut the cards four times, and give them back to me, mon."

After the fourth cut, she handed the cards back to Omar. Bowing his head in prayer, he laid the first five cards face up on the table in a cross. His eyes lingered over each card, gathering their energetic information.

Studying the spread, Omar felt his chest constrict and cold pins and needles creep up his neck. The tower, the moon, and the nine of swords lay across together; above and below, the high priestess and the queen of wands stared back at him—and both were ill favoured and reversed. The malevolence of the spread made his breath catch. He sensed this woman was at the centre of a cosmic battle between good and evil. She was in grave danger, both spiritually and physically, to herself and those around her.

He felt a great evil hovering just beyond his range of vision. A film of sweat broke out on his face, and the room seemed to turn chilly and close in on him. Picking up the ten-pound note, he slid it back across the table.

The clock on the wall chimed seven. "Time I was closin', mon," he said, getting up abruptly.

"What did the cards say?" Emma asked anxiously, rising from her chair.

Omar hurried them out of the studio, through the jumbled shop, and to the door. His reaction to the cards had freaked Emma out. He had seen something dreadful in the spread; she had seen it in his face.

Emma stopped. "Please tell me what you saw," she pleaded.

"Sorry, I have to close," Omar said gently, gesturing to the door.

"Now wait a minute. You've frightened my friend. I think you owe us an explanation," Jim said, keeping his voice reasonable. "You've upset 'er. The least you can do is tell us what's goin' on. Or do you want us to pay you more money? Em, this is probably a scam. He's tryin' to do us over."

Pulling a card from inside his kaftan, Omar said, "I an' I don't do no one over. I'm sorry for the lady. Call me," he said, thrusting a business card in Jim's hand. Before they could say another word, Omar herded them out into the street. The door slammed behind them, and the lock turned.

Emma clung to Jim's arm. "Maybe he saw my death and didn't want to tell me," she said anxiously.

Jim was just as concerned as Emma. In an effort to try and make her feel better, he said, "Now come on, Em. Stop thinkin' morbid things like that. It's more likely he's tryin' to run a scam. He knows 'e's frightened the shit out of you. That's why 'e gave me 'is card. Scare tactics, Em, that's all. Did you see all the resins in 'is shop? And he 'ad all of them biblical oils as well. Onycha, hyssop, aloe, and spikenard—spikenard was on the matchbook."

Emma was only half listening, constantly checking Jim's aura for any trace of orange.

"The club should be open by now," Jim said. "Let's go and get a drink. Maybe it'll put stuff in a different light."

Omar St Louis turned off the lights and retired to his studio. The reading had affected him badly. He was no stranger to voodoo and wickedness; it all went with the business. But this was something else—way too heavy for him. What could he have told her? She was being pursued by fiends from hell. He pitied her, though. She looked so frightened and defenceless. She had the same haunted look as . . . Hot tears trickled from his eyes. His Lucy had had the same look before the mamba came for her.

He picked up the deck of tarot cards and put them down again. They had a strange and unpleasant vibration about them, he thought, but maybe it was just a hangover from the reading. Lighting an incense stick, Omar placed it into a holder, and switching out the light, he went upstairs to his bedroom.

CHAPTER TWELVE

THE BLUE LAGOON

The road was empty with the exception of a green Mercedes-Benz parked outside the nightclub.

"That looks like the same car I saw run the halt sign at the crossroads when we left Dragonsbury Ring," Emma said. She memorised the number plate.

A sign of a go-go girl flashed from the front of the club, and they hesitated before approaching the black and intimidating entrance. Finally Jim pushed the door open.

The clubroom was dark and cool; the walls were stained a dingy yellow from the nicotine of countless cigarettes. A waitress wearing a low-cut blouse, a very short skirt, and high heels lounged on a high stool at the bar. At the back of the room was a stage with stacks of plastic chairs and a pole. A sign announced, "Exotic dancing starts at eight o'clock."

Emma sat at a table while Jim went up to the bar and ordered their drinks. While he was waiting, he asked for a light, and the barman flicked him a book of matches.

A commotion in an adjacent room jerked him to attention. There was a crash, a scream, and then silence. From a door at the back of the club, a thin, dark, middle-aged man with no chin and a receding hairline stormed past the bar and out the door, slamming it so hard that the room shook.

"Someone's in an 'uff," Jim said with a laugh to the bartender, a burly man with naked women tattooed on each arm.

"That's none of your business," he growled, putting the drinks upon the counter. "I wouldn't be asking questions if I were you. Someone might get the idea that you were snooping." He tapped the side of his nose with his index finger. "And that wouldn't be good for your health. Got it?"

Jim nodded, and the barman moved away. Picking up their glasses, Jim hastily retreated to where Emma was sitting.

"I thought for a moment 'e was goin' to pop me one," Jim said. He showed Emma the matchbook. "It's the same as the one I found on Dragonsbury Ring."

"Jim," she whispered, bending towards him, "the man who just left was the one I saw driving the Mercedes at Dragonsbury Ring."

"Are you sure?"

"I wouldn't forget his face in a hurry."

A door banged and a shapely girl with long blonde hair walked unsteadily to the bar, giving Jim and Emma a fleeting glance as she went by. Emma couldn't help but notice her tear-stained face and rapidly swelling eye.

"She came through the same door as the thin bloke," Jim hissed. "They must've 'ad an argument."

"Fucking bastard! He didn't have to punch me," the girl said in a shaking voice to the waitress sitting at the bar. "Give me a large gin and tonic, Jamie," she said to the bartender.

"You'd better put an ice pack on that eye of yours, Tina," he snarled, putting her drink on the counter. "The regulars will be here soon to see you dance, and you've got to look pretty for them."

"They're not interested in my face," the stripper said wearily. "That man's a monster, a fucking monster. He's evil."

"I'd shut it if I were you. He pays you, doesn't he?" Jamie said aggressively. "You could be back to turning tricks for a couple of quid in the back alleys opposite the pier."

"Take it easy, Jamie," the waitress spoke up, checking on Tina's eye. "The boss shouldn't be beating up on us girls; he doesn't pay us enough."

"I've told you before, kid, when Giles Kingsbury tells you to drop your knickers, you drop them."

Tina downed her drink and pushed her glass towards him. "Another one."

"And you, Sugar," Jaime said threateningly to the waitress. "You keep your beak out of the boss's business too." He glared at Tina. "And no more booze until the show is over."

"Come on, let's go and fix your eye," Sugar said. She grabbed Tina by the arm and pulled her through a side door to the right of the bar.

"Giles Kingsbury," Jim whispered to Emma, putting the matchbook in his pocket. "At least we know 'is bloody name."

At the back of the room, Jaime was setting up the chairs in rows before the stage for the dancing.

"We should finish our drinks and go," Jim said. "There's nothin' to be gained by stayin' 'ere."

Emma drained her glass and followed Jim out the door.

The Mercedes was gone and the road was empty. "It was Kingsbury's car," Emma said. "I wonder where he went."

The evening had turned blustery and cold. Emma shivered as they walked back down the steep and narrow streets to the multi-storey car park. "Jim!" she said, pointing to the right as they turned the corner to the sea front. "There's a green Mercedes pulling into the forecourt of the Star Hotel."

"The devil 'imself," Jim said as Kingsbury got out of the car and handed his keys to the doorman who came smartly over to his side.

"Come on, let's go after 'im," Jim urged as Kingsbury disappeared through the revolving glass door.

"Hang on a minute," Emma said nervously. "He might recognise us from the club, and I'm not really dressed to go in there."

"'E didn't even glance at us when 'e went stormin' by. And as for clothes, we're not goin' to the restaurant, we're just goin' into the lounge for a drink, and we are not exactly scruffy," he added, looking at his brown cords and sensible leather shoes. "Come on, we don't want to lose 'im."

Kingsbury was standing at the main desk when they entered the lobby.

"Mr Kingsbury!" the manager said. "Lady Feodora St Clare is waiting for you in your suite. She was very insistent, sir, that I let her in your rooms. I trust I've done the right thing."

"Yes, yes. I'll go straight up. We are not to be disturbed. Understand?"

"Yes, sir."

"No phone calls."

The manager took a card from a filing cabinet and made a little note.

"What now?" Emma asked as Kingsbury went up the stairs to the first-floor landing.

"We'll wait. Let's go and get a drink," Jim said, steering her through a glass door to the right marked "Lounge".

The lounge was elegantly decorated with dark panelling and red-and-gold carpet. A chandelier hung from the ceiling with beige silk lampshades covered in small teardrop crystals, bathing the room in a warm, soft light. Several groups of people were sitting at the round polished tables in comfortable padded chairs, talking in soft voices and drinking aperitifs. Jim and Emma chose a table that gave them a good view of the lobby

"I'll go and get the drinks," Jim said. "You stay 'ere and watch for Kingsbury."

The minutes ticked by and there was still no sign of him.

"Do you think 'e's upstairs for the night?" Jim asked, starting on his second pint.

"God knows," Emma answered wearily. "Are we going to sit here until they throw us out? I am so tired."

"If that's what it takes, Em. We've been to 'ell and back today, and I'm also exhausted, but I don't believe in coincidence. I 'ave a feelin' there's a reason we saw Kingsbury, so we're goin' to sit 'ere till they close."

The lounge filled up with people who had made dinner reservations. Suddenly Giles Kingsbury appeared in the crowd with a stunning woman on his arm dressed in a tight black skirt suit, black seamed stockings, and high heels. She was slim and long, the picture of haute couture. Although her features were classically beautiful, her blue eyes were cold and dead.

Sitting down at the table next to Jim and Emma's, Kingsbury clicked his fingers in the air, and a waiter came running to take their order. Emma watched Kingsbury from the corner of her eye as he checked his cell phone. A look of annoyance crept over his face, and getting up from the table, he excused himself for a moment and went out to the lobby, leaving his companion alone at the table. Feodora looked slowly round the room at the people in the bar.

Emma suddenly felt an irrational desire to get up and introduce herself to Feodora. The pressure to answer the command was relentless, and Emma desperately clung to the underside of her chair with both hands. Feodora's attention was suddenly diverted to the door. Kingsbury was back, looking pale and shaken. He nervously helped himself to one of Feodora's Sobranie Cocktail cigarettes lying on the table and lit it.

"Well, darling," Feodora said in a husky voice with a heavy East European accent. "What is so wrong that you have to leave me alone in this dump? You look a wreck. What has happened?" She reached over and wiped a smudge of lipstick from her lover's neck with a cocktail napkin.

"My suspicions have been confirmed," he said loudly. "That fucking bitch at the club has been talking out of turn, damn her."

"Lower your voice," his mistress hissed. "What do you expect? You lay with dogs . . ."

Giles Kingsbury's face contorted with rage, and his eyes narrowed into slits. "The police are on to us, but that shouldn't be a problem." He sucked on his cigarette.

"What do you mean by 'us'? I have no part in any of your doggy hobbies," Feodora snorted. "You'd better shut your bitch up. Nothing, and I mean nothing, can interfere with the ceremony next Sunday. This is the culmination of all our efforts, and now that we have the sapphire in our possession, I am not going to let some little whore interfere."

"Yes, yes. I'll see to it myself. I should have broken her fucking neck while I had the chance," he muttered.

"Is the policeman in charge one of ours?"

"No. It's a Chief Inspector Farran. He's a good guy," Kingsbury said sarcastically. "But I'll fix him. I'll teach him to interfere in my business. I'll talk to the chief constable about Mr Tony Farran and get him off the case. The chief and I share the same interests—"

"Call him now," Feodora interrupted. "We have no time for obstacles."

Giles looked at the wall clock behind the bar and hesitated.

"Right now," his mistress insisted.

"Right," Giles replied.

"Mr Kingsbury," the waiter said, "your table is waiting."

Feodora rose up like a snake, and with a last piercing glance around the room, she led Kingsbury into the dining room.

Emma heaved a sigh of relief as the couple disappeared. "They've got the sapphire, Jim. You heard what she said."

"I did. They didn't care if anyone over'eard them, either. 'Ow's that for fuckin' arrogance? Let's get out of 'ere."

Without looking back, they left the lounge. The lobby was empty and a new shift clerk was on duty.

"Goodnight," he said cheerily as they went out.

The road outside the hotel was busy, and Emma found comfort in the bright lights and the hustle and bustle of the seafront.

"Of all the luck, Em!" Jim exclaimed as they walked back to the car park. "Do you think we should go to the police and tell them what we 'eard them say about Tina?"

"Oh, come on. We're going to tell them that we overheard two people talking in a hotel lounge about murdering someone and having the chief constable in their pocket? They'll probably ask you what you've been smoking."

"We got to do somethin'," he said worriedly. "'E's threatenin' to kill that girl. You 'eard that woman, what's 'er name?"

"Feodora St Clare," Emma replied. "You mean that crack she made about the policeman on the case? 'Is he one of ours'?"

"Do you know what that means? The police got 'is back. 'E can do anythin' 'e likes, and 'is buddies in the police will cover it all up."

Emma was thoughtful. "Isn't Tony Farran Sue's friend?"

"I think 'e is. I'll call Sue first thing in the mornin' and tell 'er what we learnt."

"Feodora said something about dogs too. One of Kingsbury's police friends must have found out that Tina made a complaint against him for organising dogfights. I wonder if that's why he punched her at the Blue Lagoon."

"I don't think it was the dogfightin' business, Em. Kingsbury punched 'er at the club before 'e got the phone call at the Star."

"Perhaps Sugar was right and it was about sex," Emma postulated. "He wanted it, she didn't, so he whacked her one."

"If so, we just 'appened to be in the club at the right time," Jim said. "Another 'alf-hour and we would've missed it all. We wouldn't've known Tina's name or that Kingsbury and 'is bitch 'ad the sapphire. Now all we 'ave to do is steal it back."

"How's that for synchronicity," Emma agreed. She realised that some exterior force had guided them to the Blue Lagoon at precisely the right time. She didn't know to what or where the information they had acquired at the club would lead them, but she knew intuitively that they had been meant to hear it. She also realised that if Omar had continued with the reading and not pushed them out the door, they would have missed the pot of gold.

"You've had a couple of pints, so I'll drive," Emma said as they got to the car.

CHAPTER THIRTEEN

SUCCUBUS

"Nice clear night," Jim commented as they drove west.

"Yes, it is," Emma replied, keeping her eye on the road. "So much has happened today that it's all a blur, but it's unbelievable how everything's come together even though we were beaten to the sapphire. We would never have known who took the portal stone if someone hadn't dropped the matchbook and if you hadn't found it."

"It was a stroke of luck."

"Luck!" Emma retorted. "More like celestial intervention. I gave up on the hill but you carried on. Thanks to you, we still have a chance to get the sapphire before the gates to hell are opened."

"Some'ow we've got to get it, and that's goin' to be easier said than done. First we got to find out where Kingsbury lives." Jim sighed. "So much 'as 'appened my brain 'urts."

The miles seemed to drag by, and Emma noticed uneasily that as they got closer to home, Jim became fidgety and strangely energised. "Can you stop up 'ere for a minute?" he said when they left the motorway. "I need a leak."

When Jim came back, he opened the driver's door. "Budge over, Emma," he ordered, forcing her into the passenger seat.

Out of the corner of her eye, Emma saw a faint buzz of orange in his aura. Perspiration broke out on her forehead, and she stifled a gasp and slid her hand into her bag, grasping the pepper spray.

Just before her driveway, Jim stopped the car abruptly in the lane. "Emma, I never told you 'ow much I fancy you," he crooned, putting his hand on her leg. Realizing he was being taken over by the succubus, Emma flipped back the cover on the pepper spray. She had a moment of indecision, and then opening the car door and raising her hand, she sprayed Jim in the face. He yelped and put his hands over his eyes, and she jumped out and dashed in a panic for home. She slowed down at the entrance to her driveway and looked back. Seeing no sign of Jim following, she sprinted along the pathway to the house. She fumbled in her handbag for the key and then turned it in the keyhole, burst into the kitchen, and locked the door behind her again. Her nerve gave way, and she leaned against the door and sobbed hysterically.

"Good evening, m'dear." Trevelyan's voice rolled over her like balm, soft and reassuring.

Emma looked across the room at the kitchen table. "Trevelyan!" she cried, rushing to his side. "Thank God you're here. Jim—"

"Emma! Calm yourself," he said, putting his hand on her arm. "Come outside to the garden. There is no moon to hinder us, no prying evil light."

Following him through the door into faerie starlight, she deeply breathed in the jasmine-scented air. Arching across the velvet sky above her was a star-bow shimmering with the fantastic nameless colours of the Otherworld. Emma heaved a sigh of relief. She was safe, protected from the horror that had become her life—safe with Trevelyan in Faerie.

Emma gazed at the sky, and Trevelyan read her memories of the day. A trap had been set on Dragonsbury Ring, and Emma and Jim had fallen into it. Trevelyan blamed himself. He should have gone with them to that accursed hill and shadowed their footsteps, but Ke-enaan had sent an urgent summons to Black Head over the airwaves, and Trevelyan had gone straight away to the wizard's halls. Trevelyan knew that now, in a short space of time, the enemy's dark servants would come slithering, squirming, and walking out of every cave, mine, and shadowy place into the light of day. The battle for the Green had begun.

In the fifth density, the emerald city of Gorias was under siege. In the fourth, Niamh's twin sons, Kilfannan and Kilcannan, were fleeing north to the Crystal Mountains in Connemara. And in the third, Emma and Jim were in mortal danger. The attack was coming from all sides, angles, and dimensions. He had to act fast. Emma he had secured in Faerie, but what about Jim? Switching the focus of his attention, Trevelyan looked into the human world.

Jim was at home in the shower trying to wash the pepper spray from his face and hair. He couldn't remember what happened, but someone had sprayed him in the face. *Was it Emma?* he wondered.

No, Emma wouldn't do anythin' like that.

"Oh yes she would. And she did," a voice purred in his head. "She's a bitch. Look how ungrateful she is for all you do."

"Yes, she is ungrateful," Jim said to the voice, remembering the dinner, the roses, the champagne, and how Emma had given him the cold shoulder afterwards. All he had wanted was a kiss and a cuddle.

"She thinks she's too good for you," the voice purred again.

"Bitch!" Jim exclaimed. "Just a teasin' bitch, always flashin' those green eyes and wigglin' 'er ass."

"Emma," Trevelyan said, "'Tis time we paid Jim a visit. He is at home, and a succubus is with him poisoning his mind against you. We must be quick! If she succeeds in turning his love for you to hate, she will violate his being and destroy him. Only his love for you stands in the way of his destruction, but with the shifting of his mood, that will soon change."

Emma gasped. "Poor Jim! What can we do?"

"You must go to his house now. The succubus is in Jim's body, and she will want you to come in."

"I hope you're coming with me," Emma said, eyeing him anxiously.

"If I am to trap the succubus and banish her to her enchanted wood," Trevelyan responded, "you must first persuade Jim to invite me into his home."

"What . . . what will I say? What happens if I'm in his house and I can't get him to invite you in? I'm going to be raped and murdered!" she cried, shaking her head. "I don't think this is a good idea."

"Fear not, Emma. I will be watching you from Faerie and will put the words into your mind." Trevelyan waved his eyeglass in the air and weaved ruby rays around her body like a shawl.

Emma took in a deep breath and exhaled strongly through her nostrils. "I'm not at risk, am I?"

"Risk, there is always risk. But trust I will give you the words to say."

"What if something goes wrong?" Emma protested. "I'll be done for."

Trevelyan's face darkened and his whole being became transparent. "Did I not say that you would find the words?" His voice came from every corner of the garden and every nook and cranny in the walls. This was a strong reprimand for Emma's lack of trust, and she flushed.

"Now come, we must make haste," Trevelyan said more softly.

The garden shimmered, and in the next instant, Emma found herself on the Jim's doorstep. Taking a deep breath to steady herself, she rang the doorbell.

The door slowly opened, and Jim peered with bloodshot eyes round it. "Emma!" he said. "What are you doin' 'ere?"

Emma cringed at his use of her full name and looked warily around. "I was thinking about what happened at Sue's sanctuary this afternoon. I couldn't sleep, so I thought I'd come round and see if you were up. I saw the light on, so I rang the doorbell."

"'Ow did you get 'ere?"

She frantically searched for an answer, but he said, "Come in. I've been so miserable, I'm really glad to see you."

Following him into the sitting room, she sat down on the sofa, keeping her guard up. "Trevelyan was waiting for me when I got back to the house," she said nervously. "He had Chloe with him and he told me he can help you."

"'Elp me! What with, Emma?" Jim said, giving her a puzzled look.

"Something got inside you this afternoon and you tried to hurt me. Trevelyan's got a charm to keep . . . the thing away."

"I told you, I don't remember," he said with a frown.

"Yes you do," the voice in his head whispered. "You wanted her, like you want her now."

"This charm Trevelyan wants to give me. Where is it?" Jim asked, eyeing her hungrily.

Emma sat forwards in her seat. An orange haze was forming around his body, waxing brighter with every second, and a sweet, sickly stench permeated the room. "Trevelyan has it," she said hastily. "He would have come himself, but he didn't know if he'd be welcome. And he has Chloe with him. Your house isn't like mine, so he needs an invitation."

"Chloe!" Jim's eyes gleamed. "Trevelyan knows 'e can come in 'ere at any time."

Emma's heartbeat quickened. "Is that an invitation?" she asked eagerly.

The lights in the room flickered and went dim, and Emma's stomach churned as the odour of the succubus filled her nose.

"Yes," Jim said, "of course." But then, "No, Emma!" he shouted. "'E can't come here! All this shit that's 'appening is because of 'im."

Emma froze. His voice was mean and ugly, and a wild light flashed in his eyes. *The pepper spray*, she thought. But then she realised she had left it at home.

A tremor run through Jim's body as he sat next to her on the sofa, and she noticed with rising alarm that his hands twitched uncontrollably. "Come 'ere, Emma. I know what you came 'ere for," he muttered, his eyes blazing with lust. A dark orange glow filled the room, and the charnel perfume of the succubus clogged her nose.

Emma started to get up, but Jim grabbed her by the hair and pulled her onto the carpet. Taking her wrists, Jim forced her arms to the floor, and his mouth clamped on hers. Unseen hands pulled down her jeans, and long nails scored her flesh like razor blades. Jim wrenched her legs apart with his knee.

Trevelyan! Emma screamed in her mind. *Help me!*

The air grew hot and churned violently around her as if it, too, was struggling. Jim let out a cry and rolled off her body. Emma staggered to her feet choking with the stench of burning hair.

Sitting up, Jim looked dazedly between his legs, and seeing his huge erection, he let out a shocking scream that trailed off into terrible despair.

"Jim Lynch!" Trevelyan's voice thundered. "Get up!"

"Please 'elp me," he moaned wretchedly, stumbling to his feet, trying desperately to cover himself.

The light in the room dimmed, and Emma heard the excited bark of a dog. They were safe in Faerie.

"Trevelyan! What took you so long?" Emma asked shakily.

"Forgive me, m'dear. I had to wait until the succubus had taken complete control of Jim. Otherwise, I would not have been able to banish her."

Emma nodded. "I understand, but it gave me a bad fright."

"Methinks a drop of my special brandy is in order," Trevelyan said, bringing a tray containing three glasses and a decanter to the table. He handed the drinks round. "Slainte! Your good health!" Trevelyan reached into his waistcoat pocket and secreted something in his palm. "I have something here that belongs to you, m'dear. Your necklace," he said, opening his fingers.

"My necklace!" she cried, taking it and fastening the chain around her neck. "But how did you get it? I thought . . . I thought I'd lost it."

"Lost! Nay, the topaz is a charm that I created, and after you routed the demon Zugalfar in the cavern, the stone returned to me."

"Zugalfar?" Emma questioned.

"Yes, the arch demon Zugalfar the Red. He is fraught with poisonous design. Many have tried to defeat Zugalfar and have paid with their lives. And souls." Trevelyan smiled at her kindly. "You are very brave, m'dear. Warrior, I name you."

"Is he gone . . . forever?" Emma asked, swallowing hard.

"No, m'dear, you just sent him back to the hell worlds. He can yet be summoned with blood and human sacrifice at any time."

Trevelyan spiralled his hand in the air and presented to Jim a heavy silver ring with a brilliant green stone. "This is a peridot, a gem born of fire and air, and I want you to wear it. The succubus will not be able to draw near you while the ring is upon your finger. But," Trevelyan said as Jim slipped it on, "the peridot merely keeps her at bay. It does not remove her from your energy, and should you take off the ring, she will return. I warn you, she will try to get you to take it off." Glancing at Emma, he said, "When the succubus departed, did you not detect the smell of burning hair?"

Emma nodded. "Was it the peridot that burnt her?"

"Yes. The succubus is of the water element of the second estate, hence the orange colour that you see when she appears. The peridot is fire mixed with air, the third and fourth estates. Fire in the Heart, I name it. A love stone that turns water into steam."

Refilling their glasses, Trevelyan sat beside them in the window seat and waved his eyeglass in the air. The amethyst lens glittered warmly in the sunlight, bathing the room in a purple glow.

"Thank you for the ring," Jim said. "I saw a flash of orange light in the cellar . . . was that a succubus?"

"Yes," Trevelyan answered. "The colour orange that you saw contained not only the vibration of incubi but succubi as well. Once in the cellar, I had to trust that your love for Emma would protect you. And, your love for her prevailed. The succubus could not draw nigh. It was only later when you broke the spiral on the Dragon's Hill that she seized her chance and possessed you." He smiled kindly at Jim. "Forgive me for putting you at risk. There was no other way."

Jim gulped. "But what is a succubus? Where do they come from?"

"Let me explain. At the time of the Separation, there was a wonderful being called Agdistis, possessing male and female sexual organs. She was the mother goddess of all creation.

"The destroyer was jealous of her, so he tricked her into castrating her male parts. Agdistis fell into the lower dimensions of Faerie. In her misery, she created a male son and took him to her bed and spawned succubi and incubi. Both of you have been attacked by these creatures of myth and legend," he said, glancing at them. "Jim was attacked on Dragonsbury Ring, and you, Emma, were attacked in the space beneath your house."

"You never did tell me what happened to me down there," Emma said.

Trevelyan laid his hand gently on her arm. "You remembered what happened to you as a child, and when you revisited the place of your greatest fear, an incubus used that fear and cast a spell on you. 'Twas then that I tossed Naka to you." He gave her a reassuring smile. "I knew the incubus was there, but I had my hands full trying to close the portal to the hell worlds." He sighed. "Emma, you had to fight your darkness, the darkness attached to you from past traumas. And you triumphed! But you also were attacked by an incubus on Dragonsbury Ring."

At the mention of it, Emma shivered, remembering how close she had been to bolting down the hill. "Something came after me when I took the gannet to the car," she said. "I didn't feel anything sexual from it, just hate. That's when I called on the Faeries of Place to protect me."

"When you got to Dragonsbury Ring," Trevelyan continued, "succubi and incubi were already there, called by sexual magic to the terrible ceremony in the cavern. The great fear that came over each of you was a spell, a fear spell designed to make you flee down the hill to the safety of your car. Jim, through no fault of his own, broke the spiral, and thus he had no spiritual protection, and the succubus fastened to his energy." He smiled reassuringly at Jim. "'Twould have all been the same if Emma had broken the spiral. The incubus would have possessed her in the same way as the succubus claimed you. But Emma called upon children of the fourth ray, and being on the spiral faerie path, they immediately responded. In truth, a great evil dwells in the hill, but it does not yet have the power to draw nigh to the living green with the love of Faerie on it. In ages past, the hilltop was full of light. Earth is slow to forget her golden age of joy, and her blessed servants shall not retreat from their long home. Until the Green falls."

Perfumed sunlight streamed through the open window, and Emma listened to the sweet trilling of songbirds in the garden, their symphonies a welcome salve for her battered mind.

Making passes in the air with his hands, Trevelyan looked intently at Jim and Emma. A pot of red geraniums appeared before Jim on the table. "Geraniums will keep the succubus from your house. This flower is called the goblin bane in Faerie, for the petals burn those that reside in Lower Faerie."

"Goblin bane, eh! I mean, it's 'ard to believe in this day and age that we're bein' attacked by demons," Jim muttered.

"Demons?" Trevelyan repeated. "If you are referring to succubi and incubi, you are wrong. 'Tis only in your world that they are predators. In my realm, their faerie nature waxes strong and they are great champions of the Green. Understand! Their attack on you is not personal. They are not creatures of the abyss or mere demons; they are in a class all their own and reside in Lower Faerie. They are different aspects of the same desire, bisexual creatures that take both sperm and egg to procreate themselves.

"A short time before I arrived at your house," Trevelyan continued, "Kilfannan and Kilcannan, the last creators of the Green, were attacked by a score of goblins from the mines. The goblin chief was out to kill them both, for the enemy has put a great price upon their heads. 'Twas a succubus in her reptile form that saved their precious essence. And Emma, in Faerie you and the succubi fight together in the battle for the Green. You could say that in my realm, you are sisters."

"Sisters!" Emma was astonished, and rising from her chair, she spilt her drink on the polished wooden floor. "Oh! I'm sorry," she said. "But how can you say that we're sisters when the succubus tried to kill me?"

With a glance from Trevelyan, the brandy rose from the flooring and streamed back into her glass. "'Tis not her fault, Emma. It is her design, just as the human programme is to feed on other animals. Is her crime, in her eyes, any more than that of humans? I think not! 'Twas the fall of Agdistis into darkness that separated her male and female parts, forcing them ever to seek unity through the egg and sperm of humans in the mortal world." Trevelyan leant towards her and touched her lightly on the arm. "Close your eyes, m'dear."

Emma did as she was told and saw little orange polyhedrons appear in her inner space, and as she watched them, she saw a woman with singed long red hair and startling turquoise eyes looking out over green fields from the shadow of a wood. The figure turned to face her and smiled. Emma gasped. Budding, blooming, and then fading in her pale blue skin were small sprays of orange roses.

"Remember," Trevelyan said, "in rash judgement, there is folly."

"I've no idea how to deal with these creatures," Emma said, staring at him in amazement. "I tried to call on you for help this afternoon, but there was no trace of you on the airwaves."

"No, m'dear. Alas! I should have marked your footsteps on Dragonsbury Ring, but I had no time." His eyes held hers in a steady gaze. "Emma, you must learn to trust your faerie nature and use it. Trust! It will not betray you. There may come a time when I, too, will fall, and you will have to carry on as well as you can without me."

Emma was quiet. The thought that she might lose her greatest help in the battle for the Green frightened her. What would she do without him? "Why couldn't I find your resonance? What happened to you?"

"I was on the Burren in County Clare taking council with Ke-enaan," Trevelyan replied, getting up to refill their glasses.

"There, I tarried long, for we had much to talk about. So, for a while in your time, I was unavailable."

"Trevelyan," Jim said, "Emma 'ad a tarot readin' in Brighton, and the psychic wouldn't tell 'er what 'e'd seen in the cards."

"He basically threw us out of his shop," Emma said. "And I don't know why, or what he saw."

Fishing Omar's business card from his back pocket, Jim gave it to Trevelyan. "In view of what's happenin', I think we need to talk to 'im again. I thought about tomorrow, if 'e's willing."

Trevelyan looked carefully at the card, and for a moment Emma saw his image fade and then brighten again. "I will accompany you to Brighton," he said. "Therefore, I will see you on the morrow."

The air trembled, and the next moment, Emma and Jim were in Emma's sitting room. On the table were two pots of red geraniums. "I think one of these is yours," she said.

"I'd better go," Jim said, getting up.

"No, it's really late. You can sleep in the spare room, if you'd like."

"I really appreciate you trustin' me," he said, glancing at her. "What a bloody mess we've got ourselves involved in."

Emma smiled. "We are both victims, Jim. It could have been me attacking you. As Emily used to say, 'There but for the grace of God, go I.'"

She made two cups of cocoa, and they sat together before the glowing embers of the fire. One of the cats hopped up on Jim's knee.

"A little quiet in the chaos," Emma said, leaning back in the chair. "Jim, do you notice how different this room feels since Trevelyan cleaned out the cellar?"

"More relaxed," he answered. He sipped his cocoa. "I mean, I thought it always felt good in 'ere, but now you come to mention it, the room feels lighter."

"I just wanted to tell you that I'm sorry you've been through so much shit on my account. A couple of weeks ago, we didn't have a care in the world, apart from money, but now . . . that's all changed."

"Time to drink the philosophic wine and ale, Em," Jim replied. "There isn't a damn thing we can do about it." His tawny eyes were full of concern as he looked at her. "I can't walk away and leave you to it, can I?"

"Bless your heart," she said, giving him a hug.

Jim was a good man, one of the best. She knew he really cared about her, and she was so thankful that he was in her life. However long it lasted.

"Feels like the lull before the storm," she said.

"Ain't that the bloody truth!"

Emma finished her cocoa. "I'm off to bed now. I'll see you in the morning."

CHAPTER FOURTEEN

RASTAMAN

Jim woke up from a restless sleep. He recalled only smatterings of having a deep conversation with someone in a dream and that what they were discussing was of the uppermost importance. He had the impression it was something to do with Emma's tarot card reading. Looking at the bedside clock, he saw it was after seven, so he decided to get up and make himself a cup of tea. He'd let Emma sleep and give her a call when breakfast was ready.

He got dressed and went over to the window to gaze over the garden. The broad beans were in flower with pods already formed on the lower stems, and he understood that their vigour was due to the light of Faerie on the garden. There was also something of Faerie about his ragged dreams, and Jim heaved a sigh of frustration as the faint images of recollection disappeared. Going downstairs, he fed the cats and then put the kettle on. After he had poured it, he sat at the kitchen table warming his hands on the cup. Even though he couldn't remember the dreams, he still carried a residue of urgency and danger. It had something to do with Emma, of that he was sure.

Putting down his tea, he reached into his back pocket and looked at Omar's business card for a moment. He no longer believed that the Jamaican had been trying to take them for a ride, and he figured the reading had genuinely disturbed and maybe even frightened him. He took the phone off the wall and dialled Omar's number. The phone rang and rang, and just as Jim was about to hang up, he heard Omar's voice on the other end.

"This is Jim Lynch. My friend Emma 'ad a tarot readin' yesterday. I wanted to know if it would be all right if we came back and talked about it. She's terribly upset."

"Irie, mon," Omar said. "No problems."

"We'll been down later, if you're free . . . and we will be bringin' a friend of Emma's with us."

"Irie. I'll see you tomorrow around noon."

Jim was thoughtful as he hung up the receiver. He had expected resistance from Omar after his strange behaviour at Emma's reading and was surprised by his willingness to see them.

Breakfast was on the table when Emma came downstairs.

"You're up early," she said, sitting down at the table.

"I couldn't sleep, Em. I 'ad a strange dream. I was talkin' to someone, serious like. I think it was about your tarot readin', but I can't remember. So, I took the liberty of callin' Omar this mornin'." He looked at her sheepishly. "You don't mind, do you?"

Emma shook her head.

"'E says 'e can see us tomorrow, around noon."

"Did he say anything else?"

"Like what?"

"An explanation for why he got rid of us so fast?"

"No. I think, to be 'onest, that I woke 'im up. I told 'im we were bringin' a friend of yours."

"What did he say to that?"

"Nothin'." Jim sniffed. "I forgot to call Sue and tell 'er what we 'eard. I think after we see Omar tomorrow we'll go on to the sanctuary."

Emma nodded. "Good idea."

After the breakfast things were cleared away Emma and Jim started working in the garden. At noon they took a break. "Well, I went cradle snatchin' and picked some baby beans," Jim said. "We'll 'ave some tonight."

Emma grinned. "Cooked lightly to perfection with lots of butter and black pepper. I can't wait."

They spent the rest of the day earthing up rows of potatoes and weeding rows of beets and carrots. By seven o' clock Emma and Jim were exhausted.

Jim wiped his brow with the back of his hand. "Time we packed this in. Broad beans are waitin'. Do we 'ave any summer savory?"

"Yes. In the spice rack"

After she had gorged herself with beans, Emma leant back in the chair. "I'm mentally and physically exhausted. I feel I could sleep for a week."

"I'll wash up," Jim offered. "You go on to bed."

The following morning, Emma awoke refreshed. When she got downstairs, Jim had the breakfast on the table. "You look rested," he said, pouring the tea.

"I feel good." She smiled. "Like a weight's been lifted off me."

After clearing away the dishes, they got ready to go to Brighton.

"I wonder where Trevelyan is," Emma said as she put on her jacket. "I thought he was coming with us."

"'E'll show up. But we'd better get goin', otherwise we'll be late. We'll stop at my 'ouse on our way out so I can get a change of clothes."

Omar St Louis put down the phone. He hadn't slept. It was Jamaica all over again. The girl he had seen yesterday reminded him so much of his Lucy, his love, with those fine green eyes. Lucy's dreams had begun at the full moon, and he had pleaded with her to leave with him. But they were just dreams, she had told him. His intuition said otherwise, and four weeks later, as the sun was setting, the witch had come for her. Restrained by the mamba's helpers, he had been powerless to help her escape.

Getting off the bed, he went downstairs to his studio and lit a joint. The reading had revealed a great evil; the same black hate he had witnessed in Jamaica was now ready to engulf the world. Taking a long pull on the cigarette, he picked up the pack of cards, and holding a picture of Emma in his mind, he shuffled the deck and laid five cards face up upon the table.

The spread was a royal flush, and the cards were evil and ill favoured. Breaking out in a sweat, Omar shuddered and tears trickled down his cheeks. This was the same spread he'd cast for Lucy. In that instant he understood in his spirit that he had a sacred obligation to help Emma.

It was after ten when Emma and Jim started out for Brighton. Jim sat quietly in the passenger side as Emma drove east along the country lanes, and after a while, he nodded off.

Parking outside Omar's shop, Emma saw Trevelyan's face in the rear-view mirror. "Trevelyan!" she said, turning to look at him. "You're here. I wondered where you'd got to."

"I told you I would be here, m'dear. And here I am."

"Are we there?" Jim said sleepily, rubbing his eyes. "I must've dropped off."

"Yes," Emma said, "and Trevelyan's turned up."

They got out of the car, and Emma tried the door of Omar's shop, but it was locked.

"Hey, mon!" a voice hailed.

Emma turned and saw Omar appear from a side road eating a sandwich.

Omar stopped short and stared at Trevelyan curiously.

"Omar, this is my friend Trevelyan of Wessex," Emma said. "He's the person Jim told you about."

Trevelyan bowed. "At your service."

"Omar St Louis," the West Indian man replied, bending over to shake Trevelyan's hand.

"I have come for a divination," Trevelyan announced. Omar's dark eyes widened in astonishment, and he stared at Trevelyan anew. The loa was powerful and expansive, surrounded by outer-spectrum colours that he had never seen before. *Why would he ask a reading from a lesser seer?* Omar asked himself. It had to be about the reading he had done for Emma.

"A reading? Why, of course, mon," he said, nervously flicking back his dreads. "This way." He led the three visitors through the store and into the studio. "Welcome to my reading room."

"Mr St Louis," Trevelyan said, "forgive me, but I think 'tis best to do the reading in my world, which, I see from your aura, you are well acquainted with."

Omar nodded. "Irie, mon. No problem."

The room trembled and then rearranged itself into Trevelyan's sitting room. "Welcome to my home," Trevelyan said. He fluttered his fingers, and a round table and four padded satin chairs appeared in the centre of the room. Resting on the tabletop was Omar's pack of tarot cards and his bell.

There was a long silence, and Emma felt a tingle in the air. Glancing around, she saw Jim playing with his dog, his face suffused with delight. It made her feel good to know that he was happy. Turning her eyes to Omar, she noticed his face was expressionless, and she was suddenly aware that the tingle was a noiseless conversation between him and Trevelyan. She listened and then, finding she understood what they were saying, thought a question.

Welcome, Emma, m'dear. I am so glad you were able to join the conversation. Trevelyan beamed at her.

"Come, Jim," Trevelyan said, taking Jim's arm and steering him towards the table. "Let us see what the cards reveal."

Once they were seated, Omar picked up the bell and rang it in the four directions. He gave the deck to Trevelyan to shuffle and cut, and then he laid the first five cards face up upon the table.

Leaning forward, Trevelyan gazed intently at the spread. In the centre, the queen of swords was staring back at him. On either side were the queen of wands and the king of cups, both ill disposed. He felt the gloating malice coming from their eyes. The card above was the devil, ill dignified, and the fifth card below was the knight of swords, master of the winds and a mighty warrior.

Seeing Trevelyan's head jerk forwards, Emma followed his eyes and saw that one of the cards was moving. The queen of wands rippled like water in a pool, and an evil, sardonic face looked up from the table.

"Jah Love, protect us!" Omar shouted, jabbing his middle finger onto the card. The terrible face vanished in an instant. "I an' I nay deal wid wickedness!" he cried.

Trevelyan leaned back. "The spread has answered many questions, yet its power of divination has brought evil to us. Omar! You must destroy the pack, for it is now tainted with hate. I suspected that it might be so, and in truth, this is why I brought you into my realm. To protect you."

"Tainted!" Omar exclaimed. "What do you mean by that, mon?"

"Emma was spelled by the gannet on Dragon Hill," Trevelyan replied, "and she unknowingly carried the evil vibration back with her. When you cast the tarot for her, part of the evil transferred itself into the cards to spy on you."

Omar's eyes flashed. "I thought I felt malevolence in the deck, but I thought it was still residue from the reading, mon."

"This card represents you, Emma," Trevelyan said, tapping the queen of swords with his eyeglass. "The two on either side are your adversaries. Next Sunday is Bealltainn, and in the early hours, before the pre-dawn light, there will be a human sacrifice. Soaked in the blood of the innocent, Kingsbury will use the star-gate, and with the sapphire, he will summon his demons, and the gates to Pandemonia will open. We have to stop him!"

"Pandemonia?" Emma repeated apprehensively. "What is that?"

"'Tis the secret kingdom hidden in the Giant's Cliffs, the towering heights of Moher in the west of Ireland. In the war of Separation, the terrified emotions of the time resonated in the Cathac's dark abode in the abyss. Vibrating with the screaming

Earth field, the abomination rose." Trevelyan paused, and Emma saw a pervading sadness in his eyes. "The giant Finn McCoul was waiting on the beach as the mighty worm broke upon the shore. Such was the Cathac's hate that he let fly upon his foe, and the giant forced up the earth into a mighty barrier of rock. The great worm slammed into the blockade and became entrapped within the living stone. 'Tis said in mortal legend that a monk called Senan destroyed the Cathac, but 'tis a lie."

Trevelyan took his eyeglass from his pocket and twirled it in front of them, showering them with emerald beams. "Pandemonia is a realm wherein dwell all the creatures of your memory and myth: vampires, werewolves, wraiths, and dark things that creep from unhallowed spaces in the earth to drink the blood of men. Did you think that the horrors of legend walked not under the moon? Think again, for that is what waits at the gates of Pandemonia. When the stars are right and the foul incantations spoken, conjured with terror and with blood, the legions of hell will once more walk upon Earth. Hate there was for man and hate there is dwelling in the Giant's Cliffs."

A shadow darkened the room as clouds passed over the sun, prophetic in their timing.

"Today is Wednesday," Trevelyan continued after a pause. "We have only three days to find the location of the ritual to open the gates of Pandemonia, the sabbat. There is no time to lose." Raising his hands, Trevelyan blessed his companions. "May the speed of Gorias be with you in your search. Now, I must go to Ireland and seek council with Ke-enaan, for Kilfannan and Kilcannan are hard set to escape the clutching claws of the enemy."

The sitting room shimmered, and they were once again standing in Omar's studio in Brighton. Getting an earthenware bowl, Omar sprinkled the tarot cards with powdered sandalwood. He bowed his head in prayer and then set them ablaze. "I an' I has had these cards for many years," he said sadly as they shrivelled into ash. "They served me well. I am sorry to see them go."

"We'd better be gettin' off to Sue," Jim said, looking at his watch. "Omar, if you're free, I think you should come with us."

"I don't have any appointments, mon."

Omar gathered a few things from the studio and was just about to turn off the light when he saw a pack of tarot cards appear on the table. Picking them up, he saw that the backs were decorated with a glittering emerald octahedron. He felt a rush of warmth to his heart, and he offered a silent prayer of gratitude to Trevelyan for the wondrous deck. He put them in his rucksack with the bell, turned off the light, and followed Jim and Emma to the entrance.

Getting out of Brighton took the best part of half an hour. Finally, Jim found the road he wanted and turned left along a twisty, hedge-flanked lane. "This will take us to Greenfern," he said. "Am I glad to be out of all that traffic."

When they arrived at the sanctuary, Sue was in the yard feeding her goats. She waved as they drove down the track and went to greet them.

"Hello, mates!" she cried as they got out, and her mouth dropped open in surprise as she saw Omar wriggling out of the back seat.

"Hello! You're tall for such a little car!" she exclaimed, putting out her hand. "Sue Browne."

"Omar St Louis. Card reader, numerologist, and dealer of the mysteries. My card," he said, digging one out from his pocket.

"Omar's a friend. We met him when we went to Brighton," Emma said. "He did a tarot reading for me. He wants to help us."

Sue smiled warmly. "Why don't you all go on into the house? I won't be long, just got to finish up here. Oh, Jim, would you put the kettle on?" she called after them.

The tea was made and poured by the time Sue walked through the door. "Well, mates," she said, sitting down at the table and picking up a cup, "what's going on, then?"

Her face paled as Jim told her what they had seen at the Blue Lagoon and overheard at the Star. "I was gonna call you this mornin', but as we was comin' down to Brighton, I thought I'd tell you in person."

"I know Tina," Sue said in a strained voice.

"How do you know her?" Emma asked. "Hardly the type of person you'd hang out with."

"I met her last autumn at the agricultural show in Brighton. She stopped at my stand and wanted to talk to me about cruelty to animals. It was awkward with all the comings and goings, so we met later at a café on the seafront. She told me some dreadful stuff about Kingsbury putting up the money for dogfights and hard-core porno movies involving bestiality, torture, and the like. She also hinted that he was mixed up in other things, but despite my promptings, she wouldn't tell me what they were. I told her to contact Tony—I mean Chief Inspector Farran." Sue sighed. "I don't judge her, poor girl. She's just doing the best she can, and she's kind to animals, and that's all I care about." She paused for a few moments. "Now, hearing this news has scared the shit out of me for both of them. I'm going to call Tony. He needs to know about what you heard straight away. What night was this again?"

"Monday night," Emma replied. "All we know about Kingsbury is that he owns the Blue Lagoon, and has the sapphire. Do you know anything about him?"

"Tina told me that he stays in London during the week, at a house in Chelsea, and he's got a country house called Brising Manor near Hockham's Bridge," Sue said, taking her cell phone from her handbag.

"How far is his estate from here?" Emma asked.

"About an hour's drive," Sue answered. She got up and headed for the sitting room. "I'll call Tony now, and while I'm at it, I'll look up Kingsbury and that St Clare woman on the computer. See what I can find out about them."

Sue came back into the kitchen a few minutes later with a printout in her hand. "Tony's on his way," she said.

"So, mon! What did you find out about that wicked son of Babylon?"

"Kingsbury's lineage goes back to the Norman Conquest, 1066 and all that," Sue answered. "Feodora is a Russian countess who married Lord St Clare from Devon. I guess he died not long after they got hitched. Left her millions. Probably poisoned him with polonium and made off with his money."

"If Feodora's a black widow, 'e's lucky she didn't eat 'im. What's polonium?" Jim said. "Never 'eard of that before."

"A radioactive poison. It's quite vogue today."

"I heard somewhere that tobacco leaves collect polonium," Emma added.

Suddenly dogs barked in the yard and tyres crunched on the gravel driveway.

"That'll be Tony," Sue said, opening the door for a tall man in a black tracksuit.

"Hello, everyone," Tony said.

"Tony, these are my friends, Jim, Emma, and Omar. This is Chief Inspector Tony Farran of the Sussex Constabulary."

Tony had stunning blue eyes, dark hair greying at the temples, a lean face, and a wide smile. Emma gazed at him. He was everything she liked in a man. He was mature, distinguished-looking, suave, and very handsome with an animal magnetism that made her heart flutter. She caught herself fantasising about his sexual prowess and quickly looked away.

"Would you like a cup of tea and a piece of seed cake?" Sue asked as he sat down.

"Yes, please."

Emma noticed how Sue fussed around Tony, and how she touched his arm with her fingertips when she served the cake.

"So," Tony said, sipping on his tea, "Sue tells me that you heard my name mentioned in a conversation at the Star Hotel, and as I value her information highly, I came straight over."

"We over'eard what seemed to be a murder bein' planned, and your name was mentioned in the conversation," Jim said.

Tony looked at him doubtfully. "And who was having this conversation?"

"Giles Kingsbury and a woman . . . what was 'er name, Em?"

"Feodora St Clare."

Tony stiffened, and his slightly condescending manner vanished in an instant.

"They were in the lounge bar at the Star 'Otel in Brighton. 'E got a phone call and got all bent out of shape," Jim carried on. "That's when we 'eard what we 'eard."

"Tell me everything," Tony said tensely, leaning forwards in his chair. "I want every little detail of what you saw and heard."

Jim did tell him everything, up to the time they left the hotel.

"Are you sure that girl's name was Tina?" Tony asked when Jim had finished.

"The other girl that worked there called her Tina," Emma said quietly.

Tony rubbed the side of his face with his hand. "I have to go." he said thoughtfully, and he moved towards the door.

"Tony!" Sue said. "Wait a minute. I know Tina. I'm the one who told her to call you and report the dogfights."

"What!" Tony glared at her in astonishment. "Why didn't you tell me about this before instead of playing bloody games?" Tight lipped, he swung round on them all. "Stay away from the Blue Lagoon and Giles Kingsbury. There is an investigation going on, and I don't want you muddying the waters." He stared at those assembled for a moment, shook his head, and left.

"That didn't go down well," Emma remarked after the door slammed shut.

"Yeah," Jim said. "'E thought we was full of shit until I mentioned Giles Kingsbury."

"It's me he's really pissed off with, for keeping him in the dark about Tina," Sue admitted, "but I did what I thought was best at the time. And not telling him about her . . . well, it wasn't relevant until now."

"We'd better start takin' more care of ourselves," Jim said. "What with the break-in and all the rest of it, I think we should start payin' attention to everythin'. I'll check the boundaries of the sanctuary. We don't want to take any chances with the animals; you know 'ow cowardly these bastards are."

"I'll go with you, mon," Omar agreed. "The sun's out for a change. How about you, ladies? Do you want to come with us?"

"No, you go and have a look round. We'll get on and make some dinner," Sue said. "You'll find spare wellingtons in the barn. Go help yourselves."

"Your friend Tony is awfully good-looking," Emma said once she and Sue were alone. "I almost envy you having him as a . . . friend." She grinned. "Have you known him long?"

"About six months," Sue replied. "I was at a country fair in Spelborough last autumn and he came over to my stand, and we got talking. I didn't know he was a copper then." She smiled wanly. "Rescuing animals means that sometimes I break the law, so I try to keep away from the police. Tony adopted a dog from here, and he's been dropping in a lot lately. More tea?" Emma nodded. "Don't think that I haven't thought about going to bed with him. I think about it all the time. But you can't keep that kind of thing a secret for too long, especially around here. The postman and milkman are the biggest gossips in the village." Sue gave a wry smile. "Anyway, I should stop fantasizing about him. He's a married man and will only break my heart."

Emma smiled back. "Well, you'd better be careful if you happen to meet up with him in town."

Sue looked at her quizzically.

"You can't keep your hands off him. It's bloody obvious you fancy him," Emma said. "I noticed it straight away, and I wasn't looking for it." She held up her teacup. "Cheers! Here's to you and your handsome copper."

It was getting on towards six-thirty when Jim and Omar got back. Sue noticed the worried look on Jim's face before he was halfway through the door.

"What's up?" she asked apprehensively.

"The back gate was wide—"

"My horses! Are they in the meadow?"

"Yes, they're safe and the gate's tied up temporarily. Do you 'ave another lock and chain or anythin' to fasten it with?"

"There are all kinds of locks in the toolshed. Do you remember where it is?"

Jim nodded and left, closing the door behind him.

It was seven by the time he and Omar were finished, and they changed into their shoes and made their way to the kitchen.

"Dinner," Sue said as she put a pecan nut roast with gravy on the table, followed by oven potatoes, Brussels sprouts, carrots, and a Yorkshire pudding.

Omar's eyes widened as he stared at the spread. "Blessings, Sue," he said.

There was no talking for a while, only eating. "Mmm," Omar said, putting down his fork. "This tastes so good, it makes me want to lick the plate, mon!"

"Sue," Jim said as he wiped his mouth with a napkin, "what's your take on the lock bein' stolen from the back gate?"

"A warning," she said grimly. "I think we'll keep all the animals in their stalls until after the sabbat."

"No point in callin' the police," Jim said sarcastically. "What do you think the chief constable and Giles Kingsbury 'ave in common?"

"The funny handshake brigade," Sue replied. "They have their fingers in every pie, at least every one that matters. If you can make a phone call to the chief constable because the heat's on you and you want it taken off, and you have the pull to get it taken off, that's what's called well connected."

"That's nothin' new, mon! Black folks could have told you how the control system worked three hundred years ago. That's the privilege of Babylon."

"And psychopaths," Emma added.

"I think we should go to 'Ockham's Bridge and go in the local pubs," Jim suggested. "You know 'ow people like to talk, and we might 'ear somethin' to our advantage."

"Good idea," Emma said. "Do you want to come?" she asked the others.

"No, mon. Drop me off at home."

"And I have a dog to pick up in Market Thorpe at eight-thirty," Sue said.

Jim looked at his watch. "It's nearly seven. Time we were on our way."

"Be careful," Sue said as she saw them to the door. "Call me when you get home." She watched them drive up the track and then went to make a last check on her animals before running her errand to Market Thorpe.

It was quarter to ten when Tony pulled up outside Sue's house. "You're out late," she said as she let him in. "Tea? Or would you like something stronger?"

"Something stronger," he replied. "I'm not on duty." His voice was sharp, and she knew right away he was still pissed off. Getting the whisky from the cabinet, she poured two glasses. "Cheers!"

"Why didn't you tell me about Tina Marshall?" he asked, his eyes fixed reproachfully on her face.

"I didn't know you very well then, and my dealings with the police over the years have been pretty negative," she answered, looking him straight in the eye. "I didn't want to get involved. I suggested Tina go to you because I thought you were a decent and honest cop."

"But not decent enough for you to confide in me yourself."

"Oh, come on, Tony! Perhaps I should have told you, but there's no point in crying over spilt milk. Don't make matters worse than they already are. I'm worried about Tina after what Jim and Emma heard at the Star, and every time I've tried calling her in the last few days, I only reached her answerphone."

"Same here," Tony said. "I'll go round to her flat in the morning and see if I can find her."

"Do you think she's okay?"

"I don't know. I've kept things pretty quiet in an effort to protect Tina. Looks like I've failed." He paused. "And on top of all the bloody shit at work, I went home unannounced a couple of days ago and found my wife in bed with the chief superintendent from my station." Tony sighed and shook his head. "How could I have been so bloody blind?"

Sue didn't say anything for a moment, but a ray of hope dawned in her heart at his change of circumstances. "So what's going to happen now?" she said, trying to keep her voice steady.

"I guess I'll join the ranks of divorced men," he said. "My worry is for my daughters. They're only five and seven."

"Are you going to try and work it out with your wife?"

Tony shook his head. "No. There's no point. I don't want to live with someone I can't trust. She had an affair a few years ago and I forgave her then, but not this time. I can't keep putting myself through the emotional upheaval."

"What about the kids? Are you going to try to get custody of them?"

"With my job? No, they're better off with their mother. Have you ever been married?"

"Yes, for five years. My husband liked to drink, and things didn't work out." Sue smiled. "Once is enough."

"That's because you didn't find the right man."

"You're probably right," Sue said lightly. "No pun intended."

The air was charged with sexual energy. Sue wriggled in her seat and finished her drink. "Would you like another whisky?"

"Yes, please."

Her hand was shaking as she refilled his glass, and then on impulse, she leaned towards him and lightly kissed the tip of his nose. "Cheers!"

As they clinked their glasses together, their eyes locked, and Sue moved closer to him and looked into his eyes suggestively. Tony put his drink down, took her in his arms, and kissed her gently on the lips.

Sue melted. She wanted him so much, and now might be her only chance to show him how much she cared about him. Without a word, she picked up her drink, took him by the hand, and led him upstairs to her bedroom.

Tony left Sue's shortly after two, with mixed feelings. On one hand he was elated, but on the other, guilty. It had been years since he had experienced such tenderness and passion, and it felt good to know Sue cared for him. But he was still married. He had taken his marriage vows seriously, that was, until this evening, and in spite of his wife's infidelity, he still felt bad. *Old habits die hard,* he told himself. His thoughts turned to the information that Jim had given him. Someone had gotten access to his files at the station and tipped Kingsbury off about Tina. He thought about Kingsbury's threat against him. He had no doubt that Kingsbury would carry it through and he would be transferred to another station. He smiled grimly to himself. No doubt they'd use his marital problems as an excuse. A flush crept into his face. His colleagues would know about his wife's affair by now.

CHAPTER FIFTEEN

A LUCKY BREAK

"Are you sure you don't want to come to 'Ockham's Bridge with us, Omar?" Jim asked as they left Greenfern.

"No, mon. I don't drink, and I want to do a reading with the cards."

Jim turned into Baxter Street and parked outside Omar's shop.

"See you tomorrow, then," Omar said as he got out. With a wave to Jim and Emma, he opened the door to his premises and went inside.

Jim and Emma started south for Hockham's Bridge. Bits of leaves blew into the windscreen, and the wipers could hardly keep up with the hard rain. Emma was glad to see the village lights and the speed restriction signs. Passing the Heron public house, they carried on along the main street until they got to the Gables, an inn on the corner of the Turley Road. It was the nearest pub to Brising Manor, so they decided to try there first.

The inn was on the right-hand side of the road and set back at least fifty yards. Just four or five cars, a couple of bicycles, and a motor bike were in the car park. The building was a long rambling barn of a place with gables built in the seventeenth century. Ivy had long ago colonised the walls, and a cheerful glow shone out from the ornate diamond-paned windows. Getting out of the car, they hurried to the entrance, trying to avoid the puddles.

The door opened into a lobby with a bar on either side, the restaurant and lounge to the left and the public bar on the right.

"Let's go in the public bar." Jim steered Emma through the door. "We 'ave a better chance of 'earin loose talk amongst the local dart and domino players than some old colonel relivin' 'is exploits in the war."

Going in, Emma immediately smelled the warm aroma of hops.

"Mmm, Em. Real beer. I could do with a pint or two."

They sat on plush stools at the bar. The landlord, an affable man of about sixty years, came to the counter "What can I be getting for you, sir?"

"A pint of Tangleberry, and 'alf a stout, please," Jim replied, getting out his wallet and gazing along the row of gleaming pumps. The landlord poured the drinks and put them on the counter.

The pub ceiling was low and the walls were cream-washed and crisscrossed with beams, the old wood blackened with time and studded with gleaming horse brass. A bright copper coal scuttle and a brass bucket full of logs glowed in the light of the fire burning merrily in a large open hearth on the north side of the room. Two couples played dominoes at a long table next to the front door, and the only other patrons were a man and his wife sitting at a table by the bar complaining loudly to the landlord about the cold and windy weather.

Jim and Emma had been sitting at the bar for about half an hour when the door opened and a middle-aged man in a raincoat and trilby entered the room. He took off his wet coat and hat and hung them up on a peg by the door.

"You're late, Art," the landlord said, putting a pint of bitter on the counter. "I'd quite given up on you."

"I had to work tonight," Art said. "There's a big get-together, as Mr Kingsbury calls it, up at the manor house this weekend, startin' Friday. My wife spent all day wringin' chickens' necks and pluckin' out the feathers." He took a big slurp of beer. "You know Mr Kingsbury. He's very particular. Has to have his food organic and home-grown. The cook told me this mornin' that she was expectin' over a hundred people. I'm glad my Doris isn't doing the cookin'. Mr Kingsbury can be very awkward, especially when he hosts one of these parties. All of them are rich, and some are royal too," he added slyly, handing the landlord a five-pound note.

"So Giles is having another party," the landlord said.

"He is."

Jim and Emma exchanged a brief glance and pricked up their ears. Picking up his change, the old boy took a swig of beer and stared around. Catching Emma's eye, he came over and joined them at the bar.

"Not from these parts, are ye?" he said engagingly.

"No, we came to Brighton to go through the Lanes," Emma replied. "My friend wanted to look for semi-precious stones, and there are so many quaint little shops in the town."

"Oh! So you're a jeweller?" Art asked, turning his attention to Jim.

"No, I just make a few rings now and then. It's my 'obby. Actually, I'm a gardener."

"A gardener! I do a bit of that," Art said. "I knew there was somethin' about you I liked. The names Arthur Griffiths, but my friends call me Art. I'm the keeper up at Brisin' Manor." He held out his hand, and Jim and Emma shook it.

Brising Manor, Emma thought. *What a stroke of luck.*

Art carried on talking to the landlord about small doings in the village, and after a while he moved over to the table and for a game of cribbage with his friends.

"Fancy that," Jim whispered. "Meetin' someone who works at Brisin' Manor." He took a sip of his drink. "Do you want a toasted cheese and onion sandwich? The beer's made me peckish."

"Yes, I'd love one, I'm hungry as well."

They ordered their snacks and another drink. The bar was warm and the seats comfortable, and it was past ten before they said their goodbyes to the landlord and left.

"Will you drive, Em?" Jim asked as he unlocked the car door. "I've 'ad a bit more than I should've. Don't want to get stopped and breathalysed."

Just then, Emma saw Art going out the side door. "Jim! There's Art. I'll offer him a lift home, and then we'll know exactly where Kingsbury's estate is."

"Good idea," Jim said.

"Art!" Emma called. "I'll drive you home. Save you walking in the rain."

"That's very civil of you," the keeper said. He came over and got into the back seat. "It's a good mile to the manor. I live in one of the cottages on the estate."

Emma pulled out of the car park. "Which way is it?"

"Turn left and then right at the crossroads, and it's a mile further down the road," Art replied.

Emma turned right at the crossroads and took the lane towards Turley village. The trees were swaying wildly in the wind as she drove along the dark and narrow road. Soon a pair of imposing wrought iron gates came into view on the left-hand side.

"Pull over here," Art said. "I live in the gatehouse. A good night to ye, and thank you for the lift." They waited for a moment for Art to go in, and then Emma turned the car round in the entrance.

"The wall of the estate runs for three-quarters of a mile," Jim said as they got to the crossroads. "It must be all of seven foot 'igh."

"There's glass on the top," Emma said. "Did you see it? Kingsbury's gone to an awful lot of trouble to keep people from trespassing."

"Yes, I saw the glass glistenin' in the 'eadlights. Looks like broken bottles cemented into the top row of stones. Kingsbury really means business."

It was one o'clock when they got back to Emma's. "What a stroke of luck, meeting Art in the pub," Emma said as she opened the door. "At least, we know Kingsbury's having a *party*." She emphasised the word sarcastically. "The sabbat must be planned for afterwards, when the bastards are all buzzed up."

"I supposed I'd better go 'ome," Jim said, yawning. "I'm knackered!"

"Why don't you stay the night?" Emma said. "You can sleep in the spare room. I'm really tired, so I'm off to bed."

Jim woke up with a jolt. He blinked and caught a glimpse of the clock. It was twenty-five minutes past six. He'd overslept! Dave and Maggie would be coming for the van keys in five minutes. He got dressed in a hurry and went downstairs to pack the van.

Dave and Maggie arrived not long after he'd finished. "It's all set," he said. "I filled it up with petrol yesterday. I really appreciate you standin' in for us at the market. Em really needs a break."

"Where are you off too?" Dave asked.

"We're goin' to Brighton."

"Sin City of the South, eh? Well, you have good time, and don't worry about anything here. We've got everything taken care of."

"A good time;" the words jarred Jim. If Dave only knew the truth. He almost felt envious of Dave and Maggie and their quiet normal life. He wished things could have been like that for him and Emma.

The morning was cold and bright as Jim and Emma started out in Emma's car, a five-door Audi estate that would give them more room than Jim's Escort, especially for Omar's long legs.

"You're quiet, Em," Jim said as they left town. "What's the matter?"

"I'm just worried about the sabbat. Trying to get into Brising Manor is ridiculous," she said dejectedly. "You heard what the gamekeeper said. A hundred people! That means we'll be outnumbered twenty-five to one."

Driving through Petworth only reinforced her pessimism. The walled estate and cobbled roads reeked of feudalism and the domination of the aristocratic class. Kingsbury was one of the elite; one of the faceless plutocrats that operated outside the laws that ruled the common people. He could get away with murder.

"We 'ave no choice, Em. The whole bloody world's at stake. We 'ave to do somethin' to stop it. Even if we fail, we 'ave to try."

Jim sorted through some CDs from the console, and finding one with reggae, he slid it in the player and turned up the volume. "Positive vibrations is what we need, Em," he said. He sang along to a Bob Marley track.

It was half past ten when Emma parked outside of Omar's shop. The moment she pulled up, he came out the front door carrying a holdall.

"I've been waitin' for you, mon," he said, climbing into the back seat. "I saw somethin' strange goin' on outside the club last night. It was about midnight, and I woke up with a jolt. My loa was tellin' me to go to the front window and look out. Under the streetlight, I saw three figures at the entrance of the Blue Lagoon. One was holdin' the back door of a van open, and the other two were draggin' someone inside. They were just drivin' off when someone came runnin' out of the door. The person stood starin' after them for a minute or two, and then went back inside."

Emma shivered as she thought about Tina and the threats Kingsbury had made against her. "What was the name of the other stripper in the bar, Jim? Do you remember?" she asked as she drove on.

Jim thought for a moment. "Sugar," he said slowly. "Yes, that's it. Per'aps it was 'er than ran out in the road."

"That's what I was thinking," Emma agreed.

Sue was feeding the geese and chickens in the yard as Emma parked outside the house. "Hello, mates!" Sue said as they got out. "I didn't recognise the motor."

"We brought my car," Emma said. "It's got more leg room for Omar."

"Better than bein' cooped up in the back of Jim's little car," Omar said with a rich laugh.

The three of them followed Sue to the kitchen. "I made us some lunch," she said, putting a bowl of salad and a warm spelt loaf on the table. "Help yourselves."

Jim picked up the carving knife and cut himself two slices. "Mmm. Brings back memories. I could never resist your bread."

"That's right," Sue said, pouring out the tea. "Warm homemade bread was one of your favourite things." She sat down beside him. "You used to call it 'the hunt meet-special treat'!"

Jim laughed. "I'd quite forgotten that."

While they were eating, Omar told Sue what he had seen outside the Blue Lagoon. "Whatever was goin' on outside the club must have had some bearin' on our mission," he said. "Otherwise my loa would not have got me up."

"Could it have been a body?" Sue asked anxiously.

Omar nodded.

"That was my thought exactly," Emma said.

A gloomy silence fell, broken by the sound of tyres on the gravel outside. Sue got up and looked out the window. "It's Tony," she said, opening the door. "I hope he has some news."

Tony's face was grim as he joined them at the table. Sue put a cup of tea and a sandwich in front of him. "You look tired."

"I am," he said wearily, pushing the plate away. "Sorry, darlin', I'm just not hungry."

"What's happened?" Sue asked nervously.

Tony sipped on his tea and then rubbed his hand over his eyes. "I called at Tina Marshall's flat this morning."

"And?"

"I saw her sister. She told me Tina hadn't got back from work. I understand that it's not unusual for Tina to be late home. Depends on if she has a client."

"I saw someone being bundled into the back of a van outside the club last night," Omar said grimly. "Could have been her."

"What time was this?" Tony asked.

"About midnight."

"Her phone is still off," Sue said quietly. "I've tried her number several times. I thought she was just laying low, but I don't know now."

Tony's mouth hardened into a straight line. "I'd better be going. I'll keep you posted about Tina. And don't be jumping to conclusions."

Sue saw him out, and he kissed her lightly on the lips. "Tell your friends to keep away from Kingsbury and the Blue Lagoon," he said. "He's a nasty piece of work."

Sue closed the door behind him and joined the others at the table. Emma called Maggie to check on the cats and see how Dave was doing at the market.

"Everything's good at home," she said, shutting off the phone. "Dave was sold out by lunchtime."

"Wonderful!" Jim grinned and rubbed his hands together. "We'll be able to pay the rest of our bills when we get back 'ome."

"I don't like this Tina business, at all," Sue said, filling up the tea kettle. "And I had a strange dream last night. I was up on Dragonsbury Ring and saw a small object glowing in the grass. I saw it clear as day. I think whatever it is . . . it has to do with her. Maybe we should go back up there and take another look." She looked at the clock. "Just gone one. We could be there by two."

"I'm not goin' anywhere near that place," Jim said sharply.

"You don't have to go. You can stay here and watch the sanctuary," Sue replied. "I'll go."

"I'm with you, Sue," Omar said, stirring in his chair.

"'Ow about you, Em? You goin' too?"

"No, I'll stay. I don't want to go back up that hill either."

"Well, Omar, we'd better get off," Sue said, putting on her jacket.

"See you two later. And don't worry," Omar said as he followed Sue out.

"Well, thank God we got out of goin'," Jim said, pouring himself another cup of tea. "Want a top-up, Em?"

She nodded and pushed her cup towards him.

"I never liked that 'ill," he said. "I always used to avert my eyes when I went past it in the car."

"Stonehenge is like that for me," Emma said. "When I was small, Daddy used to take me on trips to Salisbury Plain, and I always used to hide my head when we went by Stonehenge, especially in the moonlight."

"Funny 'ow you pick up on places where bad stuff 'appens. Trevelyan 'ad it right when 'e called it Dragon 'Ill. I 'ope I never 'ave to go up there again. The place scares the livin' daylights out of me."

"I hope we never have to up there again too," Emma said, but even as the words left her mouth, she shivered with the notion that she had unfinished business there. She got up and looked in the refrigerator. "They'll probably be late back," she said. "There's a lot of eggs, so I'll make a quiche for dinner."

Chapter Sixteen

A RETURN TRIP

Sue turned into the lay-by at the bottom of Dragonsbury Ring. "Now I'm here, I don't want to go up there," she said uneasily, looking out the window at the hill. "I'm going to park in the same spot I did before. Let's hope the thugs aren't around."

"Well, mon, at least there's a break in the cloud and the sun is out. We must be thankful for that," Omar said, getting out of the car and pulling a black woollen hat over his long dreads.

Sue locked the doors, and they walked to the gap in the hedgerow leading to the footpath. They climbed over the stile and stood on the grass for a second to gaze up at the forbidding summit. The fields and downs around the mount were greening in the sun, but the sinister hill was still wallowing in shadow. Omar stared up at the ring of trees and, sticking his hand in his trouser pocket, clutched the small amethyst cluster he always carried with him for protection.

"See how that old evil from Babylon tries to weave a shade about itself?" he said, pointing to the summit. "It even tries to deny the passage of the sun."

The footpath was full of ruts and puddles, and they had to watch their footing. Sue heaved a sigh when they reached the base of the hill. "Petty slick path," she said, wiping the mud from the bottom of her boots on the grass. "I nearly went ass over titfer several times."

"Me too, mon," Omar mumbled.

Linking their hands together, they bowed their heads in prayer to the Faeries of Place for permission to ascend. A bird twittered behind them in the hedge in answer, and they began their sunwards climb.

Halfway up the hill, they stopped for a breather. "This place is a focus of dragon lines, mon," Omar said, gazing out over the countryside. "See all the mistletoe on the trees?" He waved his hand towards the south.

"A bunch of dowsers stayed at the sanctuary for a few weeks last winter," Sue responded. "They mapped some of the lines of force running across the local countryside, starting with lone high hills like this." She glanced apprehensively over her shoulder at the brooding summit. "Dragonsbury Ring lines up with Glastonbury Tor on one line of force, Avebury Circle on another, and Wayland Smithy on the Ridgeway on a third. This is a huge energy power point. And evil owns it."

Omar turned away from the pleasant scene of rolling hills and back towards the shadow. Narrowing his eyes, he looked up at the ring of trees and said urgently, "We'd better be getting to our business, mon. This is not a good place for the righteous to linger. Wicked loa are comin'. D'ya understand me?"

Sue nodded. "I do."

When they got to the top of the hill, Sue led him through the beeches to the east side of the rise. "There's the entrance to the cavern," she said, pointing to a patch of hastily piled chalky clods of earth. "Someone's been up here and filled in the doorway again, and my spade has gone."

Using his faerie sight, Omar stared through the square of earth to the space beneath and shuddered. "A young woman was tortured in the early hours of this mornin'. I see blood spattered on a pentacle in the cavern."

Sue gasped. "Oh my God!"

Omar psychically felt her revulsion, along with great pain and anger. "Sue," he whispered, "evil is gettin' to your thoughts. Be strong, mon."

Sue closed her eyes for a minute and breathed deeply.

"My loa are warnin' me," Omar hissed. "They are tellin' us to leave now. Wicked trouble is on its way."

"There's something up here, I know there is. I have to find it," Sue said, looking closely at the ground. "Help me look."

They searched the turf around the dig but found nothing. A cold wind blew, and Omar became agitated. "Sue! Wickedness is comin'. You can feel its breath in the wind. Come on!"

The sun sailed out from behind the patchy clouds, casting a beam in front of them as they turned to go. Seeing a small object glowing eerily in the grass, Sue bent down and picked it up. "This is what I saw in the dream. It's an earring," she said, putting it in her pocket.

Omar grabbed her arm. "Praise to Jah! Let's go."

They were about two-thirds of the way down the hill when the sound of a vehicle reached them.

"There's a car coming," Sue whispered. "We're lucky we're on the backside of the hill; they can't see us from the road."

They crouched down to hide and crawled forwards until the road came into view. "It's one of Kingsbury's Range Rovers," Sue said apprehensively. "As soon as they're round the bend, we'd better make a run for the car."

The moment the Range Rover turned the corner, they ran around the spiral to the bottom of the hill, and instead of taking the slippery footpath, which would have cost them precious minutes, they cut across the meadow.

"They're going to turn round at the crossroads and come back," Sue said as they rushed to the hedge. They swiftly climbed over a five-bar gate to the road and sprinted back to the car.

Sue started the engine, and as she drove out of the lay-by, she saw the Range Rover approaching in the rear-view mirror.

Realising they were going to block her in, she cut to the right in front of the vehicle, missing it by inches.

"Hang on, Omar!" she shouted. Brakes squealed and a horn blared behind them. Glancing in the rear-view mirror, Sue could see the faces of the occupants quite clearly. "That's the same crew I had the run-in with before," she said, accelerating along the narrow tree-lined lane. "Put your seat belt on, and pray we don't meet any vehicles coming the other way."

The Range Rover was on her bumper as she came to the crossroads, and a post office van coming the other way indicated for a right-hand turn. Sue put her foot down and ran the halt sign, barely missing the van.

Omar looked back as they rounded a bend. "There's nothin' behind us at the moment."

Sue took all the side roads she could find and eventually found a road to Brighton. She pulled over on the verge. "We finally lost them," she said, looking back. "What a hellacious drive. Made the back of my neck stiff." She took the earring out of her pocket and handed it to Omar. "See what information you can pick up from it."

Omar held it in his palm. "It belonged to a young woman, mon. And bad loa have touched it."

"What if it's Tina's? She might have been trying to get through to me in the dream and dropped it purposefully." Sue wiped her hand over her forehead. "Sometimes I think we're already living in hell."

"Babylon is all around us."

"Keep the earring on you, Omar. I've got a habit of losing things."

"Irie, mon."

Sue drove on, and they were silent for a while.

"We're coming into Brighton," Sue said as she passed the speed restriction signs. "I think we should go to Tina's flat and see if she's there. I know where it is."

She took her cell phone from her bag but found that the battery was dead. "That's weird. I only charged it this morning."

"It got drained by the wickedness under Dragonsbury Ring," Omar muttered.

"But I thought Emma got rid of it," Sue said nervously.

"No. That is a devil, mon. Only Jah Love can send it back to the abyss."

"So it's still under there?"

"Yes, mon. It's still under there."

Sue pulled up outside the block of rundown flats in Simpson Street where Tina Marshall lived. A bunch of youths were kicking a football around in the road, and they stared sullenly at her and Omar as they walked across the concrete forecourt to the graffiti-covered stairwell. After climbing the stairs to the third floor, they walked along the dingy terraced walkway to Tina's apartment. Sue knocked twice before the door opened on a lock chain.

"Who's there?" a pale girl about twelve years old said as she peered through the crack.

"Hello! My name's Sue, and I've come to see Tina. Is she home?"

"No, she ain't 'ome from work yet," the girl said. She looked fearfully at Omar and tried to shut the door, but Sue stuck her foot into the opening before she could.

"Don't be afraid," Sue said quietly. "I've come round to invite Tina to a gathering at my animal sanctuary. I've tried to call her on the phone but got no answer. Has she changed her number?"

Pushing back her long fair hair, the girl shook her head and then looked curiously at Sue. Sue removed her foot, and the girl took off the chain and opened the door a little wider. "Are you the animal lady Tina talks about? We wanted a cat, but we're not allowed to have any animals in the flats."

"Oh, that's a shame," Sue said. "You'll have to come to my animal sanctuary some time and see all the critters there. I have seven cats." Sue paused and then said gently, "Is Tina often late home from work?"

"No, she's never been this long before, not without phonin'. It's almost six o' clock," the girl replied, tears running down her thin face. "I've called her phone lots of times and she don't answer."

"How long has she been gone?"

"Since yesterday afternoon. It was about five when she left for work . . . and a copper called round here this mornin' askin' questions. I told 'im the same as you."

Sue smiled at her. "What's your name?"

"Lily, Lily Marshall."

Wondering how she could get Lily to invite them in, Sue glanced enquiringly at Omar, who reached into his pocket. Sue met his eyes and saw a saw a flash of purple light.

Omar said in a soothing voice, "Lily! That's a pretty name, mon. D'ya like reggae music?"

"Yes, but . . ." The door opened a bit wider.

"Would you like me to sing you a song?"

The door opened all the way, and Lily looked up at him with red and watery eyes. "Yes. Do you want to stay and wait with me? Tina will have to come home soon . . . won't she?"

"Yes," Omar said, "and if she doesn't, we'll go look for her."

They followed Lily into a small, clean room. There were no carpets on the floor, and the only furniture was a worn settee, a few threadbare armchairs, and a television set. Short shelves full of framed photographs sat along two of the walls.

"Sit anywhere you like," Lily said, sitting on the settee. Omar stood in front of her, and on the spot broke out an old Bob Marley favourite.

His sonorous, upbeat voice filled the room with the most positive vibrations. Lily watched him with wide eyes and a half smile on her thin lips.

Taking advantage of the opportunity to look around, Sue moved quietly to the shelves, and starting at one end, walked slowly along looking at the pictures. Most were shots of Tina and a few showed Tina and Lily together.

At the end of the second row, she found a picture of Tina with a glass of wine in her hand and Happy Birthday balloons behind her. She froze. In the picture, Tina was wearing pearl earrings identical to the one she'd found. Sue took a moment to master her emotions, and wiping away her tears with the back of her hand, she sat down in an armchair. At the end of his song, Omar bowed to Lily.

"Where did you learn to sing like that?" she asked, gazing at him.

"Jamaica, mon!"

"Oh!"

The happy moment didn't last long, as Lily quickly became withdrawn and silent once again.

"Lovely pictures you have on the shelf," Sue said brightly. "Tina's wearing some pretty pearl earrings in one of them." She gestured to the shelving.

"I gave Tina those earrings for her birthday two weeks ago," Lily said miserably, and she started to sob.

Catching Omar's eye, Sue nodded to the door. "Lily," she said gently, "I have to go home and feed the animals, so we're going to have to go now."

"Can't you stay and wait?" Lily pleaded.

Sue felt a pain in her heart and could barely hold back tears. "No, love. After we've finished with the animals, we're going to look for your sister, but we want you to stay here in case she comes back. We'll send someone over later to check on you."

Lily shook her head. "I don't want to stay here on my own."

Sue hastily turned away from the pitiful girl and followed Omar through the door.

"I feel dreadful leaving her like that, but what else can we do?" she said sadly as they walked down the stairwell. "She's so young. I'll call Tony. He'll know the right people to call to get her help."

"All we can do is pray to Jah to hold her in his love."

When they got back to Greenfern, Sue spotted Tony sitting in his car outside the house. She pulled up beside him and hopped out. "Go on inside, Omar. We'll join you in a minute." She went over to Tony's car, and he looked thoughtfully at her as she got into the passenger seat.

"What's up? You look stressed," he said.

"Omar and I went to Dragonsbury Ring this afternoon and found an earring. We think it belongs to Tina."

Tony raised his eyebrows. "You go for a walk somewhere and find an earring and think it's Tina's," he scoffed. "What gave you that wild notion?"

"That's just it, Tony. It's not a flight of fancy, whatever you may think. On the way back, we went to see Lily, Tina's younger sister, and I saw a recent photograph of Tina wearing the exact same pearl earrings."

Tony's eyes widened.

"There's more to this business than we've told you," Sue said. "I think you should come inside with me and hear the whole story for yourself."

He looked at her with a shocked expression. "More revelations?" he asked cuttingly.

She nodded. "Yes, Tony, more revelations."

Emma and Jim were in the sitting room playing cards when Omar came in.

"Did you find anythin?" Jim asked, putting down his hand.

"Yes, mon. We found one of Tina's earrings by the pit."

"Oh, no!" Emma cried in horror, throwing down her cards. "That's dreadful. Are you sure it's hers?"

Omar nodded sadly. "We went to see her sister, and Sue saw a photograph of Tina wearin' the exact same earrings," he answered. "I felt the energy of the pearl; it belonged to a young woman. There is no mistake," he said grimly. "The earring belonged to Tina. And she's dead."

The kitchen door creaked open. "That'll be Sue and Tony," Omar said. "Let's go and join them."

Tony and Sue were sitting thoughtfully at the kitchen table.

"Emma," Sue said, scratching her cheek nervously, "we found an earring on Dragonsbury Ring and we think it's Tina's, but Tony's sceptical. Would you tell him about the significance of Dragonsbury Ring and the hill's connection with Giles

Kingsbury?" She shot Emma a look that suggested Emma had better watch what she said.

"Well, it's private property for a start, so there won't be any walkers, just the odd one keeping the footpath open," Emma declared, "so finding an earring and dug-up earth is suspicious anyway."

"If it was private property," Tony interjected, "what were you doing up there, and so early in the morning?"

Emma searched for a plausible story.

"They were staying here for a couple of days and were walking my dogs for me," Sue said for her. "And the beagle ran off. He must have gone after the smell of blood."

"Blood! What blood?" Tony asked sharply.

"Jim, why don't you tell him? You're more objective than I am."

Jim cleared his throat and swallowed hard. "Tony, you're probably goin' to think that what I've got to tell you is a load of codswallop, I 'eard what you said before to Sue about satanism and the like, but I want you to know that what I'm goin' to tell you is the truth. I wish it weren't, but it is."

"Get on with it, man," Tony said irritably. "I haven't got all bloody night."

Leaning back in the chair, he listened with a blank expression on his face to what Jim had to say. After Jim had finished, no one spoke for several minutes.

"You found a pit and you just happened to have a spade with you." Tony gave an exasperated laugh and scratched his head, and then, looking directly at all of them in turn, he said, "Enough of this shit! I wasn't born yesterday. I want the bloody truth."

"All right," Jim said, pulling on his earlobe, "I'll tell you. Me and Em are doin' some undercover work for an animal rights group, and we got wind that Kingsbury was sacrificin' animals in an underground cavern on Dragonsbury Ring, so we went to 'ave a look."

"You lied to me about the dog running off," Tony said reproachfully to Sue.

"I did. I didn't want you to know."

"Why? Because you knew you were deliberately breaking the law?"

"The law is irrelevant when it can't protect the innocent," Emma stormed. "There's a satanic temple down there, and if that earring is Tina's, she's probably dead. Kingsbury already said he was going to shut her up, and the earring is identical to the one she's wearing in the photograph. Tina is missing. What more do you want to know?"

Tony's face paled, and he scowled. "I would like to make one thing clear. The threat against Tina Marshall, and her disappearance, are police business. Do not interfere," he said sternly. "Could you give me the earring you found? I'll take it back to the station." Taking the earring from Omar, Tony barked, "Police business is not your business." He went out the door and slammed it behind him.

"He pissed me off," Emma said. "It should be bloody obvious to a fool what's going on."

Sue sighed. "A copper's mind is a copper's mind. All hard facts and evidence."

"Anyway, enough of that. I made food while you were out," Emma said. "There's a quiche in the oven and a bowl of salad in the fridge."

Omar's teeth flashed white in his dark face, and he flicked back his dreads. "What can I do to help you, mon?"

"You can help me lay the table!"

Over dinner, Sue and Omar talked about Lily.

"How old is she?" Emma asked.

"I don't know, eleven or twelve." Sue shook her head. "I feel bad about leaving her on her own, but I've got too much on my plate right now to get involved. Damn! I should have told Tony that she's alone. I'll give him a couple minutes to cool down and then I'll phone him. He'll know who to call to get her help."

"'Ave you ever thought that Kingsbury's might be 'avin' Lily watched?" Jim said. "After all, 'e don't know if Tina told 'er what was goin' on at the Blue Lagoon."

"It didn't cross my mind," Sue said with a worried glance at Omar.

"Well, mon, if there was a son of Babylon on the watch, my loa would have warned me, but that doesn't mean to say that them sons of wickedness ain't watchin' her."

Sue got up. "Lily could well be in danger." Getting out her phone, she dialled Tony's number. "Shit! It's engaged."

"Do you 'ave an Ordnance Survey map of 'Ockham's Bridge?" Jim asked. "We need to 'ave a reccy round Brisin' Manor in case we 'ave to leave the sabbat in an 'urry."

"I think it's in the newspaper rack. Hang on a minute and I'll go and get it."

Sue was soon back with the map, and she laid it out on the table.

"'Ockham's Bridge is 'ere," Jim said, pointing at the map. "Kingsbury's estate is 'uge. Omar, I think we should 'ave a look round the place, see if there's a way in apart from the front entrance."

"Irie, mon. I'll come with you. Perhaps you girls could drop us off at the crossroads at Hockham's Bridge and pick us up later. D'ya understand me?"

Sue nodded. "Are you going to try and get in to the estate?"

"Yes, if we can find a way in," Jim answered.

"Well, you'd better have a good story ready if you're caught. A trip to the clink would be the best-case scenario."

"It ain't happenin', mon," Omar said. "We'll be as silent and swift as panthers."

"There's some camouflage gear in a plastic bag in the barn," Sue said. "Why don't you see if there's anything in there that would be useful. It's old, but it'll still do the job. In the same bag, you'll find some black sweats and hoodies as well. Bring them back with you and I'll wash them. We can wear them on Saturday night to the sabbat."

"Where in the barn?" Jim asked, getting to his feet.

"To the right of the light switch in the corner, in a black bag."

"Comin', Omar?"

"I'm with you, mon," he said, following Jim outside.

"We'll drive around Kingsbury's estate while the boys are spying out the land," Emma said, peering at the map. "I don't want to be negative, but we don't want to end up driving into a dead end if we're chased."

"My thoughts exactly," Sue said, turning her attention to the map.

A few minutes later the kitchen door opened, and Jim and Omar came in with their hands full. "Find anything to fit?" Sue asked.

"I got myself a pair of green-and-tan trousers with a shirt to match," Omar replied, showing them to her.

"Me too," Jim said, pleased as punch. "That's a little more oil to our elbow."

"We're going to drive around Kingsbury's estate while you're out and about to check out the roads," Sue said. "How long do you think you'll need to get in and out?"

"A few 'ours," Jim replied.

"What about meeting you at the crossroads at three o'clock?" Emma proposed. "That should give you plenty of time."

"That sounds good to me," Jim said. "What do you think, Omar?"

He nodded. "Three is a magic number, mon."

"I'd better take this to the car now," Sue said, folding the map. "I don't want to forget it in the morning."

After a cup of tea, they decided to call it a night. Emma was exhausted not only in body but in mind as well, and she soon fell into a deep and dreamless sleep.

CHAPTER SEVENTEEN

PUB TALK

Emma and Sue were up early the next morning and were sitting at the kitchen table drinking tea when Jim and Omar came downstairs dressed in camouflage gear.

"All ready, mon." Omar sat down.

"A very good fit," Sue remarked as she appraised the faded fatigues. "I knew they'd come in handy."

"What's for breakfast?" Jim asked, sitting next to Emma.

"Eggs from our hens with brown bread and butter. Help yourself to tea," Sue said, laying the table.

The morning was sunny and bright as Emma drove along the country lanes to Hockham's Bridge. "It's almost noon now," Jim said, checking his watch as she pulled up at the crossroads. "We'll meet you back 'ere at three."

"Be careful," Sue said. "Don't take any unnecessary risks. You're dealing with a man who can get away with murder, and who enjoys doing it."

Saying their goodbyes, Jim and Omar walked quickly along the road towards Turley village.

Emma drove on, taking a right back to the junction.

"Emma! Look!" Sue cried, pointing to the Gables on the corner of the high street. "I think that's the same vehicle we saw at Dragonsbury Ring."

There were three cars in the car park, and one of them was a green Range Rover. Emma pulled slowly past, and Sue jotted down the number plate on the back of an envelope she had found in her handbag.

"I'll give the registration number to Tony. Maybe we can finally find out who the vehicle belongs to. I'm sure it's one of Kingsbury's estate vehicles, but it would be nice to know for sure."

"I'm going to park over there," Emma said, slowing down and pointing across the road to the village green. "We'll wait for a while and see if they leave."

They had been waiting about ten minutes when four men walked out of the pub into the car park.

"That's the two assholes from Dragonsbury Ring," Sue said grimly. "The one wearing a Barbour jacket and the skinny one in the ratting cap."

"The man in the blue jumper is Jamie, the barman from the Blue Lagoon," Emma said. "I'd know him anywhere."

Neither of them recognised the fourth man. He was nondescript and thin, possibly middle to late fifties. Emma thought he looked like the policeman that had given Jim directions to Baxter Street, but it was hard to be sure. People looked different in uniform.

Three of the men stood together at the back of the Range Rover talking amongst themselves while Jamie dug in the glove compartment of a black Renault parked alongside. Emma saw the bartender pull out a roll of paper money and then furtively look round before he joined the others. After a brief discussion, he gave a bundle of notes to each of them, and the men got into their vehicles and drove away towards the crossroads.

"We'll wait for a while," Emma said, "and then we'll go and have a drink. We might hear something to our advantage."

They waited for five minutes in case the men returned, and seeing no further threat, they go out of the car and stood together in the sunlight. Emma glanced at the white stone houses clustered in a half moon around the green. The neat gardens full of spring flowers and the thatched roofs were a picture postcard of a peaceful English village.

They crossed the main street and walked quickly to the pub. The public bar was quiet, the only customers two middle-aged woman sitting at the bar eating scampi.

"Hello again," the landlord said amiably to Emma. "Couldn't keep away, eh?"

"No." She smiled. "My friend and I were in Brighton for the day, and the countryside around here is so pretty, we thought we would go for a drive."

"Well now, what can I be gettin' for you ladies?"

"A glass of red wine, please. What would you like, Sue?"

"I'll have a light and lime."

Emma paid for the drinks and they sat together at the bar.

"Sid, who was the ginger-haired fellow with Terry?" one of the women asked the landlord.

"I don't know I've ever seen him before." Sid sniffed. "Looked like a copper to me. His eyes gave him away—always looking around. Shifty like." Putting their drinks on the counter in front of Sue and Emma, Sid moved away.

Looked like a policeman, Emma thought. So she had been right. She wondered how many officers at the station Kingsbury had paid off.

"Big party up at the manor on Saturday, I hear," the other woman said to Sid. "Perhaps he's one of the partygoers come early. Makes you wonder what goes on up there. I've heard a lot of strange stories about that place."

"They do what most people do at parties, Mabel. They eat and drink 'emselves silly, except Kingsbury and his friends are hoity-toity," the landlord said. "He's a wild one all right, that Giles, but then, he can afford to be with all his bloody money."

"Do you remember that little girl that went missing? What was it, two years ago?" Mabel's friend said. "The one that disappeared without a trace. Police searched and searched. Couldn't find a clue. There was a party up at the manor that weekend too. There were rumours at the time that Giles had something to do with it. I wouldn't put anything past him."

Emma caught Sue's eye, and she raised her eyebrows in anticipation.

"I know what you mean, Jean, but we can't be judge, jury, hangman. There was never any evidence to link Giles with that terrible business," Sid said sharply.

Turning to the measures, Sid poured himself a drink and joined the ladies.

Jean continued, "Snatched from her bed, she was. Window left wide open. They found her doll in the woods bordering Kingsbury's estate. That was all." She sniffed. "Folk in the village were saying that she sleepwalked. Can you believe that! What was she, five?"

Mabel nodded.

"It was my Terry's birthday, April 30," Jean went on. "We were driving home from the pub when we saw all the cop cars with their lights flashing outside number three, just down from us. Her parents were crushed. Destroyed them. But nothing came of the investigation, as I recall. No one was arrested."

"Why doesn't that surprise me?" Sue muttered under her breath.

Mabel leaned forwards. "Julia the florist told me that Giles ordered hundreds of them white lilies. You know, the ones they have at funerals. I never could stand their sickly smell, and that's not all." She lowered her voice. "When I stopped by to buy my cat food at the pet shop this morning, the salesgirl, Jenny, told me that Giles had ordered a python for his party. What on earth would he do with a snake?" She gave her friend a dumfounded look.

"Perhaps they're going to cook it up for dinner," Jean chimed in. "Some of these rich folks have strange tastes. Remember when he ordered all them snails?"

"A snake!" Sid repeated, shaking his head in disapproval. "Whatever next!"

"Look at the time!" Mabel said, consulting her watch. "Have to be running along, Jean. We've got to make pies for the whist drive tomorrow afternoon."

The matrons said their goodbyes to the landlord, picked up their shopping bags, and headed for the door.

Sid moved along the bar to Sue and Emma. "Anything else I can get for you ladies?"

"No thank you," Emma replied.

Sue shook her head. "One's enough for me. Forgive me for eavesdropping, but I couldn't help hearing about the snake. Perhaps it's going to be a talking piece at the party."

The landlord smiled and shook his head. "Different strokes for different folks. That Giles is a weird one."

The door opened, and Art hobbled to the bar.

"Art! What have you done to yourself?" Sid asked. He poured a pint of ale and put it on the counter.

"I dropped a bloody mallet on my foot. It was so swollen all day yesterday that I couldn't put my weight on it," Art grumbled, putting his money on the bar. "Four cords of wood he wanted cut, and all I had was my son to help me. All his boys, as he calls them, were out on another job. Pretty important, mind, by the sounds of it." He sniffed and took a long swig of beer. "Then after all that, he wanted some oak planks cut. I hope it's his coffin he's a-buildin'. If I wasn't in a tied cottage, I'd have taken my axe and mallet and left! Ungrateful bugger, that he is." Picking up his change, Art turned to Sue and Emma.

"Hello!" Emma said with a friendly smile.

"Fancy seein' you back here again," Art replied before draining his glass.

"My friend and I were in Brighton," she said casually. "Nice to see you. Would you like another drink?"

The old man brightened up. "Thank you."

"Sorry to hear you've hurt yourself," Emma said, giving Art an opening.

"Slave driver, that's what Giles is. Me bein' an older man, I can't do that heavy work no more. And all that bloody nonsense this weekend. It's enough to drive a sane man mad. Almost put me in an early grave more than once, he did." Looking round the bar, Art whispered, "He ought to be careful. I know a thin' or two, I do."

The remark wasn't lost on Emma. Somehow she had to keep him talking, and she remembered he had said he was a gardener, so she asked, "Are you growing broad beans this year?"

"I am!" He smiled. "Them's my favourite. I like them cooked with butter and summer savory."

"Me too," Emma responded. "Another pint for Art," she called to Sid.

"Oh, thank you kindly, ma'am," he said with a smile as Sid put a fresh pint on the bar. "Beer is so expensive for a poor old man like me."

"So you're going to be busy this weekend," Emma said.

"Only till it gets dark," he said. "Then the master—" His eyes widened, and then he wandered off to play the fruit machines by the door.

Sue looked at her watch. "It's almost two. Let's go," she said.

They said their goodbyes to the landlord and then cautiously looked out into the street from the doorway. Seeing the coast was clear, they made their way swiftly back to the car.

"Art was scared. Did you see his face?" Emma said, starting the engine. "I wished he'd finished his sentence."

Sue nodded. "I would be scared too. If anybody heard him talking out of turn like that, and it got back to Kingsbury, he'd be murdered." She checked the map. "Let's take a quick look round the village and see if we can find a place to park on Saturday night that's out the way."

Emma drove along the high street, past the Gables, and on down the road. At the west end of the village, they came to a church. "Turn in here," Sue said, pointing to the right. "It looks like the driveway to a car park round the back."

The parking area behind the church was hidden from the road by a high hedge. "This is great," Emma said. "It's out of the way, and it'll be late when we get here, so chances are no one will be around."

"This is probably as good a place as any," Sue agreed. "Come on, let's go back to the crossroads and take the road to Turley."

"Keep your eyes peeled for any sign of the boys," Emma said as she drove past the gates at Brising Manor and along the Turley Road.

Turley consisted only of a few houses bordering the high street, a shop and post office, a couple of pubs, a fish-and-chip shop, and a church.

"Small little place," Sue remarked as they drove out of the village. "You blink and you've missed it. Take a left when you can. Hopefully we'll be able to drive around the estate in a square."

It was another three miles before Emma found a road off to the left. She turned in and then stopped. "It's hardly more than a track!" she exclaimed, looking at the ruts. "I'm not going to chance driving along it. You'd need a Range Rover to get along there. I don't want to get stuck."

"I agree, but I bet this leads to a back entrance to Brising Manor," Sue said. "Kingsbury probably owns the fields round here, as well as the estate. We've still got half an hour before we have to meet the boys, so let's drive on up the road and see if there's another place to turn left."

As Emma backed up, she felt a bump, and as she pulled back onto the road, she heard the unmistakable rumbling of a flat tyre. She stopped and got out.

"Shit! We've got a puncture."

"Where's the jack?" Sue said, getting out and taking charge. "You got a wheel brace?"

Emma put her hand over her mouth. Her mind had gone blank; she couldn't remember where the jack was.

Sue opened the back and rummaged in the boot. "I've found the jack and the tyre, but where's the brace?" she asked, putting the tools on the road next to the tyre.

"I'll look for it," Emma said, scrambling into the back seat.

She found the wheel brace wedged under the driver's seat. It took them half an hour to change the wheel. The lug nuts were on so tight it took both of them to loosen them.

By the time they got on the road again, it was past three o'clock. "This is awful, us being late like this. What if something's happened?" Emma lamented.

At half past three, they arrived at the crossroads. Jim and Omar were nowhere to be seen. "Shall we drive up the Turley Road and see if we can see them?" Emma asked anxiously.

"No, we'd best stay at the agreed meeting place," Sue said, searching the woodland with her eyes. "They'd be hiding close by if they were here."

Emma parked in a spot with a good view of the crossing, and they waited with their eyes glued to the road.

After a while, Emma became agitated and started drumming her fingers on the steering wheel. "Something's gone wrong! It's a quarter to bloody four. We should drive along the Turley Road and have a look for them."

"Let's wait a bit longer," Sue advised. "If anything has gone wrong and the boys are sussed, Kingsbury's lackeys will be on the road looking for the car they came in."

"We can't sit here all bloody afternoon," Emma said tensely.

"Okay, then—"

Gunshots rang out.

"They're in trouble!" Emma cried.

CHAPTER EIGHTEEN

RECONNOITRE

There was a cold east wind blowing as Jim and Omar walked briskly towards the estate. "The wall to the property starts about a quarter of a mile down the lane," Jim said as they slipped into the woodland bordering Brising Manor. "I clocked the distance the night we took Art back to the gate'ouse. If we walk straight ahead through the undergrowth, we should find it."

They made their way slowly through the trees and bramble thickets to a clearing. A high wall festooned with dark moss and curly white lichen reared up before them. "'Ere it is," Jim said, looking anxiously at the broken glass cemented to the top row of stones. "Kingsbury's not takin' any chances with trespassers, is 'e? That sucker 'as to be all of eight foot 'igh."

"Better put an emerald shield around us, mon," Omar said uneasily. "My loa have warned me that there are spirit watchers inside the walls. We have to be very careful."

Jim's face paled. "What do you mean by spirit watchers?"

"Demons, mon! That son of Babylon has got more than one way to protect his wicked doin's."

Jim's face blanched even whiter. "'Ow do I put up a shield?" he said in a rush.

"Concentrate on an emerald shape in front of you. My loa will help you see it, mon. See it in front of you and then walk into it."

Jim closed his eyes, and on the back of his lids, he saw a glowing emerald octahedron appear. Grasping the shape with his mind, he lowered it in front of him, and he stepped inside. Warmth rushed to his heart, and he saw an emerald glow about him. "Thanks, Omar."

Running alongside the wall was a rutted track broad enough for a vehicle. "Let's see where the pathway leads," Jim said quietly.

After pausing for a moment to make sure no one was around, they cautiously followed the track west. After a hundred yards or so, they came to a large black door set back into the stonework. "This must be one of the side entrances to the estate," Jim murmured. He walked over to it. "Let's 'ope it's open." He turned the knob and pushed. The door was locked.

"There don't seem to be any security devices, mon," Omar said. He took a couple of short steel rods of different shapes from a leather wallet in his trouser pocket and stepped up beside Jim. Crouching down, he inserted one of the rods into the keyhole and fiddled with the lock. ,

Jim watched nervously as Omar struggled with the catch. *Something's wrong,* he thought, glancing uneasily around the quiet wood. It was too quiet. Spring in the woods was always noisy. He wondered where the birds had gone.

"Got it, mon," Omar whispered.

The great door opened smoothly, and they cautiously looked around the grounds beyond for any sign of life. A footpath ran from the gate into a patch of woodland, and making sure the coast was clear, they followed it into the trees. After a few minutes, they came to the edge of another clearing with a couple of old sheds, pens of various sizes, buckets, and some feeders.

"Jesus!" Jim exclaimed. "Look at that." He pointed to a barbed wire fence hung with hundreds of bodies in different stages of decay: stoats, weasels, foxes, squirrels, cats, and different kinds of birds. "All that killin' just so a few yobs can shoot pheasants. If I'd known about this carnage, I would've rammed the glass of beer I bought the keeper right down 'is fuckin' throat."

"Jim, mon, try and calm your feelin's," Omar cautioned. "There is much cruelty and violence dwellin' in this place. I can feel it all around us. Hate is a powerful draw, and your anger only adds to the sin that is present. It will attract bad loa to us."

In dismay, Jim saw his emerald shield shrink. He concentrated and slowly formed it again, but it wasn't as vibrant now as it had been.

"I'm sorry," he muttered. "I know better. Years in animal rights taught me that like attracts like, but seein' those poor creatures displayed like that made me mad."

"Hold tough, mon."

Out of the silence raucous caw-cawing suddenly erupted. Jim looked up to see rooks, startled out of their nests by their presence, circling ominously above them. The black ring hovered over them like smoke, and Jim shivered, wondering if it was a portent of evil things to come. "Do you think the birds are evil?" Jim asked nervously.

"No, mon, but one among them is. Keep your mind neutral if you can."

Moving on slowly, they followed the road through another cover of small trees. On the other side of the copse was a sward of short green grass and a high clipped privet hedge. Set into the shrubbery was a tall, arched wrought iron gate. "This must be the entrance to the gardens," Jim said, looking through the trelliswork at the walkway beyond. Seeing no one around, he tried the latch. The gate was open. He hesitated for a moment, and then warily set off along a flagstone walkway bordered on one side by tennis courts and on the other by a stand of laurel bushes. "This must lead to the 'ouse," Jim hissed.

There was a bend up ahead, and as they rounded the corner, they both stopped dead in their tracks. Across the lawn, Brising Manor rose up before them.

Omar felt a shock of evil tingle down his neck as he gazed at the house. It lay in the centre of a shadow silhouetted by the hideous outer-spectrum colours of the lower worlds. He thought for an instant that he saw the blue emanations of the sapphire, but the ugly tints soon swallowed them.

"Whoa!" Jim exclaimed, cupping his hands over his eyes and slowly opening his fingers. "What an 'orrible sight."

Angry shouting came across the lawn, and they dived behind the laurel bushes.

A chainsaw's buzz broke off the vitriolic exchange, and then a car door banged and an engine roared. Peeping out of the shrubbery, Jim saw a green Range Rover speeding along the driveway to the house. The vehicle's brakes squealed, and it skidded to a halt in front of the entrance.

Giles Kingsbury got out of the vehicle, slammed the door behind him, and glanced quickly over his shoulder in the direction of the gatehouse. Red-faced and tight-lipped, he stalked to the entrance. Halfway up the steps, he stopped, turned around, and stared in their direction. He seemed to be listening. Then he jerked his head and ran down straight to the Range Rover.

"My loa's warnin' us to run, mon," Omar hissed. "Quick, let's go! Kingsbury's tumbled us. D'ya understand me?"

They burst out of the laurels and back along the walkway. "Run!" Omar yelled, looking back over his shoulder, "He's got a gun, and there's dogs in his ride!"

When they reached the gate, the sound of a vehicle became louder behind them.

"That son of Babylon is comin' after us!" Omar shouted, slamming the gate shut behind them.

They ran like hunted hares through the trees, across the clearing, and into the woodland.

"There's the side gate. Leg it mon!"

Bullets zipped through the trees around them, and they ducked instinctively as shots hit the wall above their heads.

"Quick!" Jim shouted, opening the side door, "'E's got an automatic rifle!" In a hail of bullets, they ran into the trees and out of the estate, and dropping low, they crawled through the thickets towards the road.

At last the road to Turley was in sight, and they rose to their feet and stumbled to the verge. Omar cautiously peered up and down the road.

"It's empty, mon. Quick! It's not far to the crossroads," he said, sprinting forwards.

The gunshots snapped Emma's nerves. "That's it, I'm going to look for them." She started the car.

"There they are!" Sue shouted, pointing straight ahead.

Two figures running full tilt towards them. Omar's lanky frame and flying dreads were unmistakable. Emma bumped off the verge, accelerated, and screeched to a halt beside them.

Gasping for breath, the men climbed into the back seat.

"Drive!" Omar shouted. "Them sons of Babylon are after us."

Pulling away, Emma checked the rear view-mirror. "Shit!"

A green pickup was speeding up behind them on the wrong side of the road, followed by a Range Rover. The truck slowed as it passed, and to Emma's horror, six rough-looking men with clubs sat in the back. The truck stopped a few feet in front of them, effectively blocking their escape. The Range Rover slowed as it came up alongside. The window slid down and the driver leaned out to look inside Emma's car. The man in the passenger seat grabbed the driver's arm and gesticulated in their direction.

"Em, back up!" Jim yelled, "The bastards are tryin' to block—"

A heavyset man with a bat jumped out of the back of the pickup and ran to Emma's car. With one blow, he knocked out the driver's window and thrust his hand through the broken glass and grabbed at the keys. Jim took hold of his arm, but the thug punched him in the face with his other fist.

Emma rammed the gear stick into reverse and accelerated backwards, barely missing the Range Rover as it moved behind them. The thug let out a howl as he jerked his hand back and fell down.

In a succession of violent swerves, Emma reversed down the twisty lane until she backed into a farm gateway to turn around. She put the car in first gear and tried to drive out, but the wheels spun in the mud.

"Jim!" she shouted anxiously.

"We're stuck in the mud." He leaped out of the car, swiftly followed by Sue and Omar. They pushed hard on the rear bumper.

"Take your foot off the gas, Em!" Jim shouted as the tyres sprayed mud in their faces. "You're diggin' in deeper. Now push!" he yelled to the others. On the second try, the car came free, and Emma shot into the road. Sue lost her balance and fell face down in the mud.

Omar picked her up. "You all right?" he asked, helping her into the car. Sue nodded.

Once they were all in, Emma took off. She didn't slow down until she passed the speed restriction signs at Hockham's Bridge.

"Take the road that runs behind the Heron Inn, the one we found earlier," Sue urged, wiping the mud off her glasses. "When we get to the crossroads, take a left towards Denhampstead, and then take the Shoreham road from there."

Emma followed Sue's directions, and they were halfway along the high street in Denhampstead when a green Range Rover pulled out behind them.

"I don't believe this! The bastards are right behind us," Emma cried, looking in the rear-view mirror. "They're speeding up!"

Sue turned to look out the back window. "Hang on, they're going to ram us!" she shouted.

There was a bump and the car was shunted forwards.

"What the fuck!" Emma shouted, swerving violently across the road.

"Never mind the speed limit or the police, just drive, mon," Omar said calmly from the back seat. His voice sounded strange and far away, and Emma put her foot down.

The Range Rover sped up too. "Watch out!" Sue shouted. "Here they come again." Expecting an impact, Emma's body stiffened, and she accelerated, but the Range Rover fell back.

"Looks like it's pulling off," Sue said. "There's steam gushing out of the bonnet." She applauded. But her alacrity was short-lived "Omar!" she cried. "Your hand is bleeding." She pointed to blood on the seat and then to his hand.

"Just a scratch from one of Kingsbury's bullets, mon," he answered grimly. "But praise and thanks to Jah Love! The loa of fire and water I command. The spirits put paid to their little hokum—the water in their engine boiled up."

The road was narrow and twisty with hedges on either side. Sue followed the route with her finger on the map on her knees. "Emma, go left at the intersection and then straight on towards Shoreham-by-Sea. The road will take us to the coast."

After they had gone a few miles along the open road, Emma pulled over in a lay-by, got out, and brushed the broken glass off her clothes.

"You're lucky, mate. It's just a small flesh wound," Sue said as she examined Omar's hand. "What the hell happened?"

"We got salted, mon. We had to run for it!" he replied. "Kingsbury had dogs, and he shot at us."

"How the hell did he track us to Denhampstead?" Sue asked in astonishment. "There is no way he could have known what route we took. No one saw us turn."

"Kingsbury has a devil with him," Omar replied. "It tagged us in the grounds and then followed us when we left. That's why they were waitin'; they knew where we were headin'."

"But you're a powerful psychic. How did Kingsbury's devil see through your protection?"

Omar shook his head and lowered his eyes.

"It was my fault," Jim said, gingerly touching his swollen jaw. "There was a vermin tree on the estate, and I got angry. I felt like murderin' the gamekeeper and stickin' 'is body on the fence." He nervously rubbed the back of his neck. "It's so 'ard not to feel angry when you see 'ow much killin' they do. What's wrong with wantin' to 'urt back? They're not fuckin' 'uman, 'urtin animals like that."

"That's as may be," Omar said, "but when you're dealin' with loa, you've got to guard your thoughts. What we're thinkin' and feelin' goes out a lot farther into the ether than you know. If your thoughts are negative, evil loa will zero in on it straight away. It's called spiritual resonance." He turned his dark, piercing eyes to Jim. "A lesson learnt, mon. We got away this time."

It was just after five-thirty when Emma pulled into Greenfern. Jim went to the barn to find a piece of plastic to cover the broken window until they got back to Basingstoke.

"I'll make some tea," Sue said as Emma and Omar followed her into the kitchen.

"Omar, would you put some wood in the Aga? Emma and I'll make a bite to eat."

"Irie, mon."

In no time, bread and butter appeared on the table with four steaming cups of tea.

"It's all so fucking unreal!" Sue said, taking off the cap of the Marmite jar. "I mean, if Omar can get tagged because of Jim's anger, that doesn't bode well for the rest of us. I'm not sure that I can handle my anger or fear. I know about protecting myself and not thinking, trying to stay in the moment, but it's a lot easier said than done."

"It's the hardest thing we will ever do, mon. Fear is programmed in. Understand what I mean?"

"I do. I really do." She gave a deep sigh. "We'll just have to do the best we can."

The door opened, and Jim came into the kitchen. "That was too close for comfort," he said, kicking off his boots. "It was certainly more than I bargained for. I mean, fancy shootin' at us in broad daylight, smashin' Emma's window. Shows 'e's got all his lackeys bought and paid for."

"We have a bit of news," Emma piped up. "Sue and I ran into Art at lunchtime while we were waiting for you. Seems he had a bit of a falling out with Kingsbury over some rough boxes Kingsbury wanted built."

"Buildin' coffins," Jim said with a shudder.

"There was also money changing hands outside the pub," Emma said. "Jamie from the club was there, and he gave a wad of notes to the three men that were with him. Jim, remember that copper we saw in Brighton, the one you asked for directions to Baxter Street?"

He nodded. "The weird one?"

"Yes. I can't be totally sure, it's hard to tell when he's out of uniform, but I think it's the same man."

"The other two were the ones in the Range Rover from Dragonsbury Ring," Sue said. "I'd know them anywhere."

"Probably bent on murder, by the sound of the coffin' buildin'," Jim commented ominously. "We're really battin' on a sticky wicket. Seems Kingsbury can do anythin' and be answerable to no one."

"The privilege of class," Sue said. "The French knights stole our land in 1066 and have held on to it ever since. Robber barons. And satanists." She glanced at the clock. "Let's take our cups to the sitting room and watch the news at six."

The breaking story was about a shocking murder at the Bishop's Stone in Epping Forest. A girl walking her dog had found the body of a young woman partially covered by leaves. The only information the report gave was that the police were investigating the death.

Sue nervously rubbed her hands. "The Bishop's Stone is a sacrificial sight, another Dragonsbury Ring," she said grimly.

A loud knock on the back door made them jump. Sue went swiftly to the kitchen to see who was there. When she came back, Tony was behind her, looking pale and haggard.

"Hello," he said hoarsely, slumping down in a chair.

Emma looked up at him. He appeared to have aged twenty years since she'd last seen him.

"Tony," Sue said hesitantly, "was it Tina's body that was found at the Bishop's Stone?"

"Yes," he said, swallowing hard. "She was sexually tortured, and then the bastards stabbed her with a pitchfork. They drove the prongs through her throat and into the earth. She was still alive when they stuck her."

A curtain of sadness fell over the room at the awful news, and Sue got up and poured glasses of whisky. "Time for a drink," she said, handing them round.

"And there's something else," Tony said, knocking back his drink in one. "The earring you found on Dragonsbury Ring . . . Tina was wearing the mate when they found her body. There's more to the story than you've told me."

Sue looked at him uncomfortably. "I had a dream that there was something lying in the grass up there . . . something to do with Tina."

"Hmm." Tony looked at the others. "Can anybody do better than that?"

"Do you think your life is in danger?" Jim asked, changing the subject. "I mean, considerin' what we over'eard, Kingsbury's already killed Tina."

"I know you're trying to lead me away from the subject. Now will you please tell me what is going on?" He sighed in exasperation. "I really wish you'd come clean with me."

"Kingsbury doesn't want to rock the boat right now," Emma said. "He has a ceremony planned and will stop at nothing to make sure there is no interference. That's why Tina was murdered."

"Stop talking in riddles. What kind of ceremony?" Tony asked.

"A black mass and a . . . human sacrifice," Emma answered. "That's what Kingsbury uses Dragonsbury Ring for."

"What!"

"Human sacrifice," Sue broke in. "Tina was a satanic sacrifice."

"What makes you think that?"

"A man was found with a pitchfork through his neck in the apple orchards a few years ago. He had been sacrificed to the gods of the orchard. His blood soaked into the earth as an offering to ensure a good cider apple harvest. Tina's murder was a carbon copy, apart from the sexual abuse."

Tony took a long slow breath. "Because Kingsbury was Tina's employer and as she was last seen at the club, I drove out to Brising Manor and interviewed him myself." He paused. "I don't really believe in evil per se, but I have to admit, I felt it in his presence. He gloated over me and made no secret of it. Of course, his alibi is watertight; he's got plenty of witnesses to back him up. All he's waiting for is the chief constable to return, and I'll be toast."

Emma glanced at Tony's worried face and felt he deserved more of an explanation. "If you think our stories are a bit strange, that's because all of us are clairvoyant. That's the real essence of our prior knowledge about Tina."

Tony stared at them and made no reply.

"So, what are you going to do about Kingsbury?" Emma asked.

"What can I do? If the chief's in cahoots with him, which he obviously is, my hands are tied," Tony replied. "Sir Giles Kingsbury is the wealthiest man in the county. He buys his way into power and out of tight corners, and he has judges, barristers, and a police chief on his payroll. His family has been at Brising Manor for hundreds of years. What he says goes, by the looks of it."

"So much for fucking justice in this country," Sue broke in angrily. "If you're in the little club, you can get away with everything."

Tony got up. "Knowing is one thing but proving it is another, especially with Kingsbury's connections. I'm walking a tightrope."

The room was silent, and pregnant with foreboding. Emma got up. "I'll make us some food before it gets too late."

"Tony, why don't you stay and eat with us?" Sue offered.

"To be honest, darlin', I don't feel like eating. I've got to figure out a way to trap the bastard. Trouble is, now I don't know who to trust at the station. Anyway, I'd better be going. I have a lot of things to do."

"There's something I haven't told you," Sue said, following him to the door. "Someone broke in here. It had to do with Kingsbury.

I think they got my address by looking up my number plate at the police station."

"What! Why didn't you tell me?"

"You have enough on your plate already. Please be careful. Watch your back."

"I will," he said. "And you had better watch yours. Call me immediately if anything happens." He gave her hug and then went outside.

Sue stood for a moment in the doorway watching him, and then she locked up and made her way back into the sitting room. The television had been switched off and Jim was building a fire.

"The wood's gettin' low," he announced. "I'm goin' outside to get some more and check on the animals before it gets too dark."

"I'll help you, mon," Omar said, getting up. "I could do with a bit of fresh air."

"Supper's on the go," Emma said, taking a nut roast out of the freezer. "It should be ready when you get back."

"Want another drink?" Sue asked when she and Emma were alone.

"Yes, please," Emma replied. She gulped the liquor down and held up her glass. "This whole damn business is ridiculous," she said dejectedly. "Kingsbury's deck is stacked against us on all levels. We don't stand a chance in hell of getting in and out of Brising Manor alive. We're going on a suicide mission. And there's the whole bloody world at stake." There was a long silence. Finally, she went on. "You can really tell now that the Green is dying. The natural world is being deliberately poisoned and no one cares. People are too busy getting for self, and checking their cellphones, to worry about a satanic takeover of the planet, even though the evidence is all around them." Emma shook her head despairingly. "But at the end of the day, we are all to blame. We've let monsters like Kingsbury and his class gain control of our world and our lives. And they're above the law."

"They've always had control, Emma," Sue said quietly. "Nothing's changed since they destroyed our tribes. That's when the slavery began. They have their fingers in every pie and every decision that matters. But Joe Public can't see it. He's too blinded by football, beer, and drama." Sue sighed and ran her hand over her hair. "I know how it is in this world. There's so much cruelty, and that's why I do what I do, try to help the creatures."

The door opened, and Jim and Omar came into the kitchen. "We've been 'avin' a little talk about gettin' into—"

The air shimmered and Trevelyan appeared in an empty chair beside Sue.

Emma reached across and touched his hand. "Trevelyan!" she said with palpable relief. "Thank God you're here."

"I have had a lucky escape, m'dear," he said gravely. "I was trying to return to you from a portal on the Burren, but it was guarded by an army of foul goblins. They were watching for me, and I was hard-pressed to get away. Evil sought to detain me, to prevent my bringing aid to you before the sabbat." He gave them a grim smile. "But chance has aided us, and I am here." He gazed at them for a moment, and Emma knew he was reading their memories of what had happened since he'd been gone.

Reaching into his waistcoat pocket, Trevelyan brought out four thin, oddly coloured bracelets. "These are made of xonite," he said, handing one to each of them. "I would like you to put them on, and keep them on, until this is over."

Emma stared at the clusters of tiny blue, lavender, yellow, and orange stones. The gems glittered with an alien brilliance, and the bronze-coloured metal was warm on her wrist.

"Xonite is magnetic, and this is how it holds the gemstones in place," Trevelyan said. "As you can see, the stones are not embedded in the metal. These bracelets will be of great help to you for getting in and out of the sabbat."

"How?" Emma asked, brightening.

"When you breathe upon the stones, you activate their power. They will bend the light of Faerie around you in an energy cloak. You will no longer reflect light and will therefore be invisible to humans and the lower castes of devils." Glancing at Jim and Omar, he said, "Like the one you fell afoul of at Brising Manor."

"Thank you!" Jim said, heaving a sigh of relief. "We'd almost given up 'ope of bein' able to get onto the estate at all, let alone into the sabbat."

"The sapphire is at the manor," Omar said. "At least we know where it is now."

"A sabbat of this import will be held on a site of sacrifice from ages past, underneath the ground. I would come with you, but I would have to use Emma's energy to transport myself, and by my radiations, she would be immediately revealed to the blackest of spirits and destroyed."

Sue thought for a moment. "Did you see a chapel on the estate?"

"No," Jim answered, "but that doesn't mean there isn't one. That's a big estate."

"These bracelets will help tremendously," Emma said gratefully. "At least we'll be protected from Kingsbury's devil sight and all his sick cronies."

"Yes, but take heed, the emanations of the stones will only protect you from minor devils. At the sabbat, no stone can shield you from the depth of evil that will be present. Only the emerald octahedron will protect you from detection then."

"How long will the bracelets keep their potency?" Sue asked.

"Under normal circumstances," Trevelyan answered, "days and even weeks, depending on the duration of their use, but at the sabbat, demons with strong magnetic fields will be present, and because of their hate-filled emanations, the cohesive energy of the bracelet will soon be undermined. For safety's sake, you should assume that the stones will disintegrate after no more than four hours. Now! Come, breathe upon the stones."

When Emma charged her bracelet, rainbows appeared around her.

"You are all now invisible, but you can see each other," Trevelyan said. "When the rainbow light around you begins to fade, you will know that the power of the stones is being drained. From that time on, you will have less than fifteen minutes before you will become visible to friend and foe alike. And remember!"

Trevelyan leaned forwards and held up his finger in a gesture of caution. "Even though the enemy cannot see you, they will still be able to touch you, as you will remain solid. So stay back until you are ready to make your move. In addition, there are these," he said, producing four woven grass bracelets and a bitter stench.

"Ugh! What's that smell?" Jim said, wrinkling his nose.

"It is asafoetida paste mixed with garlic and bitter thorn apple," Trevelyan replied, handing them each a bracelet.

"Why bitter thorn apple?" Sue asked. "I thought it was used to summon devils."

"'Tis indeed," Trevelyan answered. "'Tis true that garlic and asafoetida repel the force of evil, but for them to be effective, they need a frequency to direct them to the lower realms. That is where bitter thorn apple comes in handy. One of its potencies resonates in the dark worlds; it acts as a beacon and allows our plant allies to go on the attack."

"I'm going to get some ziplock bags," Sue said, getting up and going to a drawer. "We can put the bracelets inside until we need to use them." She handed bags around.

"Now, up, everyone," Trevelyan commanded. "Stand in a square and hold hands." When they were in position, he carried on. "I want you to relax, and take four slow breaths."

Trevelyan sang a single note, and at the same time, his voice spoke in their heads. *"Tone!"*

The sound built, surrounding them in a warm, secure vibration, and before their eyes, a green stone with eight faces, each with six points, appeared upon the table. "This is green fluorite," Trevelyan said. "It naturally forms an octahedron, the shape of the fourth order, the heart. I want you all to look at it, explore every detail of its design, absorb its energy, and then re-create the image with your mind. See it in front of you and mentally step inside. The stone is powerful, and I will leave it with you. It will dissolve your doubts and inspire you to accomplish that which seems impossible. But," he emphasised, "under no circumstances are you to take it to the sabbat, for it shines bright with the light of Faerie."

He had them practice the tone and the visualisation until they could do it in seconds. "Your lives may depend on your being able to intone the sound of Air and imagine the octahedron. Once you step into the shape, you are in a fourth-dimensional vehicle. The vibration of the geometry will protect you. Only fear will be able to undo it.

"One thing more: eat nothing between now and the sabbat, and drink only pure spring water. This will speed up your resonance, which will help to protect you from the sight of evil."

Trevelyan stepped closer, and they felt his light touch upon their foreheads. His voice said in their minds, *"Darkness awaits, and you must be ready. Your only enemy is fear and the gnawing doubt that strangles whatever hope may have. Nay! I tell thee, fear is a lie. It is an illusion. Go forth with strength and overcome the enemy. Recover that which has been lost since the Separation. May the House of the Heart protect you, now and forever."*

Emerald light flooded their minds, and with his words still echoing in their heads, he vanished.

Trevelyan stood in the faerie gate at Hillside, his mind clouded by anxiety. He wanted to stay and help them, but he knew that his frequency would betray them. Besides, he could only offer them assistance, not solutions. They had to grow into their power; he could not do it for them.

He sent his thought to Ireland, to a passage tomb in County Clare. To his surprise, the faerie gate was open.

The light shimmered as he stepped through the portal, and he heard the cries of seagulls hanging on the airwaves overhead. Standing on the limestone pavement, he looked west to the sea. There was nothing moving amongst the rocks save a hare. After blessing the orchids and blue gentians peeping from the grass, Trevelyan strode off across the Burren to the wizard's halls.

CHAPTER NINETEEN

THE PROBLEM OF FEAR

Emma felt vulnerable after Trevelyan had gone. She wished he could have gone with them to the sabbat, but she realised that the sapphire could only be stolen by human hands and hearts. She thought about Kingsbury and the power he wielded over the judiciary in Sussex and all the other controllers of men's lives ruling from their walled estates up and down the country. Trevelyan had given them instructions for spiritual protection and the bracelets, but what could the four of them do against the long arm of Kingsbury's power? The thought of what lay ahead terrified her.

Looking at the gems in her bracelet, she said to the others, "One of the stones is citrine. Any idea what the rest are?"

"The blue is chalcedony, and the orange is imperial topaz," Jim replied looking closely at his bracelet. "But I don't know what the lavender one is."

"I've got a book about crystals in the sitting room," Sue said, getting to her feet. "I'll go and get it." She came back with a large book and flicked through the pages. "Here it is," she said, turning the book so they could all see. "The lavender stones are iolite, the symbol of warriors of the spirit."

"Warriors of the spirit, eh!" Jim said, "I 'ope we can live up to that. What do the others mean?"

"Citrine is a sun stone for success, the topaz is for trust, and blue chalcedony is for courage. We're going to need all the courage we can get," Sue said, closing the book.

"Why don't we have a tarot reading after dinner?" Emma suggested. "The cards may show us things that are hidden from our conscious mind, psychic impressions that we need to be aware of."

"You took the words out of my mouth, mon," Omar said, flashing a smile.

Within a few minutes a bowl of green salad appeared on the table and a nut roast was served.

I forgot 'ow 'ungry I was." Jim cut himself a second slice of roast. "What kind of nut is this?"

"Walnut with onion and white wine," Sue replied.

"I'd really like the recipe. I'd like to take a crack at makin' it myself."

Omar gave a rich laugh. "Me too, mon, but all I can make is gunga peas and rice."

After dinner was over, Omar left the table and started rummaging in his rucksack. "Can somebody light the incense burner?" he asked. Sue lit the smudge pot, and in a few moments, the smell of frankincense billowed around the kitchen. Omar took a couple of deep breaths and then passed his bell and the new tarot cards that Trevelyan had given him through the smoke. After praying for spiritual direction, he shuffled the pack, handed it to Emma, asked her to cut it. The cards tingled in her hand with the touch of the Green, and she said a silent prayer that the unseen world would help to create a barrier against her fear.

The room was silent as Emma handed back the deck. Bowing his head, Omar sat quietly for a moment, and then he laid five cards face up upon the table in a cross. Emma looked closely at the spread. She had no knowledge of what the cards meant, but she felt a stream of ageless wisdom flow around the room.

Omar's first impression of the spread was struggle, and narrowing his eyes, he read the cards, gleaning their energetic information. After a while, he said, "The middle card is the fool, which deals with the now, mon."

Jim shifted uneasily in his chair. "I don't like the sound of that. Does that mean we're goin' on a fool's errand?"

"Irie, mon, no worry. It don't mean that," Omar said reassuringly. He cleared his throat and carried on. "At the top of the cross is the world. The card is showin' us that the future of the planet depends on the actions of the fool, who exists within the moment of the now. It's about us and our quest for the sapphire."

Reverently looking at the cards, Omar's eyes rested on the bottom one, the nine of swords. "This card symbolises the anxiety and fear we're feelin'," he said, tapping it with his middle finger. "We're all worryin' about what might happen to us and tryin' hard to push those thoughts of Babylon away. We are walkin' into hell, and chances are, we won't be comin' back."

There was silence as the others absorbed this information.

"But we have loa to work with," he carried on, "and if we can see fear for what it is and go into neutral, mon, loa can help us. The spiritual way is the only way." He flicked back his dreads. "Now, let's put this reading all together." He closed his eyes and visualised the cards.

"The chariot reveals our two minds. The charioteer represents the human bein', and the two horses he's drivin' are the two sides of his mind that want to go in opposite directions. Strength on the other side of the fool combines spiritual power with physical power, makin' us strong like the Lion of Judah, mon!" He threw up his hands. "All is about struggle to control fear, mon. We can't fight them sons of wickedness in this world; only in loa way do we stand a chance against them."

Bending his head, with a prayer of thanks on his lips, Omar put away his instruments of divination. "What the cards say is Irie, mon. Everythin's all right if we stay in the now."

"The cards are so accurate I can 'ardly believe it." Emma said.

"These are different from my old ones. They show a deeper dimension. Trevelyan's gift has the touch of loa upon it."

The waning twilight conveyed a sense of foreboding and brought the sabbat sharply into focus.

"If we get caught, we'll disappear without a trace. There will be no jail for us, just death. And no one is going to know what happened to us," Emma said grimly.

"Yeah! We'll become statistics like the other 'undred thousand people that go missin' every year." Jim stirred in his chair. "We should let someone know where we're goin'."

Sue nodded. "I'll leave a letter for Tony in the kitchen drawer telling him what we're planning. Then, just before we get to Brising Manor, I'll call and leave a message on his answerphone. It'll be too late for him to stop us then, but if we . . . don't come back, somebody will know where we went and why."

"Good idea," Emma said. "I'll call Dave and Maggie at the same time and ask them to feed the cats until we get back."

"Let me call some of the local animal rights people and see if they can come over this weekend and take care of the animals," Sue said, picking up her cell phone and going towards the sitting room. "Talking about leaving things to the last minute. I should have done this a few days ago."

The fire was burning low and the hour late when they went upstairs to bed. Emma lay down, but sleep was impossible. She was too aware of the terror that, on waking, she would have to confront. Controlling her fear would be critical to their success. Closing her eyes, she lay still, waiting for the dawn.

The day of reckoning has arrived, Emma thought as she watched the sun rise. In a few hours they would be taking a step into a world where depravity was the norm and murder no worse than swatting a fly. When she got downstairs, she found Jim sitting glumly at the kitchen table.

"Are Sue and Omar up?" she asked, sitting down beside him.

"Yeah, they're puttin' fresh straw in the stable," he answered, glancing up at her. "'Ow did you sleep?"

"The same as you," she answered, seeing the dark circles under his eyes.

"Mornin', everyone," Sue said solemnly as she came through the kitchen door. "I've got to drop something off in town. Does anyone want to come with me and get out of here for a couple of hours?"

"Yes!" Emma jumped at the chance to occupy her time.

"I'll stay 'ere," Jim said. "There's a lot of stuff needs doin' round the sanctuary so everythin's ready when your friends arrive."

"I'll stay and help you, mon," Omar said, following Sue into the kitchen. "I don't think Kingsbury saw me, but you never know. If he did, information about a black guy with dreads could well spell disaster for us."

"True enough!" Sue agreed, getting her coat. "Let's go. Emma."

Driving into Market Thorpe, Emma saw a green Mercedes parked outside the police station. "Sue!" she exclaimed in alarm. "I think that's Kingsbury's Mercedes parked outside the cop shop." Sue slowed down, and Emma peered at the number plate. "Yes, that's his car, all right."

"I'm afraid for Tony," Sue admitted. "I can't think of any other reason why Kingsbury would be here. There's a cul-de-sac just down here on the right, so I'll turn round in there, and we can park and watch. I wonder what that bastard's doing here," she said as she made the turn.

"Making a complaint in person to the chief, if he's back," Emma remarked as Sue came to a stop. "That's his style."

Sue pulled forwards until they both could see the police station and the car park. In a few minutes, Kingsbury emerged looking flustered and angry, and he marched to his car.

"He's pissed off," Sue said. "Something has definitely not gone his way. Let's get out of sight and give him a few minutes to get clear." She reversed a little ways down the road and waited. After a few minutes, she drove back to the junction and looked across the road.

"He's gone. Let's go." She pulled out and drove along the high street. "I wonder what that was all about."

A bit farther down the road, Sue parked outside the solicitor's office. "I won't be a minute. I'm going to give Mr Gittoes my last will and testament."

Last will and testament, Emma thought grimly. Fear struck her like a knife as she faced the stark reality of not returning from Brising Manor. She had pushed the idea of death to the back of her mind, but now it had hit home. Who would look after her cats? She gave herself a mental shake. *You will be coming back,* she told herself.

Sue was only gone a few minutes, and when she got back into the car, she called Tony on his cell to tell him about Kingsbury's visit to the police station.

"Damn," she said, and she left a message on his voicemail for him to call. "There's a nice little café further on. Do you want a coffee? Oh, shit! I forgot, no coffee for us. Only spring water. I doubt if there's any real spring water in town. Most bottled water comes straight from a tap!"

After Omar had helped Jim clean the stables and fill the water tanks, he went for a walk along the meadow on his own. The morning sun was warm, and when he reached the side gate, he sat down on the ground with his back against the hedgerow. From the inside pocket of his jacket, he pulled out a herbal cigarette and a book of matches. He needed to smoke, needed to commune with the spirit of the medicine. His struggle wasn't against fear, it was anger, against the destroyers of men's lives, the despoilers and polluters of Mother Earth. He thought about Jim's anger at the gamekeeper's vermin tree, his own warning that Jim's violent thoughts would bring bad loa to them. He had shared anger with Jim, but he knew both of them had to control it, for rage, like fear, was a magnet for the dark. He took a long drag on his joint, and as the sacred herb filled his lungs, he prayed to the plant loa for a shield against his wrath.

Jim was sitting at the kitchen table drinking tea when Sue and Emma got back.

"Where's Omar?" Sue asked, taking off her jacket.

"'E went out for a walk. 'E's been gone over an 'our, so 'e should be back shortly."

No sooner had the words left Jim's mouth than the door opened and Omar came into the room. "Been walkin', mon," he said, taking off his boots.

"There's tea in the pot, everybody," Jim said. "'Elp yourselves."

"Kingsbury was at the police station in Market Thorpe," Emma said, pouring herself a cup.

"What? Kingsbury?" Jim frowned. "Whinin' about Tony, no doubt."

"Whatever he went there for, it didn't go his way," Sue said. "When he came out, he had a face like a smacked ass." She took her phone out of her bag, "I'll call Tony again," she said, dialling his number. "Still getting his voicemail." Her voice was anxious. "I wonder where he is."

"Per'aps 'e's in a meetin'. God! I wish I could eat somethin'," Jim said. "My stomach's rumblin'. It's just gone two," he said, staring at the clock. "What are we goin' to do for the rest of the day? I mean, I don't want to sit 'ere all afternoon thinkin' about . . . later."

"We could have another look at the map. We can make a plan of some kind," Sue responded.

"Trevelyan told us to pray with the fluorite," Emma spoke up. "We need to practice creating an emerald octahedron around ourselves. That's what I'm going to do. Coming?" Picking up the fluorite from the table, she went into the sitting room. Her friends followed.

"We'll have one practice run with the bracelets," Sue suggested as they all sat down, "so we can see what we look like to each other. Just for a few seconds." She breathed on her bracelet and disappeared. The others followed suit. Emma noticed that when they were cloaked, the rainbows around them were continuous, as if they had been trapped inside a lustrous sphere of colours.

"Well," Sue said, when they were visible again, "the rainbows are bright enough that at least we'll surely know it when they fade."

Next they took turns praying with the fluorite and memorising its colour, texture, planes, and angles. After a while, Emma couldn't keep her eyes off the clock. The time seemed to be galloping towards the fateful hour in leaps and bounds.

"What time are we leaving for Hockham's Bridge?" she asked nervously.

"About ten o'clock," Sue replied. "That'll give us time to get there, hide the car at the church, and then make our way to Brising Manor."

"I'm going up to my room to get a bit of rest," Emma said. "We've still got a couple of hours to wait."

"We should take showers and change into clean clothes," Sue said. "Demons will fasten onto any impurities, so everything, including our bodies must be as clean as possible."

Emma got up. "Okay. I'll be down later."

She went up to the bedroom, sat at the dressing table, and gazed into the mirror. "You have to hold up," she said to her reflection. Her emotions swung like a yo-yo between fear and hope. She had to stop thinking of success or failure, to empty her mind and focus on the now.

It was after nine when Emma returned downstairs. She found the others digging in a kitchen drawer. "What are you all up to?"

"I'm going to take something to protect myself," Sue said, holding up a black leather-bound cosh. "If they catch us, they'll kill us, no questions asked, and I'm not going to go lightly. What good am I going to be to the animals that need my help if I'm dead?" She took in a tense breath and exhaled noisily. "This is going against everything I believe in frequency-wise, but the whole world is at stake. If Kingsbury's going to use the sapphire to open the gates to Pandemonia, I'll do whatever it takes to stop him. I'll take the bloody karma."

"Me too," Jim said, holding up a flick knife. "This might come in 'andy for all sorts of stuff." Grinning broadly, he put it in his pocket.

"If we could stay in Jah Love, we wouldn't need to arm ourselves, but we're human and we make mistakes, mon. Know what I'm sayin'?" Omar said, picking up a knife. "I'll take this."

"Where'd you get all these weapons?" Emma asked as she looked in the drawer. She took out a cosh and held it up. "Gosh, it's heavy."

"It's lead," Sue replied. "And I've got all this stuff because it's a dangerous world out there when you're trying to save animals. These are a few things we lifted over the years from the hunt thugs." Going over to the tap, she filled a pitcher with water and brought it to the table. "Get yourself glasses."

"Good water, mon," Omar remarked.

"It's from the spring, and it doesn't have any chemicals in it."

"Jah Love," Omar said, blessing the pitcher.

The grandfather clock in the hallway chimed ten bells. "Best be thinking about it, mates," Sue said grimly, putting a cosh and flick knife in her jacket. She took a look around. "My friends should be here at eleven," she said. "I told them I'd put the key under the flowerpot by the door." She petted her cats, made sure they had plenty of food and water, and said a silent prayer that she would see them again. On her way out, she glanced at the crucifix on the wall and the small bottle of holy water on the shelf beside it. In an impulse, she slipped both of them into her jacket pocket. She locked the door behind her and put the key under the flowerpot

"You won't need a bracelet," Jim nervously cracked to Omar as they stood outside. "Since you're all dressed in black, no one's goin' to see you in the dark!"

"Just my pearly teeth, mon!" Omar retorted, pulling his hat over his dreads.

"I'll drive, if you don't mind," Jim said, when they got to the car. "It'll take my mind off of what's ahead."

Sue nodded and got in the passenger side. "Good idea. I don't feel like driving anyway."

Jim started the engine and the green station wagon moved slowly up the track. Once they were on the road, Sue put on a Bob Marley CD and turned it up loud. She put one track on repeat, and Omar sang along in the back seat.

"I thought you'd like this song," she said.

By the time Jim got to Hockham's Bridge, they were all singing at the top of their voices, intuitively translating their fears into sound.

"This music's really psychin' me up," he said, slowing down to thirty.

"Me too," Emma agreed. "I'm ready to fight the dark!"

"Gotta focus on positivity and Jah Love."

A full moon rose as they drove through the village. "Go past the Gables straight west about a quarter of a mile," Emma said. "On your right, there's a church with a car park round the back. It's a good place to leave the car."

The church was dark save for one light flickering in a small ivy-shaded window of the rectory next door. Jim turned slowly pulled into the driveway and parked around the back.

"Let's wait for a moment," Sue whispered. "Make sure no one's around. I wish we had a bracelet for the car."

"It'd probably get rammed if we did," Jim remarked dryly.

Cautiously getting out of the car, they looked around for any sign of life, but all was still and quiet.

"We need somewhere to 'ide the key in case we get split up," Jim said as he locked the doors.

"What about over there?" Emma pointed to a row of large stones.

"Good one, Em," Jim said. Picking up the nearest rock in full view of the others, he slipped the key underneath. "You lead the way, Omar. I'll take the back and the girls can be in the middle."

"Remember, we gotta keep in the moment of the Jah Love," Omar said, setting off across the car park.

He led them past the pub to the crossroads and then turned right along the road towards Turley village. The night was cold and the ghastly moonlight seemed to track their footsteps as they walked silently along. About a quarter of a mile on, headlights shone behind them.

"Off the road!" Jim hissed.

Everyone breathed on their bracelets and jumped onto the verge. A Lamborghini rushed by.

"Phew!" Jim said as they became visible again. "That was close. Without the bracelets, we'd 'ave been seen for sure."

As they walked on, the bushes on their left gave way to the high stone wall of the estate, and the moonlight glittered eerily upon the jagged fangs of broken glass along the top. In a few yards, they rounded a bend in the road, and the entrance to Brising Manor loomed before them. The black wrought iron gates were open. Perched atop the gateposts like evil sentinels were two huge bronze griffins, their red eyes glittering in the moonlight.

The group were just about to turn into the driveway when Omar stopped and motioned them back. Holding his fingers to his lips as if he were smoking, he pointed to his left through the gateway. A man was standing in the shadows puffing on a cigarette. Breathing on their bracelets, they quietly walked in single file through the entrance.

As Emma got level with the guard, her shoe hit a stone, and it scuffed loudly on the pavement. The man switched on a flashlight, came towards them, and shone the beam on the ground where they stood. Knowing they were solid to the touch, they edged backwards across the driveway. Seeing nothing, the man went out the gate and shone his torch along the road.

"Let's split, mon."

"I think we should stay invisible," Jim whispered. "There might be guards everywhere."

Sue checked the time. "We've used up ten minutes of the bracelets," she whispered. "I'll keep track."

They hadn't gone far along the avenue when headlights swept behind them, and they jumped onto the verge. A Rolls-Royce drove past and then disappeared around a bend.

"A lot of class cars," Jim murmured.

The drive was lined with oaks, and to Emma's mind, the moon seemed to shadow them like a snooping light as they cautiously moved on. At intervals between the shadowy trees, she saw hideous bronze sculptures of satyrs raping nymphs and ugly, leering gargoyles fondling human women, all bathed in red light. *Stay neutral*, she told herself as she followed in Omar's footsteps and kept her eyes fixed on the road. As they rounded a bend, Sue gasped behind her.

Looking up, Emma saw a rambling, imposing, ivy-clad mansion of red-brick standing ghastly in the trembling moonlight. Its frowning gables like dark witches' hats and its paired chimneys reached up into impenetrable darkness. The diamond-paned windows, although totally dark, reflected the moon's rays with glittering malice. Emma gulped. The house pulsated with outer-spectrum colours, and she knew that in those dreadful hues hid the demons of legend, those that lie deep within the psyche, ready to spill out and spread like a plague across the world if she and her friends failed to retrieve the sapphire.

"Look at the porch," Sue whispered hoarsely.

The pillared portico looked more like the entrance to a Greek temple than a manor house. From the ceiling hung a red light which cast bloody shadows on the steps.

"We need to get a move on," Sue hissed. "We're spending too much time invisible."

Skirting the gravel drive and making for a stand of rhododendron bushes to the right of the front door, they hid in the shelter of the shrubs and became visible again.

"'Ow are we goin' to get into this 'ell 'ole?" Jim whispered.

"We will have to wait, mon. We must pray to Jah Love to open the way. When more guests arrive, we can follow them through the door," Omar murmured in reply. "I hope there are people comin'."

CHAPTER TWENTY

INTO DARKNESS

The moon sailed out from behind the clouds, shedding a ghostly light upon the manor house and grounds. Emma checked her watch. "We've been hiding behind the bushes for over half an hour," she said nervously, "and no one has shown up. Perhaps all the guests have already arrived and we should look for another way in."

"There might be a window we can force round the back of the 'ouse," Jim suggested, looking up at the dark ground-floor windows.

"I've got a better idea," Sue said. "Why don't we try the tradesmen's entrance? There have to be cooks and whatnot in there and a room for the chauffeurs to wait in until the ceremony is over. We can knock on the door, and whoever answers, seeing nobody there, will probably take a look outside. Then we can nip in while their back is turned. It's worth a try."

"Let's do it," Jim whispered, breathing on his bracelet.

"Wait, mon! My loa are tellin' us to wait," Omar said.

Respecting Omar's intuition, they waited a while longer, but still no last-minute guests arrived.

"P'raps we've left it too late," Jim said, looking round the empty, silent grounds.

"What's that?" Emma whispered, grabbing Jim's arm and pointing to the beam of a flashlight coming across the lawn towards the house.

"Looks like a guard, mon," Omar said, peering into the gloom.

As the light came closer, a shadowy figure appeared with a huge bull mastiff on a chain. The man paused for a moment, looked along the driveway, and then went back the way he came.

"Phew! That was close," Jim said. "Thanks, Omar. If we'd set off like I wanted, we'd've probably run right into 'im, and the dog would've sussed us for sure."

"Irie, mon."

"I think the thank you is from all of us," Sue said. "The dog would've scented us right away, and no doubt the guard is armed. At best, the dog would've made a ruckus and drawn attention to us, and that's the last thing we need."

"Someone's comin'," Omar whispered as headlights came along the driveway to the house. "Cloak up, mon, and we'll go. We'll wait at the top of the stairs in the porch and slip inside when the door opens."

Emerging from the bushes, they walked swiftly up the steps, taking cover behind the pillars of the sinister arched doorway.

Three men in evening dress got out of the car and started up the left side of the stairs, and as they gained the porch, the chauffeur drove off to the east wing. In the headlights, Emma saw that a space before the towering east gable was crammed with Bentleys, Rolls-Royces, and other classy cars, some sporting pennants and diplomatic flags. The cars were an unwelcome reminder of the wealth and power against them, and the disparity in their numbers. She took a deep breath. There was also good, she told herself, the opposite of bad, and that must be the focus of her attention.

The great black doors to Brising Manor swung open, and a thin, repellent man in an evening suit and tails came forwards into the porch to greet the new arrivals. Seizing their chance, Omar swiftly led the way through the door and into the anteroom.

Standing just inside the entrance were six pre-pubescent boys in sheer roman togas with laurel wreaths upon their heads, ready to wait on the visitors as they entered. Emma glanced at their expressionless faces and frightened eyes. They couldn't have been more than eleven or twelve years old, and she wondered where they had come from and what they were doing at a satanic gathering.

A crystal chandelier hung from the ceiling, casting a sombre light upon the large hall. Mounted on the aging cream-coloured walls were the heads of lions, leopards, and tigers, their skins stretched out beside them, and displays of butterflies and dragonflies under glass below. The room stank of death and exploitation, starkly reminding Emma of Kingsbury's disrespect for living things.

A couple of bejewelled middle-aged women sat at one of many small tables smoking cigars and sipping cocktails while their husbands talked loudly about racehorses and the sex lives of their jockeys. Other groups were sitting against the wall on padded settees smoking long, fragrant hand-rolled cigarettes.

"What do you think?" Emma whispered to the others, pointing to a dozen or more large urns of white lilies. "We can stand among the vases and wait. No one can bang into us over there."

"Good one, Em," Jim whispered as they moved swiftly across the hall to the flowers.

Above the lily display was a coat of arms. A huge sable shield bore a red cross, and coiled around the saltire was a black snake with ruby eyes. Above the shield, the placement banner read "A Posse Ad Esse".

Emma pondered the words, trying to remember the Latin she had learnt at school. *Something about coming into being, or legend comes alive. It must refer to some great work of sorcery that Kingsbury's family has been involved in for generations*, she thought. They had been hunting for the sapphire for centuries, and now they had it. At the sabbat, the jewel would be bathed in the blood of human sacrifice, opening the gates to Pandemonia. That had to be it:

"Possibility becomes reality". Kingsbury was going to let demons in and rule the earth from a satanic throne.

"Praise to Jah Love we got in, mon," Omar whispered as they secreted themselves between the vases.

The butler hissed instructions to the young serving boys.

"Drinks and enhancers are being served in the library," one of the youths said to the new arrivals. "And we . . ." his voice faltered, but catching the butler's evil eye, he went on, "We will be at your service later. If you so desire."

Running his fleshless fingers through his sparse black locks, the butler stood for a moment and slowly looked round the lobby. Emma immediately felt threatened by him, so she concentrated on the emerald shield around her and sensed his energy out of time. As she probed the ether, she was confronted with a malignant and intimidating presence, and not wanting to reveal herself, she instantly shrank back. The butler locked the front door, waved the key in the air, and looked straight at her before putting it in his pocket. She realised that he was showing it to her—no, not to her, she corrected, but to the alien presence that he felt.

After sniffing the air a couple of times, the butler scurried bow-legged across the room to the display of swords mounted on the wall. Snatching down one of the weapons, he paused, and then moved with purpose in the same awful gait towards her. A shadow hung about him as he glared at the lilies, and then without warning, he viciously jabbed the blade between the vases several times, barely missing her. Emma held her breath. The butler thrust his head forwards like a turkey, and his black eyes burned with madness as they searched the space around her. Stabbing again with the blade, he came even closer to her, and she knew that next time, the sword would find its mark. She heard Omar telepathically telling her not to move, that his loa would distract the wicked son of Babylon.

Suddenly the smell of burning filled the air, and the fire alarms went off.

"Boy!" the butler bellowed in a hollow, tomb-like voice. At his summons, a servant came running over with a bucket of water and a sponge, got on his hands and knees, and poured the water on the fire.

A sudden movement on the staircase attracted Emma's attention. Kingsbury stood halfway down in black silk pyjamas, gesticulating wildly. "What the fuck is going on?" he thundered.

"Negligence, milord," the butler answered, hauling the serving boy up by the ear as Kingsbury swiftly came over. "This stupid boy failed to clean the tables, and a smouldering cigar butt fell out of an ashtray, setting fire to the carpet."

"What's your name, boy?" Kingsbury asked mockingly.

"Tommy Smith, sir. Please . . . don't 'urt me."

Kingsbury backhanded the youngster in the mouth. "You know what happens to boys that disobey," he snarled, hitting him again.

"'E's knocked that kid's teeth out! We've got to do somethin'," Jim fumed under his breath. "I can't stand 'ere and watch this shit."

"Let it go, mon. Try and keep neutral. I told you, we're goin' to be tried and tried. This is Babylon! These are devils in human form, and if our anger betrays us, we will never get the sapphire and this will never end. It will only get worse."

Looking around the lobby, Kingsbury beckoned to a paunchy middle-aged man in a tuxedo sitting on one of the settees smoking a cigar.

"Sir Leon, I have a plaything for you. I know how you like them young," he said sarcastically. He picked the boy up by his flimsy toga, ripping it in two, and threw him on the floor.

"No! No!" the boy moaned, curling up and covering his head with his arms.

Leon got up, running his tongue over his lips, and eyed the bleeding, crying boy hungrily. "Come here, sonny," he said, grabbing the child and rubbing the youngster's body against his thighs.

"Take your toy boy to the library," Giles ordered. "And when you're finished with him, he's everybody's!" He said a few words to the butler and then laughed insanely and went back upstairs.

Emma watched as the butler examined the burn mark on the carpet and then looked straight at their hiding place again. *He knows something's wrong*, she thought. Taking a deep breath, she powered the shield around her and defiantly stared back.

One of the serving boys brought him a note, and after snarling a quick reply, the butler walked straight over to the lily display. Pausing for a moment by the vases, he made a pass in the air with his hands, and after speaking a few unintelligible words, he strode off towards the library.

When the hall emptied, Omar pointed to the library door. They moved forwards but were suddenly thrown back by an invisible barrier.

"What the fuck!" Jim snorted in surprise.

"Watch your language, mon," Omar hissed, putting his hands on the unseen wall. "We've been spelled. That son of Babylon has put a force field round the vases. We're trapped in here."

"Trapped!" Sue said. "There's less than three hours left on the bracelets. What are we going to do?"

"There 'as to be a way out," Jim said, putting his shoulder to the wall. "Ouch! It's solid as a rock."

Emma switched to faerie sight and gazed at the invisible field that imprisoned them. "I can see it," she said. "It's a black cube made of crystal surrounded by outer-spectrum colours. The only way out is through Faerie."

"It's a very dense box," Sue said. "I feel a malignant power flowing from it. It's bound to drain the energy in the bracelets. We've got to get out, quick!"

There was a moment of tense silence. Touching the amethyst cluster in his pocket, Omar felt it was hot, and he brought it out and touched it to the barrier. It sparked.

"I thought the square was too heavy for my loa to break through," he said with relief, "but the spark has given me great hope for our salvation. Let's make room so we can all stand together."

Jim and Sue moved three of the urns to make a space for them to stand in. "Hold hands around me," Omar whispered softly. "Empty your minds into Jah Love, and focus from your heart in the moment of the now."

Once they were in position, he held the amethyst cluster in his open palm, and with a silent prayer, he rubbed his other hand across the purple points and up into space.

The purple flame within the amethyst turned a brilliant yellow gold and roared as the air around them grew hot. A series of angles twisted in a stomach-sickening formation before them as a tetrahedron formed, covering them in a glowing triangle of yellow light.

"Breathe in the colour," Omar whispered in a commanding tone.

The pyramid rotated end over end, spinning faster and faster, and just when Emma thought she was about to pass out, she found herself standing with the others in the lobby.

"That was close, mon. Praise to Jah Love we got out of there," Omar said. "Now let's go take a look in the library and see what's goin' on."

The library was filled with people of all colours. Some clustered around small tables drinking cocktails while others lounged in comfortable chairs on settees and chaises longues. Young boys in the same sheer attire waited on the guests, presenting them with trays of drinks, and snuffboxes of white powder with little silver spoons.

Emma stared at the opulent and cosmopolitan assembly, their polite chatter full of social airs and graces. They looked normal enough, but she knew that underneath the suave banter, the expensive perfume, and affected accents they were monsters.

Dominating the room and frowning down upon the assembly were Kingsbury family portraits dating back to the Norman Conquest. Apart from their costumes and wigs, the centuries had done nothing to change the sinister appearance of the balding, chinless wonders that glowered down upon the gathering with thin, unsmiling mouths and cruel, sardonic eyes.

Hearing a cry and then a whimper, Emma turned her head towards an unspeakable act in progress. Sir Leon was kneeling on a daybed sodomising Tommy, cheered on by a group of flabby, older, salivating men.

With a quick intake of breath, Emma looked away. A child was being brutalised in a room full of people and no one seemed to care. It was as if it were an everyday occurrence, like opening a can of beans. *Paedophiles*, she thought, remembering an article she had read in the newspaper about pimps procuring young boys from children's homes and orphanages for the top members of society to sexually abuse. The article had reported that some of the boys had never been seen again, and although there had been a token investigation into child abduction and abuse, there had been a massive police cover-up. *To protect fiends like this from justice*, Emma thought.

Hearing a click beside her, she glanced at Jim. He had a knife in his hand and fire in his eyes. Omar flung his arm against Jim's chest to stop him. "No, mon!" he mouthed.

Turning his attention back to the library, Omar took a quick headcount. He was halfway around the room when he saw a huge black woman in flowing robes and turban lounging on a couch. Fussing around her swollen form and massaging her feet and legs were three young girls in see-through baby-doll nighties. Omar lost his count. He felt sick to his stomach, and anger blazed from his solar plexus. It was the blind mamba from Jamaica that had sacrificed his Lucy. He wanted to kill her there and then.

The nine of swords flashed before his eyes, and he heard his loa buzz a warning in his ears. "No anger, mon," he repeated to himself, knowing that the mamba would feel his hate and be alerted. Turning away, he desperately visualised an emerald light around him, and struggling with his mind, forced it into nothingness. *You will be tried and tried; you know that,* he told himself. *Pray to Jah Love, mon.*

A gong reverberated through the room, and people drained their drinks and gathered their things.

"We've got to get outta here," Omar whispered. "The front door's locked, so we can't get out that way."

They desperately looked for a place to hide.

"Come on!" Jim said, pointing at the cloakrooms to the left of the front door. "Nobody's leavin', so they won't need their coats, and we'll be out of 'arm's way over there."

No sooner had the four of them beat a hasty retreat across the room and stood back against the wall than a throng of hooded figures poured down the stairwell and into the hall.

"Just got out of there in time," Sue said, checking her watch. "Pray they get a move on. Otherwise, our bracelets will be drained."

Feeling a warning tingle down her spine, Emma looked round and saw the butler standing in front of the disordered lily urns. He bent down and picked up the amethyst cluster Omar had left behind. He jerked upwards, knocking over one of the vases.

"Boy!" he screamed, throwing down the stone like it had scalded him. "Clean up the water."

Turning on his heel, he gazed slowly round the hall and then stalked over to the door. "Get the trollop," he hissed to one of the servants standing at the entrance.

A hush fell over the room, and all eyes turned towards the staircase as Giles Kingsbury glided down. Around his neck and hanging down both sides of his magenta satin robe was a huge python. Feodora St Clare came behind him wearing a long red shift and a thin golden circlet in her hair. At the bottom of the stairs, the couple stopped.

"Red wine libation," the cadaverous butler shouted throatily to the congregation as he opened the front door. Two boys appeared each carrying a golden goblet brimming with red liquid, and as they handed the chalices to the satanic couple, the blast of a trumpet rent the air. On cue, four more boys appeared pushing trolleys to the front door full of goblets of wine for the assembly.

Passing the cloakrooms on her way to the front door, Feodora hesitated and turned her cold eyes in their direction. "What's the matter, dearest?" Kingsbury crooned.

Feodora did not answer, and Omar saw her nostrils flare and her tongue flick out between her lips. Something had disturbed the energy in the room, and she was searching for it. Glancing at Ugog, Kingsbury's devil helper, he saw the fiend clinging by its mouth to the back of his master's neck. The demon's fiery eyes looked through the door way, and Omar knew that unlike Feodora, Ugog was totally unaware of their presence. Turning his thought inwards and mentally toning on the airwaves, he summoned his loa.

Out of nowhere, a large bluebottle buzzed into Feodora's face and landed on her nose. She flicked it away in irritation. After buzzing around her head, it landed on her upper lip. She smashed her hand over her face in an effort to kill it, but it sailed out of reach with a mocking dip. Screaming obscenities, she pursued the insect across the room.

Taking advantage of the distraction Omar's loa had created, the four left the cloakrooms and hastily went outside. Veering left at the bottom of the steps, they went back behind the bushes, away from the disciples who were gathering on the lawn. Once they were concealed in the shrubbery, they became visible again.

"We've been cloaked for forty minutes," Sue whispered worriedly to the others. "Just over three hours to go. And the sabbat hasn't even started yet."

"Feodora! Come, my dearest! Our gods are waiting," Kingsbury said, impatiently lunging after her. He took her by the arm and steered her through the entrance and out onto the terrace.

"Followers of the serpent, hear me," the satanist shouted to the cloaked and cowled assembly on the lawn.

"The Old Ones are waiting! Our diligence and planning through the centuries has finally come to fruition. All is now prepared for our triumphant opening of the way. The time has come for us to walk the dragon path to the chapel." He gave the sign of the horns with his fingers to the assembled guests, who roared in acclamation. He let out a maniacal scream and dug his long nails into Feodora's wrist, and then he jerked her towards him. Pulling her head back by her hair and grinning repulsively at his followers, he opened the front of her gown, exposing her naked body in the moonlight. The snake slid from Kingsbury's neck and coiled obscenely around Feodora's body, resting its head on her mons pubis.

The crowd roared as Kingsbury held his chalice in the air. "To the lord of night and chaos," he screeched. He took a drink, spilling the liquid down his chin and robe. Then he tipped what was left of the red stuff into Feodora's open mouth, streaking her chin and neck with crimson.

"Looks like a scene from 'ell," Jim whispered.

With much pomp and ceremony, the satanic couple strode down the steps, accompanied by two servants swinging lighted silver censers. The bitter smell of thorn apple and henbane irritated Jim's nose, and he held his hands tightly across his nose and mouth to curb his body's reaction to the smoke. But the pressure became unbearable, and the sneeze burst out from between his fingers like a gunshot. He immediately stiffened. Emma peered through the laurel hedge and sighed with relief. The celebrants were too busy drinking and throwing the empty goblets on the grass to notice.

Halting at the bottom of the steps, Kingsbury and Feodora waited for torches and squawking cockerels in a basket to be brought to them.

"What's goin' on over there?" Jim asked. "I can't see much from 'ere."

"Looks like a blooding ceremony," Sue said. "Similar to the blooding at a fox hunt. The psychos kill the poor animal and use its tail to daub blood on their faces"

"That looks exactly like what they're doing with the chickens," Emma said, moving slightly to the left to get a better view. "The serving boys are ramming the chickens' heads into a funnel." She shook her head and looked away. "Too much for me."

"I'll watch," Sue whispered. "I've seen so many cruelties that I can switch my mind off at the sight."

A couple of tense minutes passed. "They're ready," Sue said as the serving boys took a bowl of blood and a handful of tail feathers to Feodora.

Raising his gown and turning round, Kingsbury bared his buttocks. Filing past, the disciples each gave him the witch's kiss and then lifted their eyes in adoration to Feodora, who splashed blood on their upturned faces.

Once the participants were all blooded, Kingsbury donned a great horned mask and then led his cowled disciples westwards along a paved tree-lined walkway.

Omar shivered. "Pray," he whispered to the others as they started after the procession. "Blood has been spilt and wicked spirits are flockin' to its call."

The moonlight tracked their footsteps again as Omar led the way down the avenue. Above their heads countless wings rushed and whirred. Owls hooted from the nearby woodlands, and other furtive, jumbled sounds conjured terrifying memories of their dim ancestral past.

"There's someone comin' up behind us," Omar said in a low voice. "Let's get off the path."

Out of the gloom, a tall figure came quickly towards them with two smaller forms scurrying behind. As they got closer, Emma saw that it was a man and two serving boys. One of the boys carried a smoking censer, and the other led a young pale girl wearing a collar on a leash. She wore only a black leather harness that crisscrossed her small breasts and strapped her wrists to her waist.

As they passed, the spectral man darted towards them, stopping only a few feet from their hiding place. As his eyes probed the verges on both sides of the road, Emma stiffened. It was the butler. Fear surged within her, but forcing her mind into neutral, she concentrated on strengthening the emerald octahedron that surrounded her. Then, as if in answer to a silent command, the butler's head jerked upwards, and after he signalled to the boys, the hellish band hurried off again after the procession.

"Omar! That's Lily on that leash," Sue said with anguish.

"We'll try and help her. Keep positive in Jah Love, mon, or we've all lost," Omar said in a low voice as they moved. "We gonna get tried and tried. Understand me?" He touched Jim's shoulder. "Anger got me, mon, just the same as you. Back there in that room, I saw the mamba that sacrificed my Lucy."

Jim patted Omar encouragingly on the shoulder. "'Ang in there."

"And the butler," Emma said. "I don't know how he knew we were hiding between the vases, but he did. Is Lily Tina's sister?"

"Yes. They call her trollop, and she's a blood sacrifice to Babylon." Omar's eyes flashed. "And the butler, he's an adept of wickedness and has bad loa with him."

"Are you all right, Sue?" Emma asked, seeing the hard set of her face.

"I'm all right. Just trying to curb my anger. I'd like to do them all a mischief, and I'm trying not to lose my cool. It's hard."

The satanists turned left along an overgrown path that led through a damp and crumbling family cemetery, and as the four followed, Emma clung to Jim's hand, trying not to look at the broken tombstones littered around them like jagged teeth.

At the end of the graveyard, they stopped and waited in the darkness. The bobbing torches had halted before a small, evil-looking chapel of grey stone that glimmered dully in the moonlight. One by one, the flames went out, swallowed by the yawning door of the chapel.

The eldritch church was surrounded by a fence of black, pointed iron rods. The gate stood ajar.

They were about to enter, an owl hooted from a nearby tree and wings rushed above them. Jim looked up. Circling above the glimmering church was a dense cloud of glowing bodies. The moon shone out from behind the clouds, and in that dreadful light, he saw that what he thought were bats had long arms and legs and horns upon their bony heads. Sinking to his knees, he covered his eyes in terror.

Omar gently took his arm and pulled him up. "Be strong, brother."

Creeping through the gate, they were in time to see the butler dragging the girl through the chapel entrance into the greater darkness beyond the door. As the serving boys followed, one slipped and fell heavily on the ground, dropping the censer, which hit the flagstones with a clang and rolled away.

The boy got up holding his head.

"I'll get it," his companion said, scrambling to pick it up.

"We must hurry, or we'll be punished! The same thing that happened to Tommy will happen to us," the other boy whimpered.

Taking advantage of the diversion, the four of them slipped into the stillness of the chapel. Past the moonlit dusty pews, a faint light at the bottom of the nave glowed like an unholy beacon. Footsteps came up behind them, and they stepped into the pews and waited as the serving boys hurried past them down the nave and disappeared behind the altar. With a click, the light coming from behind the pulpit disappeared, and they were left in darkness.

The moonlit nave was silent and charged with malice as they followed after the servants. Dangling from the vaulted ceiling were large fronds of broken cobwebs, and Sue unwittingly stumbled into one. The threads swept her face, and she shrieked. Her cry echoed around the silent church in mocking repetition. Freezing, the other four listened. Heart-pounding seconds ticked away, and then came the sound they were dreading. From underneath the stone slabs beneath their feet came muffled voices.

With another click, bright beams of light shone behind the pulpit, and two robed figures cautiously emerged into the nave wielding powerful flashlights. Pushing Emma and Sue into the front pew next to Omar, Jim crouched next to the aisle seat beside them. Hardly daring to breathe, they waited for the robed figures to go past.

"Nothing here," one said, searching with the light along the rows of pews. "That's strange. I could have sworn I heard a cry. Let's take a look outside."

The moment the men disappeared, the company moved swiftly along the nave. Behind the pulpit, they found an open trapdoor and the beginning of a flight of steep steps.

"Jim, mon, you go first with Emma and Sue, and I'll come down behind," Omar whispered.

The stairway was steep and narrow, lit on one side by flaming brands in holders mounted on the wall. At the bottom of the staircase was a narrow space before an age-blackened door. Jim gave it a push, and it eased open. Peering through the chink, Jim saw a square, torch-lit chamber. Black passages led away from it in all directions. "There are lots of tunnels we can hide in," he whispered to the others. "Follow me."

Footsteps clacked above their heads.

"The men are coming back," Emma hissed. "Quick!"

Omar joined them in the refuge of the nearest tunnel, and they waited.

"I could have sworn I heard something. I wonder what it was," a voice on the stairs said.

"Perhaps a fox caught a rabbit—they do scream so. Yes, just like a baby," a second odious voice simpered from the bottom of the steps.

The robed figures rushed passed the group's hiding place and turned left into the catacombs. Silently, the company followed them.

The passageway took a sharp right turn, and as they rounded the corner, the backs of the disciples disappeared into an orange glow. They paused for a moment in the flickering, baleful light of unreality, their eyes meeting in the common understanding of what lay ahead. Then, with a nod, Omar led the way through a low archway lit with fiery torches.

CHAPTER TWENTY-ONE

THE SABBAT

The company stood above a low, long, torch-lit cavern. Before them was a flight of worn, wide steps leading down to an arena, where the red-robed assembly stood on three graduated terraces around a large, raised stone platform. Between the disciples and the altar stone was a ring about three feet wide. At each of the cardinal points stood a naked serving boy, draped in crimson silk, his eyes closed and a wreath of leaves upon his head. The slab was draped with the same blood-red silk and surrounded on all sides by smoking black sulphur candles.

Kingsbury stood in the centre of the altar stone in front of a black, shiny phallus about five feet high. He wore only a horned headdress and a huge golden phallus strapped around his pelvis. His image cast hideous shadows on the walls. Feodora stood next to him, her hair loose and wild, with the python curled around her nude body, portraying the demon Lilith. In front of the satanic couple lay a man and a girl, naked and spread-eagled, tied with ropes to iron stakes secured firmly in the stone. Painted between them on the altar was an inverted red pentacle fashioned in the likeness of Baphomet, the satanic goat, with glowing ruby eyes.

The sight of the robed assembly gathered around the altar, the flickering torchlight, and the stench of sulphurous candles filled Emma with fresh terror.

"I can't go down there," she choked out, recoiling against the wall. Awful memories of rituals in the temple underneath her house flooded her being, and in the psychic struggle that followed, she saw herself as nothingness. Her body would die at some point, and all the thoughts, past and present, that validated who she was would also perish. She was cursed, doomed from the day she was born. There was no point in going on.

Sensing her fear, Jim grabbed her hand. "'Old up, Em," he whispered. "We've got this far. We gotta try and get the sapphire, for everythin' alive."

With a supreme effort of will, Emma forced her thoughts into the moment, and strengthening the emerald shield around her, she looked at the altar stone with faerie sight.

At first, all she could see was dirty red effulgence pulsating over the arena, but in response to her gaze, a shimmering blue glow pierced through, illuminating everything around it.

"The sapphire's on top of the pillar in the middle of the platform," Emma said. "Can you see it?"

"I can, mon," Omar answered.

"I can see it as well, but 'ow we goin' to get to it?" Jim muttered. "There are three rings of them suckers, and they're packed in pretty tight."

"We'll have to find an opportunity and go for it, mon," Omar answered grimly.

"Oh my God!" Sue gasped, peering into the gloom. "One of the sacrifices is Lily, and the other looks like Tony!" *But that's impossible*, she thought. Then she remembered the last few calls she'd made. Each time, the line was engaged, and he hadn't called her. "We have to rescue them," she said desperately, moving forwards to the steps.

"Wait!" Omar hissed, grabbing her arm. "We're going—"

A terrible note cracked from a trumpet, cutting him off, and echoed round the crypt. In answer to the signal, the disciples began a droning chant. The trumpet's whine built until the cavern vibrated with the ugly sound. It reached an ear-splitting crescendo, and the butler dragged two screaming little girls onto the altar by a rope. Pulling out a knife from his belt, he cut them free, and he pulled them by the hair into the pentagon at the centre of the star.

The cavern grew hot and tense with expectation, and Kingsbury raised his hands to begin the summoning invocation. In a high-pitched voice, he called upon the reptilian egg-born gods, those haters and deceivers of mankind, to bear witness to the opening of the way. As the foul incantation echoed round the cavern, the butler forced the girls to their knees and sexually desecrated them with a wooden phallus. Tony writhed in anguish, straining at his bonds, shrieking like a madman.

"Veni! Exercitus Malum!" Kingsbury screamed in exultation.

A foul wind swept around the cavern, fanned by the mighty flapping of unseen wings, and a low rumble vibrated through the stone beneath their feet. The butler turned his face upwards in wild abandon and pulled the whimpering girls tightly to his abdomen. Their little bodies quivered and slowly melded into his until they were consumed. The butler's flesh expanded upwards, and from the shifting mass, a hideous outline took shape. Emma felt a shock of recognition. Rising from the pentacle was Zugalfar, the demon she had routed under Dragonsbury Ring. Clutching the topaz at her throat, she felt it burn with the memory of her ordeal. Dragging her eyes away from the monstrous apparition, she focussed her attention on the sapphire.

Zugalfar towered over the cavern, flexed his leathery wings, and blotted out what little light there was. "We can't wait any longer," Omar hissed. "Let's rush 'em, mon!"

He stormed down the steps first, barging into the disciples from behind, taking them by surprise, and the back line fell into the second in a domino effect. Omar leapt onto the altar and sped towards the pillar. Zugalfar loomed above him, his red eyes swivelling grotesquely in their sockets, and with a mighty sweep of his arm, he clutched Omar in his flabby claws.

Halfway down the steps, Sue got a clear view of the altar. It was Tony who lay on one side of the pentacle and Lily on the other.

Horror stabbed her being and quickly turned into rage. She would kill Kingsbury and Feodora. They were demons in human form, parasites that revelled in cruelty and the slaughter of innocents. She vowed to save Tony and Lily or die trying. Hardening her resolve and narrowing her eyes against the fumes, she looked around the circle. Two disciples had fallen over, toppled by the sudden onrush of her friends, and taking a shallow breath of the stinking air, she ran down the last few steps to the cavern floor. Stealing behind the two robed figures still struggling to rise, she slugged them with her cosh.

She dragged first one and then the other by the cassock ropes into the shadows and stripped them, stuffing their robes down the front of her tracksuit bottoms. She turned back to the altar just as the demon swept Omar up in his claws.

Adrenaline surged, and Sue fought her way to the platform. She hurled her crucifix at the monster, hitting him in the chest. Zugalfar rocked back, slammed Omar down, and belched a stream of fire in Sue's direction. Sue dived and rolled away. The fiery blast seared the place where she had been standing. The cavern exploded with shrieking and the stench of burning flesh as the disciples in front of her caught fire. An undulating whip of snake vertebrae sprouted from Zugalfar's claws, and with a hiss, he sent the lash in her direction. The razor-sharp spine missed her by inches but ripped the flesh from the disciples in the way. Seeing the torn and burning bodies of their brethren, the horde fled in all directions. Zugalfar sent a blast of fire to consume those that had taken to the steps, rendering them to piles of ashes.

In desperation, Emma summoned her faerie nature but could find no sympathetic resonance in the ether. She grasped her necklace but found to her horror that the gem had grown cold. The topaz could not help her. She had lost her faerie power. Fear rose in her like a twisting snake. She had no weapon; she was powerless against the demon. Struggling to keep her mind in neutral, she saw the emerald shield around her shimmer and contract. Her fear was too great to sustain it.

She hesitated and, tried to bolster her courage. Finally, in desperation, she sidestepped Omar's body and jumped for the sapphire. Her fingers closed around it, and the jewel's brilliance brightened. The stone filled her mind with a kaleidoscope of images of fantastic, unfathomable worlds, and she felt she would dissolve at any second.

Regaining control, she turned to flee but found she couldn't move through the seething mass tightly clustered around the altar. The bracelet was draining, the rainbows around her now barely visible. They'd see her, and kill her. She'd failed. Looking desperately around the altar for an opening, she thought she saw a small man in Georgian dress standing in front of the pillar.

The figure was bathed in the blue glow of the sapphire, and a ray of hope leapt in her heart. "Trevelyan! Is that you?"

"Quick! Give me the jewel," he said urgently. "I can't hold the frequency much longer."

Emma hesitated. He had told her he couldn't go with them to the sabbat because his presence would reveal her. Was it a trick?

"Come, Emma, there is no time to lose! I will use the power of the prisms to take you all into Faerie. Even though their charge is waning, there is still time. Hurry! Give me the jewel."

He's putting himself at risk to save us! She gripped the sapphire tighter. Relief flooded through her as she stumbled towards him. "I prayed you come," she cried.

The moment she reached him, the figure disappeared, and in a rush of realisation, she looked down. She was standing in the pentacle. A scream welled up from the depths of her being, but the sound was strangled in her throat. The ghastly image and burning eyes of Zugalfar flashed all around her, and he swept her up in his claws into a maelstrom of malevolence. Darkness closed in, suffocating her body and battering her soul. Visions of herself naked and spread-eagled on an altar surrounded by hooded chanting figures flashed before her. From her bowels erupted the primal scream of mortal life. A vision of Dragonsbury Ring appeared. The accursed hill came closer every second. There was the stench of charnel earth and bitter incense—then merciful oblivion.

Jim, emotionally exhausted, numbly watched as Emma walked into the pentacle and disappeared in a sheet of blinding flame. The walls of the cavern shook with a deafening boom as Zugalfar exited and the roof fell in.

"Emma!" Jim screamed, seeing the pentacle was empty. Then a burning wind extinguished all the torches. All was darkness.

Grief choked his senses as he fumbled in the dark. Emma was gone and so too was his life. But he wouldn't go alone. He would avenge her death.

The disciples fled in pandemonium, pursued by the glowing bat beings that had circled the church. A torch was lit and carried to the altar. In the flickering light, Kingsbury stood over Lily's prostate body, howling an invocation to his gods. Burning with vengeance, Jim leapt onto the platform and threw himself at Kingsbury. He rained blow after blow with his cosh on the satanist's head until he lay still and bloody.

Sue ran onto the platform, stretched a cassock rope between her hands, and approached Feodora from behind. The sorceress bent and weaved over Tony's bleeding body droning an incantation. A serving boy held a metal bowl at her side. As Feodora raised the sacrificial dagger, Sue threw the rope around her neck and hauled her backwards, tightening the rope around her throat. Feodora kicked out, but Sue kept her stranglehold, tightening the rope more. After a last feeble kick, the sorceress lay still. The serving boy shrieked, dropped the bowl, and ran away.

Taking the dagger from Feodora's hand, Sue cut Tony and Lily loose.

"Can you hear me?" she said.

Tony stared into space with glassy eyes. He nodded mechanically and put on the cassock.

Lily was alive but catatonic as Sue put the robe on her shivering body. Gently taking her by the hand, Sue led her off the altar.

"Can you get up?" Jim asked Omar. "We've got to get out of 'ere."

"I think so, mon." Omar unsteadily got to his feet.

In a daze, the companions picked their way through the twisted charred remains of bodies to the steps. The mamba from the library emerged from the shadows, her stare alive with hate. In defiance of her bulk, she darted and slammed into Omar, knocking him back and smothering him. As her fat hands closed around Omar's throat, Jim stabbed her in the side with his flick knife. Her huge arm smashed his face and his teeth punctured his lip. Tasting his own blood, Jim struck her again and again until her body heaved and crashed on its side.

Gasping for air, Omar struggled to his feet and escaped with Jim through the tunnels, out of the church, and into the cold night air. A police siren wailed in the distance.

"Someone's called the cops," Sue hissed. "We'd better get as far away from here as possible. God knows, we can't trust the police. They could be Kingsbury's cronies."

Cars were erratically reversed and sped off as they came to the manor.

"Wait behind the laurels," Jim ordered. "I'll steal a car." Moving swiftly to the car park, he saw some of the chauffeurs gesticulating at each other. A black Daimler's engine was running nearby, and seeing the car was empty, Jim jumped in and drove away.

The siren came closer. Pulling up by the laurels, Jim shouted, "Quick! Get in!"

Sue bundled Tony and Lily in the back seat and got in beside them.

"Drive, mon," Omar said, jumping in the passenger side. Once they were all in, Jim took off, narrowly avoiding a police car as it swerved in through the gates.

"We'll dump this car at the church and pick up our own," he said, driving towards the crossroads with his foot flat on the floor. Swerving to the left, he raced along to the high street.

"We need to get Lily and Tony to a hospital," Sue said anxiously. "Lily's catatonic and Tony's in shock. How about you, Omar? Do you need a doctor?"

"No, I'm all right, mon. Just a few dents."

"What about you, Jim? You're bleeding."

"I'm all right," he said flatly.

Bells cracked the stroke of four at the church as Jim turned right and drove across the gravel to the car. They changed vehicles and then took off again.

"Sue! Where's the nearest 'ospital?" Jim asked as he sped along the high street.

"Denhampstead," she replied. "Turn left down here at the Heron pub."

Jim pulled up at the emergency entrance. Sue helped Lily and Tony from the car and took them inside. After a few minutes, she was back. "Let's go home," she said wearily.

The sun was rising when they pulled up at Greenfern. Their bodies ached with fatigue and their minds were numb, unable yet to process the terrible events leading up to Emma's disappearance.

Sue made a pot of strong coffee and brought it to the table along with a bottle of whisky. Pouring a good measure of liquor into three cups, she topped it up with coffee.

"No liquor for me, mon," Omar said, pushing his cup away.

"Why the fuck did Em go into the pentacle?" Jim said, draining his cup and grabbing the one she poured for Omar.

"Steady on, Jim," Omar cautioned. "Gettin' drunk won't solve anythin', mon. Wicked loa may be trackin' us, and you can't give them any chance to possess you. We have to have our wits about us."

"I don't care. What's the bloody point?" Jim gulped down the coffee and reached for the bottle. "Everythin's turned into shit. It's all washed up. There's no wakin' up to this." He banged his fist on the table. "Why the fuck did she do that? After all the shit we've been through. She just threw it all away. Now she's never comin' back—"

"Snap out of it!" Sue said fiercely. "We don't know what happened to Emma. The demon must have cast a spell over her, tricked her in some way. She wouldn't have walked into the pentacle on her own accord."

Omar nodded and flung back his dreads. "Her fear, mon. It must have been her fear the demon used to trick her. What happened to the loa Trevelyan?"

"Trevelyan! That piece of shit. It's all 'is fault. 'E got 'er into this and left 'er in the bloody lurch. Yeah, where is 'e? Not bloody 'ere, that's for sure." Jim wiped his mouth with his sleeve. He saw it all now. Trevelyan had trapped Emma and set her up for sacrifice. He'd set them all up. He emptied the whisky bottle in his cup.

"Jim!" Sue glared at him. "Don't think about driving home. Where are your car keys?"

There was a quick knock at the door, and one of Sue's friends came into the kitchen. "You're back," he said, staring at their glum faces. "Everything go all right?"

Sue nodded. "Thanks for protecting the sanctuary while we were gone."

"We kept watch in turns, but nothing happened. The others aren't up yet, but I heard a car, so I thought I'd just check. I'll go and tell them you're back."

"Come in when you're ready and make yourselves some breakfast."

Despite Omar's warning, Jim wanted to drink, wanted to drown out the awful scenes playing in his head. The rug had been pulled out from under his life. There was nothing to live for anymore. Emma was gone and the whole bloody world would soon lie in ruins. The ring Trevelyan had given him was tight, and fiddling with it, he found it would barely move around his finger. Without a word, he got up and left the table, disappearing in the direction of the bathroom.

"What do you think happened to Emma?" Sue asked as soon as Jim was out of sight.

"I don't know, mon. My loa have gone. The sabbat was too wicked for their spirits, but they'll tell us what happened when they—"

A car sped off down the drive. Sue got up and looked out of the kitchen door. "Jim's leaving!" she cried.

"Light the incense burner," Omar commanded. "We must pray that he gets home safely."

Driving back to Basingstoke, Jim was full of resentment. Everything that had happened was Trevelyan's fault. If he hadn't interfered in their lives, Emma would still be here with him. He had destroyed both of them.

The peridot ring on his finger was now uncomfortably hot, and he tugged at it, trying to slide it off, but it wouldn't go past his knuckle. He remembered there was a full bottle of brandy in the cabinet at Emma's. He was going to drink it all.

"Faerie and Chloe were an illusion," a soft voice purred in his ear. "A veil drawn across your eyes to ensnare you. You fell for it and let him banish me."

A couple of miles from Emma's, the ring burned Jim's finger, and wedging his knee under the steering wheel, he tried again to get it off, but his knuckle was red and swollen. The ring burnt into his finger, and he could smell the sweet perfume of the succubus in his nostrils. "Take off the ring," she urged.

"Yes, yes!" he cried. Overcome with passion, he gripped the ring, ripping his flesh as he pulled it over his knuckle. "I'm yours," he moaned, triumphantly throwing the ring on the floor.

The car hit a bump, and his knee slipped out from under the steering wheel. Crying out, he desperately fought for control. He swerved off the road and plunged down a bank, hitting his head on the roof. In a blur, a voluptuous woman stood in an orange robe in the trees in front of him. She beckoned to him.

The car juddered to a halt in a stand of small trees, and Jim stumbled out. The succubus stood before him and opened her robe, exposing her body.

"Emma's gone," she crooned. "And I am hungry."